I0708798

the
body thief

**BOOK TWO OF THE
SYDNEY HARBOUR
HOSPITAL SERIES**

CHRIS TAYLOR

Copyright © 2015 by Chris Taylor

(All Rights Reserved)

Without limiting the rights under copyright(s) reserved below, no part of this publication may be reproduced, stored in or introduced into a retrieval system, or transmitted, in any form, or by any means (electronic, mechanical, photocopying, recording, or otherwise) without the prior permission of the copyright owner.

LCT Productions Pty Ltd
18364 Kamilaroi Highway, Narrabri NSW 2390

ISBN. 978-1-925119-26-8 (Paperback)

The Body Thief is a work of fiction. Names, characters, places, brands, media and incidents either are the product of the author's imagination or are used fictitiously. Any resemblance to actual persons, living or dead, events, or locales, is entirely coincidental.

Published in the United States of America.

THE SYDNEY HARBOUR HOSPITAL SERIES

(in order)

THE PERFECT HUSBAND
(Book One)

THE BODY THIEF
(Book Two)

THE BABY SNATCHERS
(Book Three)

THE FINAL BULLET
(Book Four)

THE DEBT COLLECTOR
(Book Five)

Find out more about all of Chris Taylor's books, including the hugely popular Munro Family series by visiting her website at:
www.christaylorauthor.com.au/about/books

DEDICATION

*This book is dedicated to my mother Sophia Guihot
and as always, to my beautiful husband, Linden.*

ACKNOWLEDGMENTS

As usual, no book comes into being without a lot of help and support by my friends and family. A world of thanks must go to my wonderful editor, Pat Thomas. Thank you for everything that you do to make my stories even more amazing than I could ever dare to dream. To Detective Superintendent Michael Kilfoyle (ret) of the Australian Federal Police and to Scott Pearce of the New South Wales Department of Forensic Medicine, thank you for lending my story credibility. Any mistakes are wholly my own.

To Grady and all of the staff at damonza.com, thank you for yet another fantastic cover. To my sister, Nicole Guihot and to my friend, Ally Thomson, thank you for your excellent editorial comments, proof reading skills and suggestions. I hope you like the final result.

To Amy Atwell and her dedicated staff at Author EMS who are so much more than book formatters. Amy, once again, thank you for your magic.

To the fantastic writer organizations such as Romance Writers of Australia, Romance Writers of America and Romance Writers of New Zealand for all the help, support and encouragement they offer new and aspiring writers, including me.

To my readers, thank you for your support and love for my stories. Your encouragement and enjoyment make this journey all worthwhile.

And lastly, to my friends and family, especially my husband and children. Thank you for putting up with late dinners and even later conversations as I've emerged day after day from the sometimes scary but always enthralling world I've created on my computer.

PROLOGUE

Mid-September

Dear Diary,

He lies prostrate on the operating table, his skin still warm and pink. Even the intricate tattoo on his shoulder with the letters P and M interwoven around a cherub looks plump and firm. The respirator is doing its job.

His chest has been cut open to reveal the treasure trove within. I am more than certain he's had a heart attack, so that organ must remain intact, but everything else can go.

His family said he wasn't a donor, were adamant he didn't want to be one, but I can't listen. Surely, such a man would approve this final gesture. I cannot bear to see his healthy organs go to waste. So many people will benefit from his kind and generous gift. And he's dead, really. Who's to say he wouldn't have changed his mind at the last minute and been generous, if he'd lived?

I block my mind to what I know were his wishes and once again pick up my scalpel. Quickly and efficiently, I do what I do best. With each slice, I'm saving lives and furthering the cause, one lucky person at a time. It's a shame I am forced to work in secrecy and that my work is outside the laws here. How I would love for people to know who I am and what I do for so many others—and not the least among them, my family...

CHAPTER 1

Two months earlier

Doctor Samantha Wolfe bent over the corpse that lay stretched out on the steel gurney before her. The work station was one of twenty that lined the main autopsy room of the Department of Forensic Medicine, situated in Glebe, an inner city suburb of Sydney. It was the biggest and busiest mortuary in Australia and carried out the post mortems resulting from all major disasters. Most locals referred to the drab concrete-and-steel building simply as the Glebe Morgue.

Adjusting her safety glasses and mask, Samantha picked up the Stryker saw and cut through the woman's ribs. The saw squealed in protest, but did its usual efficient job. When she finished, she set the saw aside and with gloved hands, prised open the chest cavity.

"What do you have there, Sam?" Phillip Bond asked from where he stood beside the gurney adjacent to hers. His tone was conversational as he made preparations to begin the post mortem on the body of a black male that lay on the table in front of him.

Sam looked up and grimaced. "The paperwork says a suspected heart attack. She's only forty-eight. She's overweight, but not to the point of obesity. Even if it is a heart attack, I'll be doing some toxicology work just to rule out foul play. Thankfully most of us aren't that young when the heart decides to go."

Phillip chuckled and made a Y incision on his corpse. "I suppose we can be grateful for that. Every day brings us closer to the time when we'll reach the end. Let's hope we die peacefully of some immediately discernible cause." He shuddered. "I sure as hell don't want to end up here."

She threw him a teasing smile. "Oh, Phillip! We love this place! And I would take *such* good care of you! I'd make sure my scalpel cut straight and true and my stitches were neat and precise. You wouldn't find a better seamstress. Nobody would be any the wiser that I'd had my hands deep inside your belly."

Phillip grimaced and shook his head and then gave her a sideways look. "You're in a good mood today. Any particular reason?"

Samantha thought about not telling him, but then changed her mind. *What did it matter if he knew?* She was truly thankful for every day she spent on the earth. "It's my birthday," she revealed.

Phillip laughed. "Happy birthday! Dare I ask which one? Or maybe I should just guess... Oh, my God!" he exclaimed with mock surprise and horror. "Don't tell me this is the big 4-0!"

She laughed, amused at his antics. "Very funny! I bet you wish it was *your* big 4-0. I seem to recall the last birthday you celebrated started with a five and ended in a three." She used her scalpel to cut through the tissue holding the woman's lungs in place and then added, "I turned thirty-four today, if you must know."

Phillip whistled. "Thirty-four! Who'd have guessed? You look ten years younger! It must be the lack of sunlight we get, hidden away in here. It has to be good for the complexion, don't you think? I read somewhere that too much sun can age a person."

Samantha lifted the lungs out of the chest cavity and dropped them into a steel tray. The heart soon followed. She shot Phillip a wry smile. "I'm glad to hear that spending twelve hours a day, in the cold and dark we call the office, has some advantages."

"Of course! And best of all, you get to work with me!" His face reflected the innocence that filled his voice, but his eyes twinkled in merriment. He might be nearly two decades older, but she considered Phillip Bond a friend.

They'd known each other for years, from back when she'd worked at the Westmead Morgue. When she decided to move closer to the city and had requested a transfer to Glebe, Phillip was only too happy to transfer with her. They had a mutual respect and genuine affection for each other that went beyond that of mere work colleagues. For her, he was more like a father figure and right from her earliest days as a forensic pathologist, he'd taken her under his wing.

"So, how are you celebrating this momentous birthday? With some very expensive champagne, I hope?"

Phillip's questions broke into her thoughts and she glanced across at him. "I'm having lunch with my brother and I'll probably catch up with my sisters after work. That's about it."

"What? Alistair's not even taking you to dinner? What kind of brother is he?"

She laughed. "A very busy one with a lot of responsibilities right now."

"Yeah, yeah, yeah! So you say! Nobody forced him to take on the role of the Sydney Harbour Hospital's poster boy. Just because he's head of the Organ Donation for Transplantation Unit doesn't mean he shouldn't make time to take his baby sister out to dinner on her birthday."

"It's not that simple," Sam replied. "Ever since the recent joint initiative between the State Government and the Sydney Harbour Hospital to increase the public's awareness of organ and tissue donation, he's been run off his feet. Have you noticed the increase in post mortems on organ donors coming through here lately?"

"Yeah, I have." He nodded toward the body on the table. "This guy's donated his heart, lungs, liver, pancreas and both kidneys. That's a whole heap of organs. I had two similar cases last week and three the week before. That has to be some kind of record."

She nodded. "Until recently, one a week was normal. Now, it seems every other day I do a PM on a body that's missing some of its parts."

Phillip reached for his Stryker saw and went to work on the man's skull. "And those are only the bodies that come through here. Imagine how many must be hitting the funeral homes. I have to hand it to your brother, he's sure had an impact on donor numbers. He might be worth those big bucks, after all." Phillip shot her a wink and Sam rolled her eyes.

"It isn't just him," she replied, "although, I admit, he could charm just about anyone. The Sydney Harbour Hospital's now running the campaign right through winter. As the star of the show, Alistair told me he even had to attend a full-on photo shoot with models and makeup and everything. The hospital's putting up billboards around the city, encouraging people to become donors. My brother will be recognized wherever he goes."

"Lucky him. With that kind of exposure, he might even become a celebrity. Maybe you could go to one of those swanky restaurants down near the water without a reservation and demand to be seated."

Sam laughed and joined in the fun. "Yes, and then we could order the most extravagant thing on the menu and have the restaurant cover the bill. They'll be falling all over themselves to have such a megastar in their presence. It would be like something out of Hollywood." She grinned again. "I like it."

The door to the main autopsy room opened and she looked up in time to see the deputy coroner fill the doorway. Sam sent him a brief wave of acknowledgement and returned to the job at hand. With the remaining organs now in the steel tray, she began to weigh them. An examination of the woman's heart confirmed the preliminary diagnosis. A large blood clot blocked the aorta. Several smaller clots had formed in the surrounding blood vessels. Sadly, it had been inevitable that this woman's life would come to an abrupt end. Sam would conduct routine toxicology just to be thorough, even though it looked like lifestyle and hereditary factors were the leading contributors to the woman's untimely demise.

Sam's boss drew nearer and she greeted him with a smile. "Hi, Richard. What's up?"

Deputy Coroner, Richard Davis, looked from her to Phillip and back again. "What are you two so happy about?" he grumbled. "It's Monday morning and we have a backload of bodies. I don't see anything jovial about that."

Samantha smiled again because Richard's bark was always worse than his bite. It was the same every Monday.

"It's Sam's birthday," Phillip piped up and then proceeded to peel back the face of the man on the table.

Richard Davis turned to face her, his expression one of surprise. "Happy birthday, Samantha. I should have known."

"Don't be silly," she protested. "I wouldn't expect you to remember."

"I have access to every staff record in the building. I have no excuse if I forget," he replied with a smile. "Do you have any plans?"

"Ah, there we have it! A massive bleed!" Phillip announced, bending over the brain of his cadaver. "That was easy!"

Sam smiled and shook her head and then answered Richard's question. "I'm having lunch with my brother."

"Her *superstar* brother," Phillip added with a cheeky wink.

"I'm glad to see he's spending some of that hard-earned cash," Richard replied. "With his new position at the hospital, he must be raking it in."

Sam grinned. "Jealous?"

Richard shook his head. "Not at all. He deserves every cent. He has to work with the living *and* the dead. At least my job is limited to those no longer with us, and thankfully, complaints are rare. His job requires a whole lot more finesse. Having to deal with grieving relatives and convince them to donate body parts of their loved ones..." He shuddered. "Way beyond my skill set, I'm afraid. I admire him."

"So do I," Sam agreed, "and he's having a real impact. The sudden increase in the number of bodies coming here with donated organs is impressive."

Richard looked uncomfortable for a second and then his gaze sharpened. "What do you mean?"

Samantha indicated the body Phillip was working on. "Phillip's guy donated most of his organs. It's fortunate none of the ones removed were involved in the cause of his death, because they're not here and it would have been impossible to determine the way he died. I wonder who in this office authorized it?"

Tugging off her gloves, she reached across for the man's file and scanned the pages until she found what she was looking for. "Ah, here it is. The call from the Sydney Harbour Hospital Intensive Care Unit came in on Saturday night from my brother and..." She continued to scan the hospital notes and then looked up at her boss. "You were the one who gave consent."

Richard nodded. "Yes, that's right. I remember now. I was on call over the weekend. I discussed the patient with Alistair. He was of the opinion the man had died of an aneurysm on the brain. His family was adamant he'd wanted to donate his organs. Apparently, one of his children had died at a young age from a heart defect. The child could have been saved had she received a donor heart in time." He shrugged. "The story touched me. I couldn't see any harm in harvesting what was more than likely *not* involved in his cause of death. His family was beyond supportive. No need letting healthy organs go to waste, right?"

"You won't get an argument from me," Samantha replied. "My mother's been waiting for a transplant for years. I'm all for harvesting whatever can be used."

Phillip made a sound of disapproval. Sam turned to face him. "I take it you're not in agreement?"

"No way! I guess it's all right for people who don't know what goes on in a place like this, but for me..." He shuddered. "Besides, I'm a Catholic and I want to head off to the afterlife intact, the same way I came into it. Is that too much to ask? Lucky for me, my wife, Maree, feels the same way."

Sam stared at him, a little taken aback. She'd known him for years and had never suspected he felt that way. The fact that he was Catholic was hardly an excuse. The Vatican's official position was in favor of organ donation. Sam couldn't help but think of her mother. Every day without a new kidney brought her that much closer to death. Sam couldn't fathom why anyone would choose not to be an organ donor.

"Think of the number of people you could help," she replied, trying hard to maintain a calm and objective manner. "You could save a person's life, bring sight to the blind—achieve any number of worthy outcomes. Why wouldn't you want to be part of that?"

Phillip shrugged, but his expression told her he remained adamant. "I guess, but why does it have to be me? There are millions and millions of people in the world. If even a quarter of them donated organs and tissue on their death, we wouldn't have a problem. There'd be more than enough body parts to go around and we wouldn't be having this discussion."

"But there aren't enough people donating! That's the problem," Sam said, tugging on a fresh pair of latex gloves and resuming the autopsy. "Governments and hospitals do what they can, but there's no guarantee it will make a difference. Look at you! You're living in a city that's recently been inundated with advertising, countless media events about the positive side to organ donation, and more—and you're still unconvinced organ donation's a good thing."

"You're right," Phillip said. "Maybe if I got paid for it ahead of time, I'd reconsider. You can't underestimate the appeal of the dollar. It would be nice to pay off my mortgage."

Sam gasped in outrage. "Phillip Bond! I don't believe you just—"

Too late, she caught the twinkle in his hazel eyes. "Dammit, Phillip! That's not fair," she responded without heat. "You should have warned me you were joking before I got all hot and bothered. You're lucky my hands are covered in blood and body matter or I might just reach over there and grab you around the throat."

He laughed. "You'd have to catch me, first. Besides, who'd laugh at your lame jokes if I wasn't around?"

Snorting at their nonsense, Richard shook his head. "You two deserve each other. I'll leave you to it." He turned away, heading in the direction of the exit. "Happy birthday, Sam, and have a good day!" he called out as he disappeared through the doorway.

Samantha glanced back at Phillip. "You're right. Absolutely no one. But just for the record, you're not the only person in here who finds my jokes funny."

He laughed and Sam laughed with him. It wasn't her place to judge him or his beliefs. He was entitled to his opinion on organ donation and other issues too. His ideas didn't have to mesh with hers for them to be friends. If her mother wasn't in such desperate need of a transplant, Sam might not feel quite so strongly about it. She owed him an apology.

"I'm sorry," she said.

"For what?"

"For giving you a hard time. Your opinion is just as valid as mine. You're entitled to leave this world with everything you came in with."

"Just as you're entitled to leave without all your body parts."

"Agreed," Sam said and stuck out her hand.

From across the table, Phillip leaned over and shook it. "Agreed."

Sam looked down at their gloved hands, both covered in blood and gore. It should have been distasteful, but it wasn't. It was all just part of the job. A job she loved.

Chapter 2

Dear Diary,

Day after day, week after week, I see healthy human organs and tissue going to waste. Why people set limits on their generosity, I'll never understand. If they're prepared to donate body parts, why stop at just one or two? There are so many organs and tissue in a body that can be put to good use. So many lives could be saved if they gave more! So many patients could be healed! So many people could be given back their quality of life!

It doesn't seem right that the donors get to pick and choose: 'You can take this one and that one, but not that one or that one. I'm taking those ones with me to the grave.'

It frustrates me to no end. It's no wonder I've taken matters into my own hands...

———————

Sam pressed the button on the city bus to alert the driver to stop. The bell dinged over the muted conversations and the noise coming from the heavy lunchtime traffic outside. She'd planned to drive into the city to meet her brother, but the time had gotten away from her. Finding a parking space would be a nightmare and she hated to be late, so she'd opted for the nearest public transport.

Tugging her coat tighter around her, she stepped off the bus and breathed in the brisk winter air. Though the heat from the crowds and passing cars took away the bite, there was still a distinct chill in the breeze that gently lifted her hair. She glanced at her watch and picked up her pace. She still had two blocks to go. Her brother had taken time off from his busy schedule to meet her for lunch and she didn't want to keep him waiting.

With a sigh of relief, she spied her favorite restaurant half a block ahead. While it wasn't one of the swanky ones on the waterfront, the food was great and the service was friendly—and they knew her well enough that generally, she could secure a table without a reservation. She climbed the few steps that led into the restaurant and saw Alistair sitting at the bar. He turned, caught sight of her and came forward.

"Hi," she said and stood on tiptoes to give him a kiss.

"Hi, yourself," he replied and gave her a brief hug. "Happy birthday, little sis."

"Thank you. I'm always pleased to see another one come around."

Alistair laughed. "You must be one of the very few women who do."

"Well, in my line of work, you come to realize how finite life really is. The alternative to having birthdays is pretty grim."

Alistair smiled in agreement. Flinging an arm around her shoulders, he steered her back toward the bar. She looked up at him and raised a brow.

"I spoke to May-Ling when I arrived," he said, correctly interpreting her unspoken question. "She's promised us the very next table. I told her it was your birthday and that we're both on our lunch breaks. She was upset that she couldn't seat us immediately, especially on your special day."

"I guess we should have booked ahead."

"I'm sure it won't take long. You're one of her favorite customers."

Sam smiled. It was probably true. She spent many an evening collecting takeout from the Thai restaurant at the southern end of the city. Although it wasn't directly on her route home, she often made the effort to detour that way and order some of May-Ling's scrumptious fare. The spring rolls and money bags were like nothing she'd found elsewhere and the yellow curry chicken—it was beyond divine.

"What are you drinking?" Alistair asked, tugging out his wallet.

"Seeing as you're paying, let's order a bottle of my favorite champagne."

Alistair's eyebrows shot up. "Wow, you want a bottle of Moet? I take it you're off for the rest of the day."

"Perhaps I'm just feeling adventurous. It's my birthday, after all. Are you going to join me?"

"Sorry, I'm rostered on until midnight. You won't be getting drunk with me today."

"Who said anything about getting drunk? Besides, I have to return to work, too."

"Really? When you asked for a bottle of the expensive stuff, I assumed you were going to make the most of it." He smiled and gave her a wink and she was reminded how lucky she was to have such a wonderful older brother.

"Just joking. A glass of Merlot will be fine." He nodded approval and turned to give the bartender their order.

Samantha sat back on the stool and surveyed Alistair. The custom-made, charcoal-gray suit fitted him to perfection. His black hair, the same shade as hers, was thick and wavy. The small patches of gray at his temples only enhanced his physical appeal and gave him an air of experience and sophistication that was matched by his tasteful yellow-and-navy striped designer tie. Even at forty-four, he was a man people noticed. It was little wonder he'd been chosen by the Sydney Harbour Hospital to head their organ donation campaign

The glass of red wine and a Diet Coke appeared in the bartender's hands. He set the drinks before them. Murmuring her thanks, Sam took a sip of the wine, savoring the rich, mellow taste. She turned back to her brother. Alistair took a sip from his Diet Coke and then sat the glass back on the bar. Sam couldn't help but chuckle. "Watching your weight?"

"It doesn't hurt to show some restraint, especially at my age." He slapped his flat stomach. "Since I took on the role of head of the Organ Donation for Transplantation Unit, I don't get time to work out like I used to."

She shook her head, but refrained from commenting. Alistair had never been overweight. "How's work?" she asked instead.

He shrugged. "Busy, you know how it is, especially at this time of year."

"Yes, winter can be such a bitch and unfortunately, it hits the most vulnerable hardest: babies and the elderly. You'd see it even more than me. Bronchitis and chronic chest infections deteriorate into pneumonia... And then there are the accidental deaths. Elderly people who don't turn up the thermostat and consequently freeze; or they leave a heater on and their house burns down. I've lost count of the number of autopsies I've done on fire victims over the years."

"Yes, it's tough and this winter's been longer and colder than most. Frosts nearly every day this week. The deaths are tragic, but there is a silver lining. It means more potential organ donors." He winked at her, but Sam's thoughts were distracted. She was reminded of her earlier conversation with Phillip.

"I wonder if that accounts for the recent trend," she said slowly.

"What trend?"

"The increase in donor deaths."

"What do you mean?"

"There's been a noticeable rise in the number

of bodies coming through the morgue with donated organs removed. Phillip and I were talking about it earlier today. Your comment made me think the increase might be due to nothing more than the unseasonably cold weather."

"Phillip's one of the pathologists you work with, right?"

"Yes. We've worked together for years. I knew him out at Westmead. He surprised me today by—"

May-Ling's arrival cut short their conversation. After greeting Sam with exuberant birthday greetings and a warm hug, the owner of the restaurant escorted them to a table.

"Your usual, Miss Samantha?" the old woman asked with a twinkle in her eye.

"Yes, thank you, May-Ling, but seeing as my brother's paying, let's double it and I'll take a serving home for dinner."

May-Ling's smile widened and she glanced at Alistair. He waved away her unspoken question. "Whatever my sister wants. After all, it's her birthday."

Samantha grinned. "I like the way you think. Have I told you lately you're my favorite brother?"

"Gee, thanks," Alistair replied, his voice dry. "Considering I'm your *only* brother, I feel beyond special."

"Oh, don't get yourself all worked up over that. It's a tiny, insignificant detail. I'm sure if I did have any other brothers, you'd still be my favorite." She lifted her wine glass to her lips. Giving him a wink over the rim, she swallowed a healthy mouthful.

Alistair picked up his drink. "Here's to my favorite little sister," he said and clinked his glass with hers.

Sam smiled in surprise. "Wow, considering you have *two* other little sisters, this is quite a coup! Wait until I tell Jessie and Ava," Sam said, referring to their siblings. "They might never speak to you again."

"Of course they will," Alistair replied with a lazy smile. "They love and admire their older brother as much as you do and they'll forgive me. It *is* your birthday, after all."

Sam screwed up her napkin and tossed it at his head. He caught it before it connected and set it down on the table, the corners of his eyes crinkling with laughter. Her heart warmed. It had been awhile since she'd seen her brother so carefree. The financial stress of providing the best possible education and opportunities for his children, and starting his new job had left him with little time to laugh and joke with his family. She was even more grateful that he'd taken the time to be with her now.

"Thanks for taking me to lunch, Alistair. I really appreciate it. And...it means a lot."

He averted his gaze, but she could tell he was pleased.

"No problem, Sammie. I'd do it for anyone."

She looked around for the napkin to toss it back at his head, but he still had it in his hand. Reading her mind, he smiled at her and made a point of setting it out of her reach. She made a sound of mock frustration and took another sip of wine.

Alistair's expression sobered. "Sorry I didn't make it to Mom's dialysis appointment last week. I got caught up in surgery. How did it go?"

Sam thought of their mother, fighting to stay alive, and her chest tightened. She drew in a deep breath and eased it out. "Not so good. You know how it is."

Alistair nodded, shadows darkening his brown eyes. "Yeah, I called in to see her over the weekend. She's going downhill fast." He cursed aloud. "It's ironic, isn't it? I work in the Organ Donation for Transplantation Unit at Sydney's most prestigious hospital. I'm the head surgeon of the retrieval team. With a college education and all those fancy titles and yet, I can't help my own mother. I can't save her from her pain. If she doesn't get a transplant soon, she'll die."

He slapped his hand on the table in frustration. Startled, Sam jumped, but remained silent. She didn't blame him for losing control. She knew exactly how he felt.

"Why is it so hard for people to make the decision?" he asked, his cheeks becoming flushed. "Why do so many of them leave their wishes unstated? Do you know how hard it is to approach a grieving relative and ask them to donate their loved one's body parts? Who wants to think of something like that at a moment when their world has been turned on its end and they're saying their good-byes? Nobody. And that's the problem.

"Demand for organs and tissue far outstrips supply. There are thousands of people like our mother all over the world, waiting, just waiting for someone to die. And not just to die, but to donate their organs and tissue to another. Why is it so hard for some people to contemplate donating their organs? What does it matter if they go to a stranger? A friend? An enemy? Surely the fact *someone* is going to benefit is what counts?"

He blew out a breath laced with frustration. Sam reached across the table and squeezed his hand. "It's not your fault the rates of donors have historically been so low, Alistair. You're doing the best you can. And it's not your fault you weren't a match for Mom," she added quietly. "Just like it isn't mine or Jessie's or Ava's."

His expression showed he remained unconvinced and she tried again to reassure him. "There's no denying it sucks, Alistair, but that's the way it is. The only thing we can do is hope and pray a donor's found in time. I just hope your campaign has more success with other Sydneysiders than it has with Phillip," she muttered.

Alistair frowned. "What do you mean?"

She sighed. "After working together for years, I found out this morning that Phillip's dead against organ donation. Despite everything, he's unconvinced."

"Why?"

She shrugged. "Religious beliefs, mainly. He wants to maintain his body's integrity for its journey to the afterlife."

Alistair shook his head in disbelief. "But the Church—"

"Yes, I know. It doesn't seem to make a difference."

Alistair swore under his breath and his expression turned bleak. "What the hell are we supposed to do when intelligent people hold such stupid, uninformed opinions?"

"Not necessarily uninformed or stupid," Samantha countered gently. "I don't agree with him, but everyone's entitled to their opinion. The body parts are theirs, after all."

Her brother took a deep breath and blew it out on a heavy sigh. "Yeah, I guess you're right. But that's also the problem, too."

He fell silent. To Sam's relief, after a moment, his shoulders relaxed. He picked up his glass and drank and then turned to look at her again.

"I'm sorry, Sammie. I shouldn't have said anything. It's your birthday! We should be talking about happier things."

"Like what?"

"Like...your love life. That's always an interesting topic. How's the online dating thing going?"

Sam pulled a face, wishing she'd never told him. "Do we have to talk about this?"

He grinned. "Of course we do! I love hearing about all the weirdoes and freaks you converse with online. It brightens my day."

"They're not all weirdoes and freaks!" she protested. "Most of them are just lonely men and women looking for the love of their lives. You ought to read their bios. Some of them are hilarious at the outset, but gradually, you can't help feeling sorry for them and hope they find what they're after."

"Why did you join?"

She averted her gaze, uncomfortable with the turn of the conversation. "I don't know. I thought it would be fun and I'm tired of being single."

"What happened to meeting men the old-fashioned way? I'm sure I could hook you up with one of my colleagues."

"No offense, Alistair but the guys you hang out with are mostly your age—old."

He pretended to look hurt. "Ouch! You're being a little harsh, Samantha. They're not all as old as me. Besides, someone's better than no one, surely? You're thirty-four, Sammie. Time's slipping away."

She grimaced. "You don't need to remind me. It's my birthday, remember? But it's easy for you to say that. You met and married the love of your life in college. You didn't have to look around and wonder if it would ever happen for you." She paused and took a sip of Merlot. Determined to steer the conversation back to more comfortable ground, she smiled at her brother and asked, "How is my favorite sister-in-law?"

Alistair offered her a wry grin. "Nancy's your *only* sister-in-law, Samantha."

"Oh, so she is. She's still my favorite."

He laughed aloud and shook his head. "You're incorrigible, Samantha Wolfe. Has anyone told you that?"

With a finger up to her lip, Sam pretended to think about his question. "Um... Now that you mention it, I think the answer's yes and I'm almost certain the last person to say it was you."

"Yes, and I meant it then and I mean it now. But

to answer your earlier question, Nancy's as beautiful and sweet as ever. Busy with her charity projects and ferrying the kids around. You must come over one of these nights for dinner. Lexie and Brendan would love to see you."

Sam smiled. "How are they? It feels like ages since I saw my gorgeous niece and nephew."

"Brendan is busy with football and girls. He'll be sixteen in a couple of months. Lexie is thirteen going on thirty and giving her mother plenty of grief. Puberty and teenage girls are another thing altogether. I don't know how Mom survived with three of you."

Sam laughed. "I'm sure we weren't that bad. Jessie and Ava weren't exactly difficult and I was, of course, the perfect angel. At least with us all so close in age, she got it over and done with quickly. Some people have it drag on for years. Phillip has four girls and each of them are five years apart. Imagine having four daughters going through puberty, one after the other—for the better part of twenty years!"

Alistair looked horrified. "Oh, my God! That poor guy! What's his wife like?"

"Maree seems nice. I don't know her well, but they've been together forever. They were high school sweethearts. Phillip even has a tattoo on his shoulder with the first letter of their names entwined in a cherub. It's very sweet."

"Well, I'm glad it's them, and not me, raising four women. How old are the kids?"

"The oldest has left home already. She graduated with honors from the University of

Technology. I think she studied fashion design, or something like that. She scored an apprenticeship with one of the top Sydney designers, so she must be good. The next one is studying veterinary science at Sydney University. I think she's in her final year. Then there are the two youngest girls. They're still at school—fifteen and ten, respectively. Phillip's always bemoaning the cost of their school fees."

"Tell me about it," Alistair said. "Between Brendan and Lexie, I pay more than one-hundred-and-twenty grand a year and that doesn't take into account all the incidentals like uniforms, excursions, pocket money, sporting engagements and the rest. By the time they finish their education, I could have bought a small apartment in Bondi."

Sam shook her head and chuckled. "Is it worth it, then? The private school education? You and I attended a public school. So did Jessie and Ava. It didn't do us any harm. Look at you, the Sydney Harbour Hospital's most celebrated surgeon. I'm a doctor, too. Jessie's on the way to making partner at her law firm and Ava's psychiatry practice is going ahead in leaps and bounds. I'd say the public education system didn't do us any harm."

"You're right," Alistair said thoughtfully. "I guess it's seeing Mom struggle so hard to provide for us, and despite all her efforts, she was never able to give us all that... The fact is, I can. And I want to make her proud. I guess I also like the prestige that comes with sending your kids to a top-rated private school. It's a heady feeling when you realize you're in a position to give your kids the best."

"I suppose so. Anyway, it's your money. Do what you like with it. If giving your kids a private school education makes everyone happy, it's money well spent."

He looked at her quizzically, a tender smile hovering around his lips. "When did you get to be so wise?"

Sam was prevented from answering when May-Ling and one of her helpers arrived with steaming trays of food. As Sam filled her plate, her stomach reminded her it had been hours since breakfast when she'd chewed on a piece of toast spread with Vegemite.

"*Mm*, it smells delicious," she said and then took her first fragrant bite. The spring roll was everything it promised to be and she quickly finished it and reached for another. Alistair watched her with amusement.

"When was the last time you ate?"

The fact that he still worried about little things like that warmed her through. It had been years since she'd left home and yet, he still looked out for her. She couldn't have asked for a better brother and that was the truth.

More food arrived. They continued to eat in silence and Sam finished her glass of wine. She longed to order another, but she hadn't been lying when she'd told Alistair she needed to return to work. There were three more autopsies waiting in the fridge and then there was the paperwork. Regretfully, one glass was her limit.

"Don't give up on him, will you?" Alistair said quietly, setting his fork aside.

Sam stopped eating mid-bite, a little confused. "Who?"

"Your Mr Right. You'll find the perfect someone. He's out there. I'm sure of it."

She blinked back a sudden rush of tears and marveled again about the caring and sensitivity of her brother. "Thanks," she whispered, her voice husky with emotion.

Alistair stared at her a moment longer and then glanced at his watch. Wiping his mouth with the napkin, he pushed away from the table. "I'm going to have to go, Sammie. Duty calls."

She opened her mouth to protest his early departure and then closed it again. He wouldn't leave without good reason. He was crazy busy. She was grateful for the time he'd given her. She'd seen more of him over their short lunch date than she had in the past month. He leaned over and kissed her on the cheek.

"You need to get out more, little sis. You're looking way too pale. Too much time spent working in the cold and dark with all those dead bodies. You could always switch your specialty and come over to the lighter side. Our patients talk and respond to jokes and sometimes even thank us and we actually get to see the sun for more than a snippet of time. I could look into a vacancy for you, if you're interested. There would always be room at the hospital for someone with your skills."

She was shaking her head back and forth, even

before he finished. "Thanks for the offer, but I'm more than content where I am. The dead need help, too. I like to listen to their stories, help their families find peace. Someone has to care enough to do it. Besides, haven't you heard? Too much sun isn't good for the complexion. I'm thirty-four. I don't need to hasten the ageing process." She grinned and was relieved when he grinned back. "Call Mom soon, okay?" she added gently. "She worries when she doesn't hear from you regularly."

"I saw her on the weekend, remember?"

"Yes, but none of us know how much longer she'll be here. You're her first born child and only son. She needs to hear from you more often," she repeated.

He leaned over and gave her another peck on the cheek. "Okay. Just for you. Because today's your birthday and I love you and I love our mom. Is that good enough?"

She nodded, unable to speak over the lump that had lodged itself in her throat.

"I really have to go, Sammie. Nancy and I are attending a black-tie function at the Hilton tonight. Another joint effort between the government and the hospital. I'm expected to meet and greet and smile for the cameras and all the while do my best to increase awareness about organ donations. So, though I might not call Mom as often as I should, I'm doing my bit. You're not the only one who wants to see her well."

"Of course not. You care about her as much as any of us. We all know that."

"When is she due in again for treatment?"

"Jessie sat with her this morning. She'll be back in the Dialysis Unit again from nine the day after tomorrow."

He nodded. "Good. I'll do my best to drop in and see her."

She smiled her gratitude. "Thank you."

"I'll fix up the bill on my way out. Happy birthday, Sammie. I'll talk to you soon." And with that, he was gone.

CHAPTER 3

The sound of Detective Sergeant Rohan Coleridge's siren was as deafening as the pounding of his heart. Another rush of adrenaline surged through him at the thought of what lay ahead. A call had come over the radio about a two-car pile-up that also involved a fuel tanker. He didn't want to imagine what might happen if the tanker was leaking and they didn't get there in time.

He glanced across at his partner. Detective Bryce Sutcliffe looked equally grim. The scratchy reports they'd obtained from dispatch had filled them both with dread. At least one car had passengers trapped in their vehicle. Emergency response teams from all over the city were, right now, accelerating toward the accident. As luck would have it, Rohan and Bryce had been interviewing a witness to an unrelated matter only a few blocks away. Closest to the site of the accident, they now expected to be the first responders on the scene.

Another wave of adrenaline flooded Rohan's veins. Mentally, he began to think about what might need to be done. A leaking fuel tanker was a time bomb. The first thing was to ensure the safety of any passengers who were still alive and pray to God it wasn't too late.

"There it is!" Bryce called out, tension in his voice.

With a squeal of tires, Rohan swung the squad car onto the sidewalk and braked hard. Shoving it into Park, he leaped from the vehicle with Bryce on his heels.

"You take the white Toyota. I'll check the Nissan," Rohan shouted and took off at a run.

Racing toward one of the sedans, Rohan was relieved to see the tanker driver had made it out of his truck and was now stumbling across the grassy verge that adjoined the pavement. With his heart in his throat, Rohan skidded to a halt beside the passenger door of the Nissan.

Peering through the window, he made out the shape of two people in the front of the car. The sound of a baby screaming reached his ears. He wrenched open the front door and came up short. The front of the Nissan had folded in on the occupants. Steel and plastic lay twisted and broken, leaving the inside front compartment of the vehicle almost unrecognizable.

"Hey, can you hear me?" he shouted to the adults in the front of the car. Both the driver and passenger were covered in blood. Neither of them responded. Rohan checked the passenger for a pulse and found none. Reaching across the mess of metal wreckage, he searched the driver for signs of life. Again, nothing.

Pulling back, he stood upright and the sharp smell of gasoline scorched his nostrils. His heartbeat kicked into overdrive. Any minute the tanker could blow. He looked across at Bryce and saw that he was dragging someone out of the Toyota.

"How many?" he shouted, his panic increasing with every passing second.

"Only the driver. He's pretty badly hurt, but I've managed to pull him free. How about you?"

Rohan shook his head at the same time he tried to wrench open the back door. It was stuck. "It's already too late for the occupants in the front, but there's a child in the back."

The baby's screams increased in intensity, along with the wail of more sirens. Rohan looked up and spied two fire engines bearing down on them. It seemed like there were blue and red strobe emergency lights everywhere. He pulled hard on the door handle again and finally felt it give. With a shout of triumph, he tore the panel open and bent down to rescue the child.

The baby was strapped into a car seat that was wedged hard up against the front seat. No matter what Rohan did, he couldn't seem to free the straps. The baby's screaming pierced his eardrums and yet he continued to work at a frantic pace. The smell of gas grew stronger and he knew it was only a matter of time. As if reading his panicked thoughts, Rohan heard one of the fire captains shouting at the crowd.

"Clear the area! Everybody get back! This tanker could blow at any minute."

Working even more feverishly, Rohan cursed when the straps continued to hold. The only way to free the child was to cut through them.

"I need a knife!" he shouted. "For Christ's sake, someone bring me a knife!"

Bryce materialized at his elbow with a blade in his hand. Rohan didn't question where he'd gotten it from. He was just relieved to have it.

"Rohan, we have to get out of here! That tanker's going to go!"

The urgency in Bryce's voice and the panic in his eyes told Rohan all he needed to know. This wasn't some training exercise where any minute the drill sergeant would blow his whistle and call it off. This was the real thing and peoples' lives were on the line. His, included.

Sawing through the thick straps that held the baby in place, Rohan's heart thumped so hard it felt like he was about to die. The baby screamed, his face a bright red, but Rohan continued to work away.

"Rohan! For fuck's sake! You have to get out of the way!"

Ignoring Bryce, he cut through the last strap and almost collapsed with relief. With no time to linger, he snatched up the baby and hauled the child out of the car. Running faster than he ever had in his life, he headed for safety, away from the tanker.

It seemed like only seconds later that he was deafened by an enormous explosion. The ground shook from the force of it. He stumbled and almost fell. Covering the baby's head with his jacket, he shielded the child from harm.

"Get down, Rohan! It could blow again!"

Rohan nodded at Bryce to show him he understood and half-crawled, half-ran toward the row of ambulances parked well clear of the danger zone. It seemed like a lifetime passed before he finally reached the safety of the emergency vehicles, the baby still in his arms. Paramedics ran toward him, reaching for the child. He handed the screaming bundle over with a grateful sigh.

"It's all right, Detective. We have him. You can let go now."

Rohan prised his fingers open and stepped away. Residual shock set in and he began to tremble uncontrollably. Another paramedic came toward him and he could see the concern on her face. A moment later, everything went fuzzy and he fell face down on the ground.

―――――――――

Alistair stared at the computer screen in front of him and scanned through his emails. Many were from pharmaceutical companies and other medical supply businesses, flogging their products. He looked at them briefly before consigning them to the trash.

As he'd promised Sam at her birthday lunch, he'd sat with their mother earlier in the day while she underwent one of her thrice-weekly dialysis sessions and had done his best to distract her from what was happening. Though it had only been a few days, he'd been shocked at her appearance. Thin and sallow, she looked like someone close to death. Sadness and panic filled his gut. He didn't want to believe they wouldn't find a donor kidney, but time was fast running out.

He cursed under his breath and a surge of frustration flooded through him. What he'd told Sam was true. It aggravated him beyond measure that he was the head of the Organ Donation for Transplantation Unit in the largest hospital in Australia and couldn't find a single kidney for his dying mother.

Pushing the depressing thoughts aside, he continued to scroll through his emails. One in particular caught his eye. It had been sent from a company purporting to be in the business of supplying human organ and tissue to international agencies, who then supplied the donated body parts to medical facilities who undertook the transplants. Perhaps they could help locate a kidney for his mother... Alistair frowned and scrolled down further, reading as he went.

According to the email, Biologistics was a company based in the US and had received approval for its business from the American Food and Drug Administration. The FDA was responsible for overseeing the legitimacy of such companies and they'd apparently given Biologistics five stars. Doctor Charles Shillington, the CEO of Biologistics, had contacted Alistair with a view to making him a proposal: *Would he be interested in helping them to supply the market?* The email implied that if his answer was in the affirmative, he'd be extremely well compensated.

Compensated? An interesting idea. Up until now, he'd been the one doing the compensating. It had been tough, in addition to paying all the bills for his children, but he'd considered the added expense an acceptable sacrifice for the worthy work he'd been doing. To receive financial gain would make it even more satisfying.

Alistair's heart began to pound. Trafficking in human tissue was illegal in most countries, including Australia and the US. What the hell was Shillington getting at? Was the email even legitimate? And if so, how, and why had they chosen to contact *him*?

Typing the name "Biologistics" into Google, Alistair waited for the search results and was surprised to discover the company had a website. Until he found it, he'd been sure the email was a hoax. Clicking on the link, he read through the details on the homepage.

Like the email claimed, the company was not only legitimate and FDA approved, it had been established ten years earlier and there were pages of testimonials from doctors lauding the service provided by the company. A page dedicated to its CEO, Charles Shillington, indicated the doctor had established the company in order to fill a need. He wanted to help facilitate the business of organ and tissue harvesting by sourcing good quality body parts and making them available to those in need.

And those who could afford them, Alistair thought dryly.

Knowing he'd probably regret it, but curious to know more, Alistair shot off a reply. Within minutes, he received another email.

Doctor Wolfe,

I'm so pleased to receive your email. I appreciate you have several questions about our business and exactly what we do. To answer your first question, we found your contact details on the Sydney Harbour Hospital website. For some time, we've been looking for more people to join our team. And not just any people. We need the right kind of people. People who understand our goals and who are willing to work with us to help us achieve them.

In the US alone, more than two million products derived from human tissue change hands between suppliers and medical facilities each year. We are in an industry that promotes treatments and products that literally allow the blind to see and the lame to walk. Who wouldn't want to be a part of that?

We are a legitimate, FDA-approved company and while you quite rightly point out that it's illegal to buy or sell human tissue, it is permissible in the US to pay service fees to cover the costs of finding, storing, and processing human tissue. I understand the same rules might not apply in your country and it is important that you weigh up any potential risk against the benefits. Pleased be assured, the benefits are many.

Apart from the immense satisfaction members

of our team receive knowing they are a part of something almost miraculous, Biologistics rewards its suppliers very generously. We are prepared to pay a handsome sum for good and useable human tissue. All you have to do is let us know that you would like to be part of this exciting venture.

The email had been signed: Charles Shillington, CEO, Biologistics. Alistair reread the email twice more and was filled with a growing sense of excitement. He did his best to keep it in check, but he couldn't deny the possibility of contributing to a tissue donation scheme on such a magnificent scale was mind-blowing. The fact that he could make a little money from it was an added bonus. If luck prevailed, it might even cover some of his kids' annual school fees. With fingers that weren't quite steady, he shot off another reply.

What kind of money are you talking?

Once again, he received a reply in minutes.

To put it more plainly, for every five pounds of disease-free human tissue you provide, we will pay you the sum of $50,000 US dollars—deposited directly into your nominated account. All you have to do is say the word. We'll handle pickup and transportation—the logistics.

Alistair's eyes bugged out of his head. *Fifty grand?* For five pounds of tissue? How could they afford to pay him that much? He had no idea there could be so much money involved in the human tissue industry. *And, why would he?* Trafficking in human body parts was illegal in Australia. Even human tissue imported into Australia was regulated by the government and closely scrutinized. There was no possibility a company such as Biologistics could be established here. *Was it possible to get away with such a thing in the US?*

Becoming more and more curious, Alistair conducted further research via the Internet. More than an hour later, he'd discovered the trade in human tissue was not only allowed in the US, but flourishing. Like Charles had stated, it was illegal to buy and sell the tissue, but it appeared millions of dollars were made by compensating those people supplying, storing and processing it—and there appeared to be little, if no, government scrutiny.

Though tissue banks were required to be registered with the FDA, it meant no more than filling out a form and waiting for an inspection. From what Alistair had read on the Internet, at least thirty-five percent of active, registered US tissue banks had never been inspected and of those that had been, the FDA had yet to shut a single one down over concern about illicit activities.

Could it really be that simple? Human tissue went to waste in Alistair's hospital every single day. For a long time, he'd mourned its loss, frustrated that nothing could be done. Was this the answer he'd been searching for? Illegal or not, the process ensured that any useable tissue would be recycled and used again.

Like Charles Shillington had said, it meant making the blind see, helping lame people walk... And that was only the beginning. It might not help Alistair's mom, but someone would get the benefit. Many someones. *How could he not want to be part of that?*

And if he made a little—okay, a lot of money—on the side, where was the harm in it? Desperate people got the transplants they needed and he got to put his kids through school with less financial strain than otherwise. It seemed like a win-win situation. Besides, it wasn't like he hadn't already broken the law in the name of the greater good.

The idea of harvesting organs in addition to those they had consent to remove, struck him late one night when he was suturing closed a legal donor's chest. He'd silently bemoaned the fact that so many useable organs were heading straight for the grave and wondered what could be done about it. It was late May. Winter had been fast closing in and with it came a naturally occurring increase in the number of deaths. The timing couldn't have been more perfect. It was then that the idea formed into a plan. By early July, he'd recruited Richard and had been acting on it ever since.

When Samantha mentioned she'd noticed the rise in the number of donor bodies, he'd almost choked on his Diet Coke. While most of the bodies he illegally harvested from went to funeral homes and crematoriums scattered around the inner city, a small number of them ended up in the Glebe Morgue. He'd hoped that they'd slide by unnoticed; that with the number of forensic pathologists on staff, the rise in donor bodies wouldn't cause anyone to become alarmed, but it appeared he hadn't been so lucky.

Either that, or Richard Davis hadn't done as he'd promised. The deputy coroner had assured Alistair at the outset Richard would make certain the bodies Alistair handled would personally be autopsied by him. That way, none of his staff would be any the wiser. After Sam's comment, it was now obvious that hadn't happened. The last thing he needed was to have his own sister asking questions, or even thinking about it, at all.

If he accepted Biologistics' offer, he'd be forced to illegally harvest the tissues of many more patients in the future. The company expected him to sign a contract and a quota would be specified. Now that Samantha's suspicions had been raised, it would be safer to ignore the autopsy cases and concentrate his efforts only on the bodies being sent directly to the funeral homes and crematoriums. There was much less likelihood an undertaker would put his mind to the fact that he was seeing way more bodies with surgical scars than he had in the past—if he thought about it at all. As well, there was no call for any paperwork to accompany those bodies.

The more Alistair pondered it, the more it seemed like a good idea. He'd have done it from the outset if Richard hadn't promised he'd look after him, in return for a small fee and Alistair hadn't taken him at his word. As far as Alistair had been aware, the arrangement had worked and they'd both walked away satisfied. Alistair had quietly and illegally set about increasing the donor rates and Richard had endorsed them and collected his money.

But for now, with Samantha possibly asking questions, it was just too risky to continue to involve the city morgue and its staff. He'd call Richard and tell him the deal was over and hopefully that would be the end of it. The deputy coroner might wonder about Alistair's change of heart, but if Alistair threw in a couple extra thousand in the final payoff to his friend, it would hopefully do the trick and keep the man quiet. So far, the deputy coroner had gotten more than ten thousand dollars out of him—money Alistair's family could have used. The man had no cause for complaint.

––––––––

"What do you mean, you're quitting?" Richard Davis demanded several hours later.

Alistair looked quickly around him at the dozen or so patrons scattered around the dimly lit, inner city bar, but thankfully, no one appeared to be listening to them. "Keep your voice down!" he ordered in a harsh whisper. "We don't want the whole world to know."

Richard glanced to his left and right and then leaned closer over the small round table that separated them. "I'm not ready for you to quit. I need that extra money. You can't get me involved in this and then, out of the blue, tell me you've had enough. It isn't fair. I won't let you do it!"

Alistair stared at the man and saw the weakness

in his chin. *Why hadn't Alistair remembered what a poor excuse of a man the deputy coroner really was?* He bit down hard on a sigh. It was too late for regrets.

"If you stop, I'll go to the police."

Richard's words penetrated Alistair's brain. He tensed. *How the hell had he managed to get himself into this situation?* He and Richard had gone through med school together. They'd been good friends, almost inseparable until Alistair met Nancy. Then love and life got in the way and the two friends had drifted apart. Richard had gone into forensic medicine and Alistair had become a surgeon.

Although they'd lost touch over the years, when Alistair came upon the idea to harvest additional organs from donor patients, Richard was one of the first people that came to mind to become his accomplice. The deputy coroner's father had died from liver cancer when Richard was still a child. Richard knew firsthand that a transplant might have saved his dad if a donor liver had been available. He'd grown up a passionate supporter of organ donation.

"You need me, Alistair, and you know it. That's the reason you came to me in the first place."

Alistair's jaw clenched. What Richard said was true. When a deceased organ donor required an autopsy, the senior doctor presiding over the death had to obtain the coroner's, or one of his deputies' authorization prior to any organ harvesting going ahead.

Of course, Alistair could have simply bypassed

the coronial cases and concentrated on those donors headed directly for the funeral homes and crematoriums, but at the time it seemed like such a waste of good organs to let even those few donors go. Having a college buddy in the coroner's office seemed too good an opportunity to let slide. Knowing Richard's attitude toward organ donation was what cemented the matter.

But circumstances had changed. With Samantha's curiosity piqued, it had become too risky and Alistair had hoped to shut down the morgue arm of their operation. But now, Richard had dropped a bombshell. *Was he stupid enough to carry out his threat and go to the police?*

With a sigh, Alistair squeezed his eyes shut for a few moments and ignored the pounding in his head. Opening his eyes, he stared at Richard across the table and tried to gage the other man's sincerity. Richard refused to meet his gaze.

"I mean it, Alistair. If you stop harvesting those extra organs and don't continue to throw a little money my way, I'll go to the police and tell them everything."

"Why would you do a silly thing like that?" Alistair asked, working hard to keep his voice even. "It would destroy both of us."

"I don't want to, but if you quit, you'll give me no choice. I need the money and... It makes me feel good knowing more people are benefiting from our actions. You can't stop now. Besides, I'll tell the police it was all your idea and that you forced me to go along with it."

"You're bluffing. The police will hardly believe a

mere surgeon had the wherewithal to intimidate the deputy state coroner."

"Then I'll tell them I knew nothing about it. That you called, I authorized it, but you gave me false information. I'll tell them you told me the next of kin had consented; that they were supportive of their loved ones' wishes. It will be your word against mine and if the police interview the families..." A sly look came into Richard's eyes and Alistair cursed aloud.

He hadn't thought of that.

Anger surged through him and he gave it its head. "You listen to me, Richard and listen well. If I go down, we'll both go down. You'll spend just as many years in a jail cell as I will. Is that what you want?"

Richard lifted his glass of beer and drank quickly. His schooner was half-empty by the time he set it back down. "Of course not," he replied, wiping the back of his hand across his mouth. "But what other option do I have? Like I told you, I need the money. I have a few...debts I need to pay."

"So pay them. It can't be that much. You must earn a fortune in your job. You don't have a wife or kids draining every cent faster than you can earn it. What's your problem?"

A dark red flush started at the base of Richard's neck and worked its way across his cheeks. He lowered his head in shame. Alistair gritted his teeth and braced himself against what he might hear.

"I like to have a flutter on the horses and the dogs once in a while. You know, a harmless bet here and there. The problem is, they add up and the bookkeepers are at me to pay." Richard swung his head back and forth and Alistair was aghast to notice there were tears in the other man's eyes. "I can't help it, Alistair. It's out of control and I don't know what to do about it."

"How much do you owe?" Alistair asked quietly, his anger slipping away.

"Sixty thousand."

He reeled back against his chair in shock. "Sixty *thousand*! How the hell could you have gambled away that kind of money?"

"I don't know! I don't know! It just happened. I was shocked when they told me how much. But now they're threatening to break my arms and legs—or worse—if I don't find the money soon. That's why you have to keep on doing it, Alistair."

"Even if I do, you're never going to make that kind of money. What are you going to do?"

Like the wall of a dam had suddenly been breached, Richard collapsed into a noisy bout of sobbing. Tears streamed down his cheeks. Alistair looked around them, embarrassed, but only one or two curious stares were thrown their way. Most hotel patrons ignored them.

Alistair thought back to the time when Richard had helped him with chemistry in college. It had been the one subject Alistair had struggled to master. For Richard, it had come easily. For hours and hours on end, he'd patiently walked Alistair through the concepts. Without Richard, Alistair might never have made it through. Alistair owed Richard his career. And that was the truth.

With a sigh, Alistair reached into his back pocket and pulled out a clean handkerchief. Passing it over, he urged the man to get ahold of himself. "Stop crying, Richard. Nothing's as bad as all that. I'll think of something to do."

Richard lifted his head. His eyes were red and swollen, but hope flared briefly in their depths. "Really? You'll come up with a plan?"

Alistair nodded, knowing what he was going to do. "Yes, I'll come up with a plan. In fact, I might already have one. Listen close. I recently received a very interesting email..."

CHAPTER 4

Rohan Coleridge took a moment to wipe the sweat out of his eyes. It was nearing the end of a cold August, the last month of winter, but he still managed to elevate his body temperature with each swing of his arms.

"Whew!" he said, leaning on the ax so that he could catch his breath. "This is hard work, Dad."

His father chuckled and scratched at the hank of white hair that hung over his eyes. "You're going soft, lad. It must be all that time you spend sitting on your ass."

Rohan smiled and took the jibe in the spirit it was intended. He didn't need to be told how proud Bill Coleridge was of his oldest son. Rohan only had to walk into his father's den and see the evidence of his career since he first entered the police academy at the ripe old age of eighteen, to know how his father felt.

"I don't know how you do this every winter," Rohan said. Choosing another log from the wood heap, he lifted the ax again. With a crack that sounded like gunfire, he brought the blade down hard.

"I don't work as rigorously as you do, son. I only cut what we need for the night. You've been at it for an hour. No wonder you've worked up a sweat."

"It's the least I can do after you invited me to dinner. I can smell Mom's chicken pot pie from here. With a serving of her famous mashed potato and fresh garden peas on the side, I could die a happy man."

"You need to find yourself a good woman, Rohan. One who knows how to cook."

"I'm not sure that kind of woman exists anymore, Dad. They're all too busy with their careers to spend time getting up close and personal with the oven."

"Yeah, I'm afraid you're right. I only have to look at your younger sisters to see that. Where did your mother and I go wrong?" he asked in mock dismay, shaking his head.

"Lucky Mom insisted on showing us the basics. At least we can all cook bacon and eggs and I do a mean barbeque. I have you to thank for that."

He shot his father a grin and turned back toward the woodpile. Bringing the ax up over his shoulder, he drove it once again into the log. This time, it split open and he bent down and added the pieces to the growing pile.

"A couple more should do it," his father commented. "It should see us through to warmer weather. Thanks for that, son. It's much appreciated."

"No problem, Dad. I'm glad I can help out. I don't get home as often as I want to. It's nice to be able to do something for you and Mom, when I can."

"Too bad you moved closer to the city. It's a fair commute for you to come out to Cronulla now."

"Yeah, that's the down side, but I'm so much closer to work and I spend a hell of a lot more hours there, let me assure you. Mostly sitting on my ass," he teased.

"They don't give officers bravery medals for sitting around, Rohan."

Rohan looked at him in surprise.

"It was all over the news."

"Of course." Rohan accepted the comment quietly.

"I saw it on the television. You pulled that baby out of the car only moments before that tanker blew sky high. Someone uploaded a video to YouTube. I lost count of the number of times I watched it. You could have been killed, son."

Rohan shrugged and ducked his head, uncomfortable with the praise. He'd done what had to be done. He'd attended the accident in the course of his job. There was nothing special about him or his so-called courageous actions in those circumstances and he couldn't forget how, despite his mammoth efforts, the baby's parents hadn't survived.

Forcing the sad memory aside, he grimaced,

stood another log on its end and brought the ax down hard. A couple more swings and the log split in half and the pieces joined the others in the laden wheelbarrow.

"Did they ever find out what caused the accident?"

Rohan swallowed a sigh and wearily set the ax aside. "The tanker driver's blood alcohol level was well over the legal limit. He should never have been behind the wheel. Forty-eight years old, he has a wife and three children. He'll be doing some serious time."

"What happened to the baby?"

"He was put into the care of relatives. I guess the courts will sort out that one, too."

Throwing the last two pieces of wood into the wheelbarrow, Rohan moved to pick up the handles. His dad beat him to it.

"I'll do that, Dad. It's way too heavy for you."

"It's all right, son. I'm as strong as an ox." Bill took a moment to set the wheelbarrow down and flexed his muscles. His long-sleeved flannel shirt rode high, exposing a generous belly that hung over the top of his jeans.

"Of course you are," Rohan agreed, "but you're not as young as you used to be. There's no harm in taking it a little easy, especially since I'm here and can do it for you."

"Yeah, I guess you're right," his dad muttered and stepped out of the way. Rohan took his father's place in front of the wheelbarrow and pushed it to the back door. Without being asked, he began unloading it, stacking the wood in a neat pile against the side of the house.

"I'm worried about your mother," Bill said, taking Rohan by surprise.

"Why is that?"

"Her blood pressure's a little higher than her doctor wants it to be and she's got that awful cough. She's had it a couple months. If anyone needs to take it easy, it's her. Every time I turn around, she's heading out the door. Between the charity projects she's involved in, the bingo and her lawn bowls, she hardly draws breath."

"Do you want me to talk to her?"

"Would you?" Bill asked with a grateful expression on his face. "She'll listen to you. Whenever I say anything, she just accuses me of interfering and fussing over her too much."

Rohan chuckled. "Well, Dad, I have to agree with her there. You do tend to hover."

Bill had the grace to blush. "It's only because I care about her, son. She has a few years on me. I don't want her leaving before me."

Rohan's smile faded and a rush of emotion tightened his chest. He loved his parents and knew they had something rare and special. Nearly forty years they'd been together and they loved each other now, as much as they had when they'd married. He couldn't help but hope he'd find a woman whose heart would remain so true.

"I'm sure Mom's not planning to die anytime soon, Dad. She's almost as fit as me. Is she still jogging around the esplanade every day?"

"Yes, of course she is. I'd never hear the end of it if she wasn't well enough to do that! She says it's the highlight of her day. Watching the freighters way out in the ocean and the people milling around on the shore... Depending on the season, sometimes she's even spotted a pod of dolphins."

"See, there you go! Does that sound like someone heading toward their grave?" Though Rohan spoke lightly, he couldn't help but notice his father's expression remained troubled.

"Wintertime is hard on old folks," Bill murmured. "The cold seeps into our bones. We get aches and pains that we don't even notice in the summer. This cough your mother has just doesn't seem to want to go away."

"When was the last visit to her doctor?"

"Earlier in the month. She was so breathless, I insisted she go and see him."

"What did he say?"

"He said she had a bout of bronchitis and gave her a prescription for some antibiotics. She finished the course a week ago, but the cough hasn't eased."

"Perhaps you ought to take her back? Or phone for a repeat of the medication?"

"Yeah, I guess so. I just can't help feeling there's more to it. You know what I mean?"

Rohan stared at his dad and his gut slowly filled with dread. "What are you saying, Dad?"

His father held his gaze for a long moment and then lowered it and picked up a log. "Nothing, son. Forget I said anything. I'm sure you're right. Your mom's as fit as a fiddle. She'll probably outlive me."

Before Rohan could respond, Bill turned away

and added the split wood to the stacked pile. Wiping his hands on his jeans, he pulled open the back door. "Let's wash up for dinner and then go and enjoy your mother's pie."

Rohan stared after his father's departing back. All of a sudden, eating pie was the last thing on his mind.

Samantha checked the toe tag against the paperwork in her hand and proceeded to pull the body off the wire shelf of the fridge where it lay. She rolled it onto the gurney. The blue plastic sheeting that covered most of what used to be Natalie Piccoli crackled with the movement. Positioning the body so that it wouldn't fall, Sam hurriedly pushed the trolley out of the fridge.

It was a Saturday and she shouldn't have even been working. The fact that she'd been called in put her out of sorts. She was rostered to work the weekdays, but the usual pathologists who covered the weekend were both off sick, including Richard. Staffing had phoned her in desperation, asking if she'd come in and deal with the backlog of cases. The day was winding down. Soon it would be dark and she still had another two cases to go, including Natalie Piccoli.

With a sigh, she wheeled the body to her usual workstation and quietly and efficiently prepared her tools. When all was as she liked it, she picked up a scalpel and turned to make the Y incision. A fresh surgical scar gave her pause.

In the notes Sam had scanned earlier, there had been no mention that the woman had undergone recent surgery in the hospital and yet it was obvious she had. Reopening the incision with her scalpel, she noticed the woman's ribs had already been sawn through. Prising open the chest cavity, Sam did a preliminary search for Natalie's organs.

Which weren't there. At least, not all of them. The heart, lungs, liver, kidneys, intestine and pancreas were missing.

They'd obviously been donated. It had been a few weeks since Sam had autopsied a donor body. When she'd noticed the evidence of recent abdominal surgery, harvesting of organs hadn't immediately come to mind. But now, there was no other explanation, though it was unusual for someone to donate almost every organ they had. Most chose to limit their donation to the heart and the lungs.

According to the report the police had prepared for the coroner, Natalie Piccoli's suspected cause of death was a brain aneurysm. Sam hoped that the doctors who'd treated the woman were right because there was very little else for her to examine. Tugging off her gloves, she reached for the paperwork again.

Flipping through the pages, she searched for the consent form that was usually signed by the deceased's next of kin, giving permission for the organs to be recovered. She couldn't find it. Frowning, she went through the pages again, more slowly, and still she couldn't locate it.

With an impatient curse, she went through the paperwork a third time. This time, she loosened the clip that held all the papers together and went through them individually, checking both the front and the back. The consent simply had to be there.

And yet, it wasn't.

Perplexed, Sam took a moment to flip back to the start of the notes and looked for the doctor who had signed off on the death certificate. Her brother's name and signature were there in bold black ink: *Doctor Alistair Wolfe*. He'd also done the organ recovery.

There was no surprise in that. He was the head of the donation for transplantation team. Much of the organ recovery surgery was carried out by him. His name had also been on the paperwork for the donor bodies she'd autopsied the previous month.

She checked for the letter of authorization that would have come from the coroner's office and found it. A quick scan of its contents showed that Deputy Coroner Richard Davis had authorized the removal of the donor organs prior to the autopsy.

Again, there was nothing unusual about that. Richard must have taken Alistair's call from the ICU, just prior to the patient's death. It had happened before. In fact, she seemed to recall Richard had also consented to the last donor body she'd autopsied.

Perhaps the consent form had been misplaced or simply gone astray somewhere between the hospital and the morgue? It wasn't unheard of.

Though the morgue workers took care to ensure nothing was lost in transit, nobody was perfect. It could have happened.

Satisfied that was the only reasonable explanation, Sam made a mental note to speak with Richard about it on Monday morning and let him know that the consent form was missing. If the relatives of the deceased ever questioned the organ donation, the consent would become important. Besides, she didn't like to think of any paperwork being mislaid.

Swallowing a sigh, she once again set the paperwork aside and pulled on another pair of latex gloves. If she didn't get on with the PM, she'd be there half the night. Working quickly, she used the scalpel to make the incision, then peeled back the woman's face. The Stryker saw made short work of the skull and a moment later, Natalie Piccoli's brain was exposed.

It was immediately obvious the woman had suffered a severe bleed. The dark, clotted blood filled almost half of the right rear quadrant and left Sam in no doubt as to what had caused the woman's death. After taking note of the size and position of the infarction and recording the weight of the brain, Sam returned the organ to its original location and fitted the skull back in place.

Returning to the woman's chest cavity, Sam retrieved the few organs that were still present in Natalie's abdomen and carefully examined, weighed and returned them to where they'd come from. With neat stitches, she sutured closed the woman's chest and wheeled her back to the fridge where she'd soon be collected by staff from the appointed funeral home.

Sam cleaned up and headed to the tea room. Pulling open the door to the staff drinks fridge, she retrieved a can of Diet Coke. Taking a grateful mouthful, she sat and rested a moment. Conducting any autopsy was exhausting—both mentally and physically. It was essential she communicate with the body on the table and find the answers that had eluded the person's doctors in life. If nothing else, it gave closure, and quite often peace of mind, to the relatives left behind— and to Sam that was important.

She prided herself on being thorough—and the fact the consent form hadn't been with Natalie Piccoli's other hospital papers had put her out of sorts. It was an irritation, like a burr under her skin, that wouldn't go away and she was annoyed someone's carelessness had ruined her Saturday evening. She just knew she'd be thinking about it all night, probably for the rest of the weekend.

With a heavy sigh, she finished her soda and tossed the can into the trash. There was one more autopsy to go. Hopefully, it wouldn't offer up too many surprises. She'd had enough for one day.

A *ding* from the vicinity of her handbag snagged her attention. She stood and retrieved the bag from where she'd left it on the counter near the sink. Pulling out her phone, she checked the screen. There was a new message from her best friend, Hannah Langdon.

"Damn," she muttered, remembering she was

supposed to be meeting Hannah for dinner. With work commitments getting in the way of Sam's social life, it had been the best part of a month since she'd seen her friend, but she'd been looking forward to catching up. Now, it looked like, yet again, work would interfere.

Finding Hannah's number, she selected it and waited for it to dial out. It was answered by her friend in her trademark cheery voice.

"Hi, Sam. How are things? Did you get my text? I was just checking to see if you're still right for dinner."

Sam bit her lip, hating to disappoint her. "I'm sorry, Hannah, I've been called in to work. I still have one more PM to do before I can consider getting out of here."

"Bummer for you! As if you don't work hard enough during the week. Why were you the one to draw the shortest straw?"

"I'm not sure, but so be it. I've been here all day. I'm exhausted."

"Why don't I meet you at your place? We can order pizza and drink beer. That way, you don't have to go to any trouble dressing up and heading back out."

The idea was tempting. "Are you sure you don't mind? I thought you wanted to check out that new bar in George Street?"

"I did, but we can do that another time. It's been ages since we got together. I... I really need to talk to you."

Sam frowned at Hannah's somber tone, so different from her usual cheerfulness. "Is everything all right?"

"Yes, of course. I mean... Why wouldn't it be? It's just that...I need someone who'll listen when I whinge and whine about work. You're the only one who understands."

Hannah was an embalmer at one of the inner city funeral homes and not everyone understood her choice of occupation or her fascination with the dead. But Samantha did and she understood exactly where Hannah was coming from. Sam suffered from the same problem. The thought of a hot shower and a relaxed night on the couch, catching up with her best friend over beer and a pizza, sounded like heaven. All of a sudden, she couldn't wait to finish up at the office and go home.

"I'm happy to listen for as long as you need, Hannah. I'll be another hour or two here, if all goes well. How about I meet you at my place at eight? That should give me plenty of time."

"It's a date." Hannah giggled and Sam couldn't help but smile. "See you soon," she said and ended the call.

The front doorbell rang and Sam hurried to open it. She'd showered and changed at work and not long ago had put a six-pack of beer in the fridge. Glancing at her watch, she noticed it was bang on eight. Hannah was punctual, as usual. With a quick check through the security keyhole, Sam spied her friend waiting on the other side of the door and opened it.

"Hi, it's great to see you," Hannah said and enveloped Sam in an enthusiastic hug.

"You, too," Sam replied and meant it.

She'd met Hannah not long after she'd started at the Glebe Morgue. While the pair of them spent most of their waking hours working with the dead, it wasn't actually work that had brought them together. Whenever Sam found the time, she liked to attend a yoga class, held at the University of Sydney. The college was within walking distance of Sam's work and after a long and stressful day in the morgue, she liked to treat herself to a wind-down. It was at a yoga class that she'd met Hannah.

They found themselves lying with their yoga mats side by side on the floor. While Sam attempted the various positions, she couldn't help but notice the girl beside her who seemed so graceful and at ease with the class. Tall and slender and at least five or six years younger than Sam, Hannah's long, straight blond hair, held in a high ponytail, was just as elegant as her frame. Sam couldn't help but feel a tiny bit envious of the girl and the kindness Mother Nature had bestowed.

But when Hannah turned and smiled at her, Sam forgot all about the green-eyed monster. The girl's smile was warm and friendly and genuine kindness shone in her eyes. Sam couldn't help but respond and before long, they were the best of friends. When they discovered they both had similar occupations, it seemed like fate had brought them together.

Now, Sam reached for the pizza box Hannah held in her hands and headed toward the kitchen. "Are you ready to eat now, or would you rather wait?"

"I'm starving," Hannah answered, following her inside. "I got busy at work and skipped lunch. I figured since we were supposed to be going out to dinner, I'd work up an appetite."

Sam turned and grimaced. "Yeah, I'm sorry about that. We're short staffed. I didn't have a choice."

"Hey, it's no biggie," Hannah smiled. "I know how it is. I've had to cover for more than my fair share of no-shows."

Sam reached for the plates and set them alongside the pizza on the kitchen table. It was only big enough to seat the two of them, but as Sam lived alone, it suited her just fine.

"Help yourself," she said and reached inside the fridge for two beers. Handing one to Hannah, she sat down across from her friend and took a grateful sip. "Ah, there's nothing quite like the taste of a cold beer after a hard day's work."

Hannah grinned and opened the pizza box. The mouthwatering aroma of pepperoni, onion, olives and melted cheese permeated the air. Sam lifted a piece of pizza out of the box and took a generous bite.

"*Mm*, that's so good. And still hot."

"Yes, I just picked it up from the pizza shop on the corner. Giuseppe says hello, by the way."

Sam laughed. "He laments the fact I don't buy

pizza often enough. I don't have the heart to tell him my weakness for takeout is serviced by May-Ling's Thai."

"Oh, yes! She has the best Thai food in Sydney! It's been ages since I ate there."

"I was lucky enough to have lunch there with Alistair when he took me to May-Ling's for my birthday."

"I'm sorry I missed it. I was out of town."

"No problem. I'm sure there will be others. At least, I hope so."

Hannah smiled. "And how is the Sydney Harbour Hospital's poster boy? I couldn't help but notice the enormous billboard picture of him as I was driving down George Street the other day."

Sam giggled. "It's amazing what a little airbrushing can do! He looks younger than me!"

"He looks younger than *me*!" Hannah grinned. "It's a good shot, though," she added, "and it seems to be having an impact. The number of bodies coming through the funeral home with donated organs has skyrocketed and most of them are coming from the Sydney Harbour Hospital."

Sam stared at her and her heart began to pound. "Really?"

"Yes, before the advertising campaign, we'd see three, maybe four a week. Now we're seeing ten or twelve. I think there are more bodies coming into the funeral home with organs and tissue missing than those who've remained intact." She shrugged. "I'm not complaining. It makes my job quicker and easier. There are far less body fluids to extract. In fact, there's less leakage all round."

Sam swallowed a smile. For anyone not comfortable with the messy side of death, the discussion, especially over dinner, would probably be distasteful. To the girls, however, it was like discussing the weather.

"This is really good pizza," Hannah mumbled around another bite. "You ought to get takeout from Giuseppe more often."

"And give up May-Ling's Thai?" Sam asked in mock dismay.

"Hey, there's no rule against having both. Maybe you could alternate?"

Sam rolled her eyes and smiled, but her thoughts returned to Hannah's earlier comment and she grew serious.

"It's funny you mentioned the increase in donor bodies. I've noticed the same thing," she said. "At least, it appeared that way last month. They seem to have gone back to their usual number of late, or maybe they're simply not coming to me? Whatever it is, the extra donors are a good thing. More donors means more organs available for transplant and less time on a waiting list."

"How's your mom?" Hannah asked, aware of Enid Wolfe's fragile health status.

Sam shrugged and blinked hard to ward off a sudden surge of tears. "She's okay. Still getting treatment three times a week. Her kidneys are hanging in there, but only just. We've all had to accept that if she doesn't get a transplant soon, it's only a matter of time."

Hannah's eyes filled with sadness. "How old is

she?"

"Sixty-nine."

"Way too young to die."

"Yep." Sam drew in a deep breath and let it out on a heavy sigh. "But there's nothing we can do about it, short of praying for a donor kidney to be found." Silence fell between them as they concentrated on their food. Hannah was the first to break it.

"So, how's your love life?"

Sam chuckled. "Wow, this conversation goes from bad to worse." She cleared her throat. "To answer your question, my love life is non-existent. My last blind date was a disaster!"

"Did you meet him online?"

"Yes. His bio sounded so good and his photo was really nice. I finally scrounged up the courage to go out with him and it was the most uncomfortable couple of hours of my life."

Hannah laughed. "What happened? It sounds hilarious."

"Oh, yeah. Hilarious. Easy for you to say. You weren't the one having to sit across from him and pretend you had even the tiniest bit of interest in what he had to say. To make things worse, he barely resembled his photo."

"Oh, boy!" Hannah shrieked, with laughter in her eyes. "What did you say?"

"What could I say? He'd aged twenty years and had put on thirty pounds since it had been taken—if it was even him at all. I seriously have my doubts on that score."

"You poor thing!" Hannah sympathized. "What

did you do?"

"There was nothing I could do! We met outside the restaurant. He'd reserved a table. It was a nice restaurant, too. I could hardly turn tail and run when I saw him, despite the fact he looked old enough to be my father."

"So you stayed and had dinner?"

"Yes, although I went straight to the main meal, declined dessert and coffee and got the hell out of there as quickly as I could."

Hannah giggled. "Did he ask if he could see you again?"

"Yes."

"Oh, no!" Hannah laughed, throwing her hands up in the air.

Sam screwed up a napkin and threw it at her. "You're making fun of a very traumatic experience. Have some sympathy for your best friend."

"I'm sorry," Hannah responded, looking anything but. "So, does this mean you're staying away from online dating sites?"

Sam closed her eyes briefly and sighed. "It's all right for you. You're young and beautiful and sexy. You could have any man you choose! I'm thirty-four, not so beautiful and definitely not sexy. It's not so easy for me. I want to fall in love and get married and be a mother to a handful of children. I've dreamed of it since I was a little girl."

Hannah's expression softened. "For a start, you're not old. Thirties are the new twenties, haven't you heard? Nobody finds the love of their life in their twenties anymore. We're all too busy with our careers and climbing the corporate ladder. Girls and guys who marry in their twenties are *so* yesterday." She rolled her eyes and Sam couldn't help but grin.

Hannah continued in a no-nonsense tone. "What's more, what do you mean, you're not sexy? You're gorgeous! All that dark, wavy hair and big brown eyes and your skin—it's flawless. I'd die to have skin like that. Well, maybe not die, but you know what I mean. I only have to be out in the sun for ten minutes and my nose turns pink. You look like you have a tan all year round and I know it doesn't come from a bottle. Give yourself a break, Sam. Take a moment and look at yourself and see what everyone else does."

"Then why haven't I found my prince charming yet?" she asked, unable to keep the whine from her voice.

"Have patience, honey. He's out there, I'm sure of it. Maybe you're trying too hard?"

"What do you mean?"

"I mean, stop putting so much effort into online boyfriends and go out and live your life. In the *real* world. With *real* men who you can tell even from a distance whether they're going to appeal. It's old fashioned, but guess what? It's worked for hundreds, maybe even thousands of years! Give it a go, girl! What do you have to lose?"

Sam stared at her friend for a long moment and slowly nodded. "You're right. I've been so busy it feels like all I ever do is get up, go to work and come home again. I can't expect to find someone like that. It's time I brought back a little balance in my life. We could go dancing or even to a live show. Or maybe even just to one of those hip city bars we talked about, where the professionals like to hang out."

Hannah beamed. "Exactly! Now you're getting into the spirit!"

"Will you come with me?"

"Of course! What are best friends for?"

The girls fell into another companionable silence, each lost in their thoughts. Sam picked up her beer and took another drink. Hannah chewed on another slice of pizza. When they were finished, Sam collected the leftovers and tossed them into the trash. Hannah rinsed the plates and left them to dry.

"Would you like another beer?" Sam asked.

"Thanks, it would be nice."

"It might even be warm enough outside to sit on the balcony."

With drinks in hand, the girls headed to the sliding door that connected the living room to a small balcony. A light breeze greeted them, but the air temperature wasn't cold.

"It feels like spring already," Hannah smiled.

"Yes. Soon we'll be complaining it's too hot!"

Hannah merely smiled again and took another sip from her beer. Sam sat in a deck chair and Hannah took a seat opposite. For a moment, the girls enjoyed the silence until Hannah let out a heavy sigh.

"My, that sounds ominous," Sam teased.

"Maybe it is."

Sam straightened in her chair, a little alarmed

at the solemn expression on her friend's face. "Don't tell me Aaron is giving you grief again? Sorry, I should have asked earlier how things were. When will that man face the fact that the two of you are over and you're never going back?"

"No, it's not Aaron. I haven't heard from him in weeks, thank God. I think he's finally gotten the message we're through."

"Then why do you look so troubled?"

Hannah stared at her and then sat forward in her chair. Her shoulders slumped on another heavy sigh.

A sense of foreboding crept through Sam's veins. "Hannah... You're scaring me. What's going on?"

"You know when we were talking about the increase in the number of bodies coming in with missing organs?"

Sam grimaced. "Donated organs. They're not exactly missing. I assume someone knows where they are." She attempted a smile at her joke, but it fell flat. Hannah's expression remained serious.

"I don't receive any paperwork, except the patient's personal details and the name of the hospital that sends them. I only assume the organs and tissues have been donated because, what else would have happened to them?"

Sam frowned. She stared hard at Hannah and her pulse picked up its pace. "What are you saying?"

"I'm not sure, but yesterday I had a body that was missing nearly everything."

"What do you mean, *everything*?"

Hannah spread her arms out wide, sloshing her beer. "Everything."

Sam shook her head in confusion. "Like, all of the organs?"

"I couldn't tell just by looking at the suture lines which organs were gone, but from the position and length of the incisions, I'm guessing most of them had been removed. On top of that, there were no tendons or ligaments; both corneas and sclera were missing; even a large piece of skin. I didn't immediately realize the skin had been removed too, because it had been taken from the deceased's back. It wasn't until I'd turned the body over to clean it that I saw the fresh wound." She shook her head. "It was awful. I think there's something weird going on."

Sam stared at her in shock, her heart now thumping double time. She could barely believe what she was hearing. Never in her years as a doctor and pathologist had she heard of people donating their ligaments and tendons, or even pieces of skin. Though it was possible to reuse that type of tissue, most people weren't aware of that and didn't pay them any heed. She thought back to Natalie Piccoli and the missing consent form and unease trickled like icy water down her spine.

"I'm thinking about going to the police."

Hannah's quiet words jerked Sam out of her troubled thoughts. "The police?"

"Yes. I've got a bad feeling. This patient was eighty-six. Who gives consent for that kind of carnage on behalf of someone who's eighty-six?

Something's not right."

"I agree. Have you spoken to Max?" Sam asked, referring to Hannah's boss and the owner of the funeral home.

"Yes, but he barely listened. He doesn't care and he doesn't want to get involved, particularly if it might affect his business. A body's a body as far as Max's concerned. 'There's no bringing them back, so why worry about how they went out?' That's Max's motto."

"Empathetic right to the very end, isn't he?"

"Yep, that's Max," Hannah responded, her voice dry. She took another mouthful of beer and looked out across the city. Thousands of twinkling lights from distant houses and shop fronts lit up the night. She turned back to Sam. "How about you? Have you noticed anything strange lately?"

Sam frowned and shook her head. "Apart from the rush of donor bodies last month, not really. But now that you mention it, today I autopsied a woman who was missing all of her major organs...but the tissues you mentioned were still there. I must admit, at the time I found it a little strange that someone would donate so many organs. It's not the usual thing we see."

"Where did she come from?"

"The Sydney Harbour Hospital."

"Who authorized the organ removal prior to autopsy?"

"Richard Davis."

"Have you spoken to him?"

"No. I only conducted the PM this afternoon. Staffing told me he was ill, along with a couple of others. That's the reason I was called in. I'm sure he wouldn't take kindly to me contacting him."

"What did Richard think about the sudden increase in donors last month? I assume you spoke with him about it."

"Yes, I did. I can't remember exactly what he said. He didn't seem too concerned. I also mentioned it to my brother, but he suggested it could simply be a response to the fact we were in the middle of a harsh winter and that time of year, we always experience an increase in the number of deaths and correspondingly, an increase in the number of donor bodies. And of course, there's the success of his campaign to consider."

Sam pursed her lips in thought. "At the time, his explanation seemed reasonable. Of course, I didn't know about what you were seeing at your work, and what you're still seeing."

Silence fell between them as they were once again caught up in their thoughts, but this time, it was far from easy. Sam finished her beer and set the bottle down on the small cane table that squatted on the balcony between them. The breeze had picked up and now had a distinct chill to it. She shivered and hugged herself.

"It's cooling off. I might go in," she said, standing and then moving toward the sliding door.

Hannah looked up at her with a troubled expression. "I still think I should go to the police."

Sam stopped and turned. "And tell them what?"

"I don't know! But something's not right. I can

feel it in here," Hannah said, placing a hand over her heart. "I owe it to the deceased to make sure they're treated with respect, right to the very end. It's my job to protect them, to make sure that happens and right now, I'm horribly afraid it's not."

"We're talking about people who were mostly patients of the Sydney Harbour Hospital. What if my brother's involved?" Sam whispered, hardly daring to give the awful thought voice.

"We don't know anything for sure."

"All of the cases that came to my attention had Alistair noted as the surgeon," she said, feeling more and more concerned.

"He's the head surgeon, Sam. The fact that his name was on a few cases doesn't mean anything."

Relief surged through her. "Yes, you're right. I'm being silly. Of course Alistair's not involved."

"The only way we're going to find out what's going on is to go to the police and let them know what we've been seeing. If they take this on, the hospital will have to provide them with the records. You and I aren't going to be given access to them. They're confidential."

Sam nodded, knowing what Hannah said was true, even though the last thing she wanted was to draw attention to their suspicions.

"Will you come with me?"

"To the police?" Sam asked, even though she hadn't misunderstood. She wanted to buy time, even a few seconds, to decide what her answer would be.

Hannah looked at her solemnly. "Yes."

"I... I..."

"Sam!" Hannah cried in exasperation. "Something's not right. You know it as well as I do. It could be any number of doctors in that hospital. There's nothing to say it's your brother."

"And if it is?" Sam whispered, hardly able to lift her gaze from her feet.

"Then so be it," Hannah softly, with sadness and resignation in her eyes.

A sudden surge of anger rushed through Sam's veins and she clenched her fists. "No! No, it isn't that easy! Alistair's the best brother a girl could ever have! My dad died when I was a baby! Alistair took on all the responsibilities of the man around the house. He carried me across the burrs when I went outside without my shoes; he helped change my dirty diapers; he even threatened to beat up Sandy Packer when he refused to take me to the prom. He's always been there for me! He's my brother and I love him!"

Hannah pushed away from her chair and moved to stand close to Sam. Her eyes were solemn, her face was beyond sad. She reached out and squeezed Sam's shoulder. Sam flinched from the contact and Hannah's hand dropped away.

"I understand, Sammie. I understand about all of those things. Your brother's a saint. He's the nicest man I know. Of course he isn't involved in something so horrible! He's good and kind and compassionate. He loves his patients! But someone *is* responsible. And families of the deceased have a right to know. People planning their deaths need to know we don't take their wishes lightly. At the very least, it needs to be investigated. If Alistair's innocent, you have nothing to worry about."

Sam stared at her friend, suddenly wishing she'd never agreed to meet. She should have simply declined Hannah's dinner invitation and gone home to bed. Now it was too late. The conversation had happened and it couldn't be undone. It was clear Hannah intended to report what she'd discovered to the police, with or without Sam.

With resolve firming up inside her, she held Hannah's gaze. "And if he isn't?"

Her friend stared right back at her and Sam could tell Hannah was silently pleading with her to understand and do the right thing. A long moment later, Sam cursed under her breath, pushed past Hannah and headed back inside.

CHAPTER 5

Dear Diary,

What have I done? I'm terrified I've created a monster. I've sold my soul to the devil and there's no telling he'll ever give it back. And what is anyone without a soul?

———

The phone near Rohan's elbow rang and he leaned over to answer it.

"Detective Coleridge."

"Detective, it's Constable Foley downstairs. I have a couple of women here who wish to speak with someone about the illegal harvesting of human organs and tissue. Are you available?"

Rohan bit back a sound of surprise. It wasn't every day he took a call like this. He glanced at his watch. He was intrigued and there was still an hour before his shift ended. Besides, he was the only one around. "Sure," he replied. "I'll be down in a minute."

Replacing the phone on its cradle, Rohan pushed away from his desk and headed for the stairwell that connected the first floor with the ground level. Taking the stairs two at a time, he then strode across the worn linoleum and punched his security code into the panel on the door that divided the entry to the stairs from the reception. The door beeped and he swung it open and stepped into the public waiting area.

His gaze was immediately drawn to a striking, tall blonde who stood closest to the door. With bumps and curves in all the right places, she wore her Levis and long sleeved T-shirt with casual panache. The other woman had her back to him. She was as dark as the blonde was fair. Shorter in stature, but with a tidy figure that was in proportion to her height, there was something about her that seemed familiar. He stilled, trying to place her in his memory. She turned to face him and it came back to him in a rush.

He shook his head in surprise. "Samantha Wolfe? Is that you?"

Surprise and recognition flared in her familiar brown eyes before it was quickly replaced by an expression that bordered on angry. With her lips compressed, she reached up and pushed a length of wavy, dark hair from her eyes. Her expression was far from friendly.

He frowned and wondered at her strange reaction. As far as he could recall, the last time he'd seen her she hadn't been upset, and yet it was clear she was now. Perhaps it would be better for another detective to conduct the interview? The woman was obviously already on edge. Getting to the bottom of any story was always more difficult when the interviewee was hostile.

But what excuse would he give? He didn't have a clue about the cause of her antagonism. Besides, there was no one else upstairs. The other rostered on detectives had left in a group to enforce a search warrant on the headquarters of one of the city's most notorious biker gangs. They wouldn't be back anytime soon.

The only reason Rohan had been confined to his desk was because he was still recovering from a football injury he'd sustained the weekend before. Detective Superintendent Holt Denman had refused to allow him to take part in a raid that could quite possibly turn physical. His boss had enough to worry about without concerning himself with an officer who wasn't at his peak. At least, that's the excuse Holt had given when he'd ordered Rohan to stay put.

So now he had the dubious pleasure of interviewing a blonde who looked like she could grace any catwalk and the angry woman from his past who stood defiantly beside her. A woman who was even now watching him through narrowed eyes. With no other option, Rohan stepped forward and held out his hand to the blonde and shot her a friendly smile.

"Good afternoon, I'm Detective Rohan Coleridge."

"Hannah Langdon," the blonde answered and shook his hand firmly.

Rohan turned to her companion. "Samantha. How nice it is to see you again. It's been awhile."

To her credit, she took his proffered hand, but gave it the most perfunctory handshake. Hannah looked from one to the other, a questioning look on her face. "You two know each other?"

Rohan noticed Samantha did little more than offer the tiniest of nods. He wasn't quite so reticent.

"Yes, we knew each other years ago, back when Samantha was still in college. It must be ten years or more since we've seen each other, right?" His gaze snagged hers before moving lower. Without conscious thought, he paused at the swell of her generous cleavage where it peeked out from the opening in her shirt. She tensed under his perusal and fresh anger flared in her dark eyes. He cursed silently under his breath.

What the hell was he doing? It was obvious the woman had a gripe with him. What did it matter that he didn't have a clue about what he'd done to put her off side? And why did he care, anyway? The odds were after today he'd never see her again.

Hannah appeared oblivious to the tension. "Wow, what a coincidence," she said with a brief smile and turned to her friend. "It must be our lucky day. Sharing our concerns with someone who's at least familiar to you will hopefully make things a little easier."

Rohan suddenly recalled the women were supposed to be there to report something about illegal organ harvesting. With his gaze trained on the cute blonde, he said, "Follow me. We'll go upstairs. We can talk in private up there."

Turning his back on them, he re-entered his code into the security pad and then held the door open for the women. Samantha followed more slowly. As she passed through the doorway, she kept her head averted, as if unwilling to look him in the face.

Rohan caught a whiff of her perfume and ancient memories bombarded him from all sides. He was twenty-four again and had just made detective. To top it off, he was in love with the girl of his dreams. A girl who happened to be Samantha Wolfe's roommate.

Samantha took a seat beside Hannah in the stark interview room and once again cursed under her breath. Of all the people to run into, it had to be a man she despised from her past. And Hannah thought it was a good thing that Sam could confide in a familiar face. *Huh!*

She couldn't believe the irony. She'd agonized over her decision to accompany Hannah to the police station. It was only after her friend made it clear she was going to the police to report her suspicions with or without her, Sam had finally agreed to come along. At least if she were present, she might have a hope of downplaying Alistair's role. She still refused to believe he might be involved in anything illegal, but as the head of the organ retrieval team, his name appeared on at least some of the paperwork and it was feasible the police might view him as a person of interest.

She had to admit, she was curious to hear Rohan's take on the evidence, if one could call it that. A big part of her hoped he'd dismiss Hannah's concerns as coincidence and then both of them could put it out of their minds. She wished she'd known being present for the interview meant she'd cross paths with Rohan Coleridge again. She might have seriously reconsidered.

He'd told the truth when he said they hadn't seen each other since college. Sam was surprised he'd mentioned it at all. He must surely know Daphne had told Sam all about the baby and how Rohan had abandoned them. When Daphne broke down in tears one night and told her all about it, Sam had been so furious, she didn't know if she'd ever feel calm again. It had been up to her to console her friend and reassure the devastated girl that she and her unborn child were better off without Rohan Coleridge, a low life who lacked the courage to face up to his responsibilities.

Daphne had left college right before the baby was due and had returned to her hometown in the country. Gradually, she and Sam had drifted apart. Sam had heard via mutual friends that Daphne had given birth to a little boy.

Sam might not have seen or heard from her roommate since college, but that didn't mean she'd forgotten about her, or the unforgivable way she'd been treated. And now, a decade later, the cause of Sam's angst sat across from her with nothing but a scarred, modest Formica table between them, looking calm and relaxed and way too good looking for any woman's peace of mind.

He'd always been an attractive man. He might have been her former roommate's boyfriend, but that didn't mean Sam had been blind to his assets. Even back then, there were many. Tall and broad shouldered, his blond hair was sun bleached in summer and darkened to a tawny golden color in winter. It matched the color of his skin. Daphne had once told her Rohan had French heritage on his mother's side. His eyes were bluer than the ocean on a bright and sunny day and right now, they contemplated her with a mixture of wariness, curiosity and confusion, as if he weren't quite sure what to make of her prickly attitude.

Renewed anger surged through her at the thought that he was pretending not to know about the source of her antagonism. He couldn't honestly believe Daphne wouldn't tell her? They'd been roommates. Not even Rohan could believe Sam wouldn't notice her friend's pregnancy or the sudden absence of her boyfriend.

No, he must know. The fact that he once again chose to shrug off responsibility infuriated her. She wondered how long she'd be able to stay in the same room as the cad. Before she was able to consider the thought further, Rohan drew a notepad toward him and pulled a pen out of his crisp, tailored shirt pocket. He cleared his throat and directed his first question to Sam.

"The constable downstairs indicated you were here to report illegal harvesting of human organs. Is that correct?"

His gaze drilled into hers and without warning, her throat went tight with nerves. So in police matters, he could be direct. Fine. She could do direct. She licked her suddenly dry lips and cast around for a response that wouldn't implicate her brother.

"Yes, that's correct," Hannah answered firmly.

Sam frowned and tried to make eye contact with her friend, but the girl either steadfastly refused to look at her or was unaware of Sam's efforts. Sam couldn't help but suspect it was the former.

"What makes you think that?" Rohan asked, this time speaking to Hannah.

Hannah finally glanced at Sam, but quickly looked away. "I work as an embalmer at the Max Grace Funeral Home in Balmain. Sam is a forensic pathologist at the Glebe Morgue. I'm sure you can appreciate that between the two of us, we come across a fair number of the deceased persons who resided in or around the inner city. Over the past couple of months, we've each noticed an unusual increase in both the number of bodies with donated organs and the volume of organs and tissue that have been removed."

"You mean, bodies where the deceased has donated organs prior to their death?" Rohan asked, looking at Hannah.

"Yes," Hannah replied.

"When you say an unusual increase, how many do you normally see?"

"Three or four donor bodies a week, on

average with the majority of donors limiting their donation to two or three major organs," Hannah said.

"And now?"

"More than double that," Hannah replied.

"And what about you?" Rohan asked, directing his gaze at Sam.

She held his stare without flinching. "Usually one a week, if we're lucky and like Hannah said, it's normal practice for donors to put a limit on the number of organs donated."

"I take it you're an advocate for organ donation?" he asked dryly.

"Yes. Are you?"

Rohan appeared to consider her question and then replied, "I guess so. I haven't given it a lot of thought."

She compressed her lips in disapproval, even though she had no right to judge. Not everyone had a loved one in dire need of a transplant. Like Phillip, Rohan was entitled to his opinion. It was only fair she concede her personal circumstances had a great influence on her attitude toward organ donation.

"You should," Sam managed between gritted teeth, still unable to let it go. "It's important to give it consideration before it becomes an issue. You never know..."

Ignoring the tension in her voice, he nodded and gave her a wink. "You're absolutely right, Doctor Wolfe. Of course, I don't plan on keeling over any time soon, but as you say, you never know."

He grinned and she felt it all the way down to

her toes. Warmth coursed through her and to her dismay, heat washed over her cheeks. She averted her gaze and silently cursed her body's traitorous reaction.

The truth was, she reminded herself harshly, Rohan Coleridge was a coward. He'd turned his back on his pregnant girlfriend, abandoning her without a second thought. As far as Sam knew, he'd never taken responsibility for the child. Somewhere, there was a ten-year-old boy growing up without a father and it was all Rohan's fault. She'd best remember it the next time she went all warm and gooey at the sight of his way-too-sexy grin.

As if finally sensing her disapproval, Rohan's expression sobered. He cleared his throat. "Let's get back to the reason you're here. What makes you suspect illegal organ and tissue harvesting? It's a very serious allegation. I assume there's a protocol that's followed when a person donates their organs?"

"Yes," Sam answered, fighting to keep her voice on an even keel. "If a deceased person, who has made a request prior to their death—to have their organs and tissue donated—requires an autopsy, the treating doctor must first contact the coroner or one of his deputies and obtain authorization to carry out the recovery of the donated organs prior to the post mortem."

"I assume the coroner or his deputy makes a decision based upon the likely cause of death? Whether or not there are suspicious circumstances, that kind of thing?" Rohan asked.

Sam held his gaze and nodded, feeling slightly less angry as she focused on their reason for being there. "Yes, all of those things are taken into account."

"For example, if the doctors suspect Mary Jane has died from complications arising from brain surgery, I'm guessing the coroner would be okay about her donating her heart and kidneys. Would that be a fair assumption?" Rohan asked.

"Yes," Sam replied.

Rohan made a few notes on the paper in front of him and then turned to Hannah. "And how does it work in the funeral homes? Is there a similar procedure in place?"

"Well, of course, there are protocols that are followed, but anyone coming directly from the hospital to the funeral home doesn't need permission from the coroner for the donation to take place. The doctors obtain the necessary consents from the donor's next of kin and the removal of the donated organs and tissue occurs while the patient is still in hospital. We don't receive any notification or even any paperwork concerning the donation process and we don't need to. The body is prepared for burial in the usual way."

Rohan acknowledged her explanation with a nod. "I get how Samantha would be aware in her line of work that a body is minus a few organs, but how do you know?"

"It's usually a matter of recognizing the signs that the body's been operated on just prior to death. There's no need to use keyhole surgery on someone who's as good as dead. Depending upon which organs and tissues are being donated, the doctors cut across the abdomen or straight down the chest. It's reasonable to assume when you come across those kinds of incisions on a body that the deceased has been an organ donor."

"I see," Rohan replied with the slightest shake of his head. "Fascinating."

Sam bit down on her impatience. "Can we please get on with it? I have other things to do."

Rohan looked up at her. "Of course, but it's important for me to understand the basics before I can decide whether your suspicions warrant further investigation. Getting up close and personal with dead bodies might be an everyday occurrence for you ladies, but it's something I am thankfully a whole lot less familiar with."

"Afraid you wouldn't have the stomach for it?" Sam smirked.

Rohan stared at her, his expression unreadable. "Absolutely. Quite frankly, I don't know how either of you manage it. I admire your resilience and courage."

"Someone has to do it," Sam said in a dismissive manner, uncomfortable with his praise.

"I enjoy it," Hannah said. "It's more than just a job. It makes me sound weird, but it gives me pleasure and a wonderful sense of satisfaction knowing I've made someone's journey into the afterlife a little more comfortable, not to mention a whole lot less smelly. Let's face it, death can be a messy affair."

She smiled with genuine humor and Sam was reminded what a wonderful person she was. Determined to finish what they'd come for, Sam straightened in her seat and spoke again.

"The fact is, both of us have noticed an unusual spike in the number of donor bodies and the volume of donated tissue. We're not sure if it's the result of the raised awareness about organ and tissue donation because of media coverage and the advertising campaign by the Sydney Harbour Hospital, or if there's something sinister going on."

Rohan kept his gaze on Sam. "What makes you think the latter?"

Sam closed her eyes briefly and drew in a deep breath. Easing it out, she cast around for the right words. "Apart from the fact we're seeing at least double the usual number of affected bodies, we've noticed a few other anomalies."

Rohan's gaze didn't waver. "Such as?"

"I autopsied a patient on the weekend who had all of the major organs in her abdomen and chest removed, which as you know, is unusual. But what concerned me even more was that the consent form for the organ donation wasn't there with the patient's notes."

Rohan's demeanor became more alert and he leaned forward in his chair. "You mean no consent was given for the organ harvesting?"

"No, Detective, that's not what I'm saying. I don't have a clue whether or not the consent was obtained. All I know is that the consent form was missing from the paperwork I received."

"Has that happened before?" Rohan asked.

Sam retained eye contact. "Occasionally. We're a busy place, Detective. We deal with two hundred or more bodies a week. Now and then, paperwork gets mislaid. But, I've never known something as important as a consent form to go missing."

Rohan stared at her a moment longer before switching his attention to Hannah. "So, Ms Langdon, missing paperwork hasn't been your concern. Why do you think there's something suspicious going on?"

Hannah blew out her breath on a soft sigh. "Like Sam said, I've seen a huge increase in the number of bodies that've exhibited signs of having organs harvested. Obviously, I have no idea how many or which organs have been removed, but last week I came across something very strange." She paused and Sam could tell she was remembering what had happened.

"Go on," Rohan encouraged.

"This body not only had recent suture lines, there were also deep cuts across both wrists and ankles. It appeared the ligaments and tendons in all of the limbs were missing."

Rohan's eyebrows shot upward in surprise. "I take it that isn't usual?"

"No, it's not. In fact, in the five years since I've worked as an embalmer, I haven't once come across wounds like that. And there was more."

"More?" Rohan asked.

"Yes. When I turned the body over, I discovered large tracts of skin had been removed from the patient's back and the back of the legs." She shook her head. "It was very, very strange. I've never seen anything like it."

Rohan's expression turned grim. Gone was even the slightest hint of humor. A frown line marred the smooth expanse of his forehead. As Sam waited for him to speak, she couldn't stop the icy dread that slid stealthily into her stomach. At last, he looked up at them.

"You're right. It does sound odd."

Sam's breath caught in her throat. Her heart pounded and blood rushed through her ears. She had to strain against that noise to hear what else Rohan had to say.

"A sudden increase in the number of donors and the volume of donated tissue, missing consent forms, highly unusual donations... I'm going to confer with my colleagues as soon as possible. This needs to be investigated further." He looked at Sam. "I assume you're able to identify which hospital the bodies have been transferred from?"

"Yes, of course, it's on all of the paperwork."

"Including details of the treating doctors and the persons responsible for obtaining the consents?"

The dread inside Sam grew into a cold, hard lump, but she looked Rohan in the eye. "Yes."

He turned to Hannah. "What about you? Are you aware of where the bodies were sent from?"

She nodded somberly. "Yes. We're contacted by relatives of the deceased and then attend upon the relevant hospital to collect their loved one.

That's about the extent of the information we get, apart from the patients' personal identification details."

In silence, Rohan made a few more notations on the notepad, his lips compressed. "I'll need your contact details," he said, looking from one to the other. "Home address, work and cell phone numbers."

Sam bit her lip and then forced herself to relax. It wouldn't matter that Rohan Coleridge knew where she lived and how to get ahold of her. It was the fact he'd confirmed their suspicions that had her tense. Something strange was going on. The fact that it might involve her brother was something she didn't want to contemplate.

———

Rohan took down their details and then slipped his pen back into his shirt pocket. Glancing at his watch, he noticed it was almost the end of his shift. He hadn't heard any of his colleagues return from the raid and could only assume they were still caught up in that drama. Not that it mattered. The information Samantha and Hannah had relayed to him was disturbing, but didn't require urgent attention. It could wait until the regular briefing held prior to the next shift.

He pushed back his chair and opened the door to the interview room. The women followed him into the corridor and back to the stairwell. When they reached the bottom, he entered his security code and opened the door before turning back to face them.

"Thank you for coming forward with this. I'm sure you didn't do it lightly."

Hannah nodded. "It's kept me awake for some time now, that's for sure."

"Well, I appreciate your courage. You've done the right thing. I'll be in touch." He indicated for them to precede him. Hannah brushed past and gave him a brief smile of farewell. Sam went to follow behind her.

"Samantha? Do you have a moment?"

She tensed and then reluctantly turned back toward him. "Is there something else?"

"I'll catch up with you later, Sam," Hannah called out on her way toward the exit.

Samantha looked like she wanted to scurry off with her friend, but Rohan closed the connecting door. She stared at him and once again he caught the flicker of anger in her eyes. Determined to find out the reason for her animosity, he got straight to the point.

"It's quite clear you're angry with me, but for the life of me, I can't work out why. I've scoured my memory and I've come up blank. How about you tell me why you look at me like you want to stab me in the eye?"

If anything, the anger in her eyes burned hotter. He even took a step back and then cursed under his breath. He had nothing to feel guilty about.

"I can't believe you're standing there, pretending it never happened!" she hissed.

Rohan frowned in confusion. "What the hell are you talking about?"

Her cheeks flushed and her breath came faster. She looked like she might explode. Once again, he searched through his memory for something that warranted her extreme reaction and came up empty.

"You know what I'm talking about!" she said, her tone full of contempt.

He drew in a deep breath and did his best to hold his patience in check. "No, Samantha, I don't. Now, are we going to stand here like this until nightfall, or are you just going to tell me what you're so riled up about?"

Her stare turned lethal. "I'm talking about *Daphne!* Remember her? Your college girlfriend? The one you promised to love forever?"

He stared back at her, still confused. *What the hell did Daphne have to do with any of this?* Until Samantha appeared at the station, he hadn't thought about his ex-girlfriend in years. If he were honest, he could barely remember what she looked like. They'd dated for a year-and-a-half before he ended it. What was so maddening about that? It wasn't like he'd broken Daphne's heart. In fact, he'd been the one brokenhearted.

But, instead, he said, "Of course I remember Daphne. What does she have to do with anything? We've been over for more than decade."

"Oh, you're unbelievable! It's so easy for you to wipe your hands of it, isn't it? You ought to be ashamed!"

"Of *what?* For Christ's sake, get to the point. I don't have a clue what you're getting at!"

"Of abandoning your responsibilities, that's what!"

He shook his head and anger started to rear its head. Never in his life had he been accused of shirking his responsibilities. It irritated him to hear Samantha accuse him of such now. Suddenly impatient, he got up in her face. Her head only came up to his shoulder, but she continued to stare at him defiantly, refusing to be intimidated.

"Cut the crap, Samantha. Spit it out. Tell me what the hell you think I've done and why you're so furious!"

"Oh, yeah, I'm furious all right," she replied, pushing him in the chest.

He tensed and snatched at her hands, holding them away from him. "Talk. *Now.*"

Her eyes narrowed. "I'm talking about your *son!* The baby you made with Daphne and then callously abandoned because the pregnancy didn't fit in with your plans. You promised to love her forever and that's how you treated her! Like I said, you ought to bow your head in shame and beg forgiveness from the mother of your child."

Rohan reeled back in shock and let go of Samantha's hands. He could barely hear over the roar of blood in his ears. Of course, he'd known about the baby. It was the reason he'd ended it. Daphne obviously hadn't told her roommate that the baby wasn't his.

He stared at the angry flush that stained Samantha's cheeks and was stunned she could think so badly of him. After all the nights they'd double dated and sat around the girls' apartment sharing pizza and drinking beer... He couldn't believe she hadn't defended him. Or bothered to wonder whether the man she'd considered a friend really could behave in such an appalling manner.

Hurt and disappointment surged through him and his chest went tight. He turned away from her, unwilling to let her see how much her assessment of his character mattered. He'd always liked her and had found her fun to be around, even though at the time, he'd only had eyes for Daphne. To discover that Samantha, a person he respected and liked, could believe he was capable of such selfish, irresponsible behavior rocked him to the core.

With an effort, he unclenched his fists and steeled his heart. His pride refused to allow him to explain. If that's how little she knew and thought of him, then who was he to argue? Turning back to face her, he unlocked the connecting door in silence.

"It's obvious you're convinced you have the story right. I think it's best that you leave." It was all he could manage.

Chapter 6

Sam made her way home in the early evening traffic and thought about her meeting with Rohan. She'd known he was a police officer, of course. He'd made detective not long after he started dating Daphne. At that time, he'd been stationed at Cronulla, a southern suburb of Sydney and a long way from the station in the city. She hadn't imagined she'd run into him when she accompanied Hannah.

The years had been kind to him and the knowledge irritated her. Somehow, it would have made her feel better if she'd discovered his hair had disappeared off his head and the athletic body he'd sported a decade earlier had given way to fat. A near-sighted squint would also have gone a long way to soothing her annoyance. But it wasn't to be. He looked as good, if not better, than he had ten years ago.

Although she wouldn't admit it to anyone, he also appeared competent in his job. His questions had been insightful and he'd been genuinely determined to get to the bottom of their complaint. She almost wished they'd met with a buffoon who couldn't care less about what they had to say. The knowledge that Rohan would investigate the matter until he was satisfied with the answers meant she now had to deal with the growing sense of unease that weighed her down.

Her phone rang in the car kit to the tune of a Bruno Mars song, distracting her from her thoughts. She glanced across at the screen. *Alistair.* All of sudden, the dread in her stomach grew wings and took flight. Swallowing, she moistened her dry lips and answered.

"Hi, Alistair, how are you?"

"What's the matter? You sound weird."

Sam groaned under her breath. *Trust her brother to notice.* She forced a smile and did her best to lighten her tone. "It must be the noise of the traffic. I have you on hands-free. I'm on my way home."

"I just thought I'd call and see how you were now that you're a week older."

"I'm fine, Alistair. Just getting on with life: work, sleep, sitting with Mom, more work. You know how it is."

"Unfortunately, I do. Nancy and the kids complain they barely see me these days."

"So does Mom."

"Hey, I was with her in the Dialysis Unit two days last week when Ava and Jessie couldn't make it."

"And what about this week? It doesn't just stop, you know."

"Of course. I'll do what I can. Who kept her company today?"

"Ava did. She moved around a few appointments. Got the time cleared."

"Ava's such a good daughter," Alistair replied, sounding genuine. "You all are."

"Yeah, yeah, yeah," Sam replied with a wry chuckle though her mirth was forced.

"Are you sure you're all right?"

She bit her lip against a sudden rush of tears. *No, she wasn't all right.* Her mother was dying and she was facing the possibility her brother might be involved in something so awful she couldn't even think about it—and yet, she might be completely and utterly wrong. The worry and doubt and confusion and uncertainty was doing her head in.

A car cut into her lane in front of her and she cursed aloud and blasted the driver with her horn.

"What happened?" Alistair asked.

"Just another stupid Sydney driver impatient to get home. Doesn't he realize we've all had a long day and we're all desperate to get home? Talk about selfish. The idiot could have caused an accident!"

"How do you know it's a male?" Alistair teased.

"You're not helping, Alistair," she replied through gritted teeth.

"I take it you had a rough day?" His voice was full of sympathy. Another rush of tears pricked Sam behind her eyes. She blinked hard to hold them at bay.

"Yeah," she admitted quietly. "It was tough."

"Was it a kid? Doing an autopsy on a kid would have to be the worst."

"No, it wasn't a kid and it's not work that has worn me out."

"Then, what?"

Sam bit her lip and debated silently over what to say. She wanted so much to tell him about her fears—about what her and Hannah had found—and she wanted to tell him about going to the police and how an officer she'd met ten years earlier, might be giving him a call.

And then, all of a sudden, she wanted to hear what he had to say. If he had nothing to do with it, surely he'd be just as curious and concerned about the findings as she was.

"I accompanied Hannah Langdon to the police station this afternoon," she blurted out. "We wanted to talk to someone about our uneasiness over the recent high influx of bodies that had donated organs." Her announcement was met with shocked silence.

Finally, Alistair spoke. "Wow! I... I'm speechless. When you mentioned it last week, I didn't realize the numbers were so high that you'd go to the police."

"Well, they are and Hannah felt the same way. I had dinner with her on the weekend. She's also noticed a significant increase. She had a deceased come through her funeral home recently that had not only donated organs, but ligaments and tendons and even tracts of skin removed. Don't you think that sounds strange?"

She held her breath and waited for her brother

to answer. Her hands tightened around the steering wheel.

"Absolutely! You're right, it sounds very weird. I pride myself on being good at my job and I can't remember the last time I convinced a relative to give consent for all of those things. I wish I was that persuasive. For sure we need those kinds of tissues as much as any of them, but it's rare for people to agree. I wonder who the doctor was who managed to secure the consent?"

Sam's breath rushed out of her body in relief. Her brother sounded just as bemused with the whole thing as she was. If he'd had any prior knowledge or, heaven forbid, intimate knowledge, surely he'd be on the defensive?

"I don't know any details, other than the body came from your hospital," she hastened to tell him. "Hannah only receives the most basic information about her clients."

"Of course. Do you have a name? I could look them up in our records and see who dealt with them."

"No, but Hannah does. I could call her and ask."

"Don't bother her tonight. Besides, I've already called it a day. I'm at home, kicking back with a scotch, watching the rugby game I taped earlier."

"Lucky you," she teased. "I have another three miles to go."

"Well, I'll leave you to concentrate on the road. I don't want you arriving home in pieces. Or worse still, not arriving at all." His tone was light, but Sam appreciated the concern behind his words. She was lucky to have a big brother like him watching out for her. Not everyone was so fortunate. With a promise to take care and talk again soon, Sam ended the call.

There, she'd done it and Alistair had reacted exactly as she'd expect. Curious, concerned, wanting to investigate further and get to the bottom of it. There was no way he was involved. She was sure of it.

CHAPTER 7

Dear Diary,

I woke up last night from a nightmare. I was trapped in a bottomless pool of blood. It was all over me—sticky, warm and wet. I wiped myself clean over and over, but by the time I'd finished I was covered in blood again.

It hung from my hair, it dripped in my eyes; it filled my mouth and ears. I was drowning in blood. At any moment, I could disappear, swallowed up by the metallic tasting fluid, never to be seen again...

"All done, Doctor Wolfe?"

Alistair was focused on the patient who lay on the operating table. The only thing keeping the woman alive was the respirator that sent artificial, measured breaths into her lungs. Soon, even that would be gone. Registering the nurse's question, he looked up and nodded. "Just about, thank you, nurse. Feel free to leave. It's way past late. I'll finish up here."

"Are you sure?" the nurse asked, unable to keep the hopeful note out of her voice.

"Yes, of course. The excitement's over. All I have to do is suture her up and unplug the machine. Then I'm done. I don't need you for that. I'll talk to the family and make sure she's sent to the morgue afterwards."

The nurse nodded and smiled gratefully. She'd been on her feet for hours. Alistair was sure she wouldn't argue with him about leaving the operating theater a little sooner than the end of her shift. He was counting on it.

"Thank you, Doctor Wolfe. I'm rostered on again first thing in the morning, so I really appreciate being able to get away a little early. I'll barely have time to put my head down on the pillow before I have to be on shift again."

Alistair tossed her a sympathetic smile. "Yes, those back-to-back shifts are a bitch. I hope you don't live too far away?"

"No, about twenty minutes from the hospital. Long enough, though, when I'm following a late shift with an early."

"Go, and don't think anything more of it. I'll see you in the morning."

She flashed him another grateful smile and then turned and headed toward the exit. Alistair waited a few minutes, to make sure she'd left the suite. When he heard the outer door open and close, he returned his attention to the patient.

The woman's heart, liver and kidneys had been

harvested in accordance with the consent Alistair had obtained from her next of kin. The transplant teams had been in attendance and once the organs were harvested and placed inside insulated containers, the teams evaporated with their precious cargo, to be couriered under police escort to the various hospitals around Sydney where the transplants would then take place.

It was an exciting, tense, nervous time where every minute counted. Somewhere in the city, even now, patients were being prepped for surgery. They would have received the call they'd been waiting for—a donor organ had become available, giving them another chance at life. He couldn't help but send a little prayer heavenwards that one day soon his mother might be so lucky.

The entire organ donation process filled Alistair with indescribable hope. It was almost like playing God. And now, if it meant he made a little extra money on the side, who could argue with that? It was an excellent outcome for all concerned, but right now, the woman on the table had so much more to offer and Alistair was just the man to take advantage of it. Working quickly, he removed the lungs, intestines and pancreas.

Next, he pinned the woman's eyelids open and removed both corneas and the sclera. A lot of people didn't pay any heed to what they considered such insignificant tissues but for Alistair, the thought that he might be responsible for helping a blind person see was far too important to overlook. Besides, Biologistics paid good money for eye tissue.

He thought of the terms of his contract with the US corporation and frowned. He was only in the second month of his arrangement and already, he risked breaching its terms. August was all but over and with temperatures rising, he was way below his quota.

He'd overlooked the fact that, as the weather got warmer, the number of deaths decreased. As spring set in, fewer people burned down their homes with faulty heaters or crashed their cars driving over icy roads. Of course, there was always the possibility of a heatwave in summer, cutting short a few extra lives, but even if that happened, it wouldn't be until January. There was no way he could wait that long.

While the CEO of Biologistics had been amenable up until now, Charles Shillingworth had made it clear that the company took its contracts seriously. There were plenty of doctors around the world who were clamoring to be part of their team. If Alistair failed to measure up to his promise, he'd quickly be replaced.

The thought of losing a second, substantial stream of income put him into a slight panic. He'd used half of the first payment bailing out Richard. His act of goodwill had bought him unlimited access to the deputy coroner and Alistair didn't ever have to worry about risking refusal of an authorization from that quarter, but it also meant he'd seen less than he'd like of the promised windfall. If he could meet the terms of his contract long enough to secure his long-term financial future, he'd be more than pleased.

The problem was finding and harvesting the amount of tissue to fill his quota when fewer and fewer patients were dying. It had become almost impossible to achieve. Even recovering additional tissue that wasn't included in the consent hadn't fully closed the gap.

Alistair continued to justify his actions by relying on the fact that the patient or their relative had agreed to donate at least some of their organs. He was sure they wouldn't object to him taking all that was of use. What was the difference between donating a heart or lungs or liver and the other things? After all, what was the deceased going to do with them? If there was one thing Alistair couldn't stand, it was waste.

Every day, people were dying around the world from diseases or damage that could be repaired if there was enough donated tissue to go around. It didn't make sense to him to cremate healthy, useable organs or put them in the ground. Skin from deceased persons could totally transform the lives of victims suffering from severe burns and protect them from life-threatening bacterial infections and it had done wonders for breast reconstructive surgery. As far as he was concerned, there were only positive gains to be had from increasing the supply of human tissue.

Moving to the feet of the patient, he ran his scalpel across the woman's ankles. With an efficiency that came from experience, he stripped away the tendons and ligaments. He did the same to her wrists and carefully stored the tissues in the special containers that were used for that purpose. He could only hope the woman didn't end up at the funeral home where his sister's friend worked.

Thinking of Sam and Hannah and the fact that they'd gone to the police gave him a moment's pause. Ever since Samantha had told him, it had been playing on his mind. He was more than concerned that at least two individuals had noticed his handiwork.

He should have known better than to illegally harvest tissues from a patient tagged for an autopsy, but after Sam's birthday, when she'd first mentioned the increase in donor bodies, he'd talked to Richard and the man had assured him again the only pathologist to handle Alistair's bodies would be him.

That obviously hadn't happened, or Sam wouldn't have seen what she did. He remembered the patient she spoke of. He'd been at work when he'd been paged by the ICU. In accordance with the State law and hospital protocol, he'd called Richard and had obtained his authority to harvest prior to the post mortem. At that time, Richard assured Alistair he'd conduct the PM himself. To make things worse, Alistair now had an embalmer from a funeral home taking note of the number of donor bodies coming her way. To have Hannah Langdon question the anomalies was just another thorn in his side.

The best thing to do would be to stop the illegal harvesting, at least until the interest in it had died down. Hell, thanks to his sister and her friend, even now he might have an over enthusiastic police sergeant about to knock on his door asking questions. He had no way of knowing how serious the officer had taken the girls' concerns, but even so, it would be wise to keep a low profile for a little while.

He could always start up again in summer, but it would mean breaching his contract and that could be the end of the money until things picked up again. Furthermore, there was no guarantee Biologistics would rehire him. In fact, more likely the opposite. Charles Shillington probably wouldn't want anything to do with him if he couldn't come up with the contracted goods.

With a sigh, Alistair sutured the woman's wounds closed and then covered her with a sheet. He was still in a quandary about what to do. Switching off the respirator, he waited a little while and then called a porter to transport the body to the hospital morgue. She'd be collected by whatever funeral home or crematorium the family had arranged, and with a bit of luck, that would be the end of it.

He wished he believed deep in his gut that it would be that simple. When had life become so complicated...?

Rohan swung the unmarked squad car alongside the curb and killed the engine. A large, bold sign fixed to the fence bordering the nearest property announced to the world that it was

Forsyth's Funeral Home. He glanced across at his partner who sat beside him.

"Have you ever been inside a funeral home, Bryce?"

"Nope, but it can't be any worse than the morgue and I've pulled that short straw on more than one occasion."

Rohan chuckled. "There are close to fifty funeral homes in the vicinity of the Sydney Harbour Hospital. For this stage of the investigation, I've chosen the five that are closest. I want to determine whether any other funeral homes have noticed an increase in donor bodies or other anomalies over the past few months."

Bryce nodded. "It'll be interesting to hear what they have to say. I can't imagine that a rogue doctor, illegally removing body tissue, would take the time to enquire about where the bodies are to go for services and burial. In fact, that kind of information generally wouldn't even have been decided upon at that time."

"Yeah, that's the way I see it, too. If it's going on, I won't be surprised if the majority of the undertakers, if not all of them, confirm Hannah Langdon's story. But it doesn't hurt to gather additional evidence and get a clearer picture about what we're dealing with. The more information we're armed with, the more pressure we can bring on the hospital to cooperate."

Rohan had used the time since Samantha and Hannah attended the police station to get a clearer picture of the organ and tissue donation process before bringing his boss up to speed and he was surprised at what his research had revealed. Worldwide, it seemed the majority of people simply didn't put their mind to organ and tissue donation and for those who did, most of them didn't favor the idea. The reasons were many and varied, but Rohan understood them.

He glanced at Bryce. "Do you know the major barriers to people wanting to donate organs and tissue on their death?"

Bryce nodded. "Believe it or not, I do. Chanel raised the topic not long after the triplets were born. I must admit, I hadn't given it any real thought before then. Chanel told me decisions not to donate are often because of a lack of understanding about brain death and how it's determined, or because of a general mistrust of doctors."

Rohan grinned. "Considering your lovely wife's a doctor, it must have been tough for her to share that."

"Not at all. She understands better than most why some people act with caution around the medical profession. She says it's mostly from ignorance and fear. Most of us don't have anything to do with hospitals and doctors and medical stuff unless we're sick or injured and it's then that we're at our most vulnerable. Vulnerable people don't trust easily. It's just the way it is."

"True. I've never spent any time inside a hospital unrelated to work. I'd probably be one of those freaking out if I was unwell enough to be admitted. Until Samantha Wolfe raised the issue of organ donation the other day, I hadn't given it any real thought."

Bryce shot him a wry smile. "Like thousands of other people."

"I guess so. I've never been personally touched by the issue; never known anyone who faced certain death without a transplant. But I can see now how important it is to have the conversation with loved ones. From what I've read, it's so much easier to deal with the issue of consent when everyone knows where they stand, particularly if you're the next of kin."

The men climbed out of the squad car and met on the pavement adjacent to the funeral home. The business was conducted in a federation-style house squatting among similarly ancient neighbors. A few streets over, the original buildings had been replaced with newer structures, all sporting an excess of style and glass, but modernization hadn't yet made it this far.

There had been an attempt to keep up a garden, and a scattering of small flowers grew beside unenthusiastic patches of grass, but the building's paintwork had been recently refreshed and the heritage colors of heavy cream, dark green and maroon contrasted nicely.

Rohan figured it wouldn't matter what the place looked like. To grieving relatives, struggling to deal with the effort of arranging a funeral, any type of building more than likely evoked nothing but dread—if noticed at all. He turned to Bryce. "You ready?"

Bryce drew in a breath and squared his

shoulders. "Hey, it's a funeral home. How bad can it be?"

Rohan smothered a grin and pushed open the white picket gate that led up a concrete path to the front door. The gate squeaked in protest.

"It mustn't see a lot of use," Bryce mused. "Who could stand putting up with that kind of noise all day?"

"I can't imagine a place like this is overrun with eager staff and it's not likely they'd receive many repeat complaints from clients."

Bryce offered a slight grin and then followed Rohan up the two steps that ended at a porch. The weathered boards creaked under their boots. An ancient doorbell was situated beside the front door.

"Let's see if this works," Rohan murmured as he pressed the button. He heard the sound of a bell echoing inside the house. Stepping away, he waited with Bryce for the door to open.

"How are Chanel and the girls, anyway?" Rohan asked in an attempt to fill the silence.

This time, Bryce's grin was unrestrained. "They're good. Chanel's going crazy trying to juggle work and three two-year-olds, but she insists she can do it all. I tell her she's mad. She should wait until the girls are at least in school before resurrecting her career, but she loves being a doctor and doesn't want her skills to go rusty. It would drive me to drink if I was trying to do even half of what she does."

Rohan chuckled. "That's why God made women the mothers. They're more naturally skilled at multi-tasking. It's a proven fact. Besides, work might provide some relief for her if you have good child care."

"Yes, we're lucky in that regard and you won't get any argument from me about my wife's ability to multi-task," Bryce replied, shaking his head ruefully. "I've seen her in action."

"She works at the Sydney Harbour Hospital, doesn't she?"

"Yep. She won't hear a bad word said about the place, despite what went on there a couple of years ago."

Rohan frowned. "That must have been before my time. I was still stationed out at Penrith. What happened?"

"I was the lead detective on the investigation. It was how I met Chanel." Bryce smiled at what was obviously a fond memory.

"Forget that mushy crap. What happened?"

Bryce's expression turned grim. "One of the medical staff decided to play God. Doctor Leo Baker was murdering patients indiscriminately using poison from castor beans. My grandmother came very close to being one of his victims."

At the mention of Leo Baker, Rohan's foggy memories of the event suddenly returned. "I remember seeing reports in the media. He was a bigwig in the hospital. Right?"

"Yeah, it was a huge shock to everyone who knew him, including Chanel."

"She knew him?"

"She trained under him. She was the first person to bring it to our attention. She turned up at the station looking like she'd just stepped off a fashion shoot and told me one of Sydney Harbour Hospital's most respected surgeons was doing away with his patients. What could I do?" Bryce grinned. "A girl who had both looks and brains and boundless courage to boot. I had no choice but to marry her."

Rohan smiled. He'd met Chanel on a few occasions at staff functions and found her charming and pretty and smart. Bryce was lucky to have fallen in love with a girl who had it all. Rohan wondered if he'd ever be so fortunate. That triggered thoughts of his parents and the conversation he'd had with his dad about his mother's health and Rohan gave himself a mental reminder to call his father again and get another update.

The sound of the door opening snagged his attention and he focused on the short balding man who stood in the doorway. A pair of thick black-rimmed spectacles, reminiscent of something from the fifties, perched on the man's bulbous, red nose. Gray whiskers dotted his face.

"Can I help you?" The man's voice was scratchy, as if from lack of use. Bryce couldn't help but think the man probably didn't engage in too much conversation during his working hours.

"I'm Detective Sergeant Rohan Coleridge and this is Detective Sergeant Bryce Sutcliffe. We're making a few enquiries about some of the bodies you've had through here the last couple of months."

The man frowned and his face clouded with

suspicion. "Detectives? Why would two detectives be interested in what I do?"

"Are you Mr Forsyth?" Rohan asked, ignoring the man's question.

"Yes, I'm Melvin Forsyth."

"So you're the owner of Forsyth's Funeral Home?" Bryce asked.

"Yes, I inherited it from my father and his father before him. We've been in the undertaking business for more than one hundred years."

Melvin thrust back his thin shoulders and behind his thick glasses, his eyes gleamed with pride. Rohan wondered what it would be like to grow up knowing you were destined to spend your days working in a funeral home.

"Do you mind if we come inside and ask you a few more questions?" Bryce asked.

Once again, the man looked reticent. "Why?"

"We're investigating a complaint," Rohan explained patiently. "We'd like to talk to you about whether you've noticed anything strange about the bodies you've recently embalmed."

Melvin looked affronted. "Complaint? Who's made a complaint? I bet it was that big fat daughter of Eloisa Jackson. That woman insisted on choosing the very cheapest coffin for her mother and then had the hide to bargain me down on the price! She accused me of stealing money from people when they were at their most needy.

"*Humph!*" he scoffed. "From the size of her, she's never been needy in her life. I tell you what, I wouldn't want to be paying for *her* coffin. She'll need one custom made. There won't be a coffin off the shelf that will fit the likes of her!"

By now, the man was quite worked up. His breath came faster and his cheeks were flushed. He looked more alive than he had when he opened the door. Rohan hurried to reassure him.

"It's nothing like that, Mr Forsyth. The complaint's not about you. Do you mind if we come in so we can discuss it in more detail?"

With a dramatic sigh, Melvin turned and headed down a short corridor. To the right was a small waiting room. It was gloomy with heavy red velvet drapes that covered the floor-to-ceiling windows and blocked all but the tiniest glimmer of light. At the end of the corridor, there was a closed door with a "Staff Only—Do Not Enter" hand-printed note taped to its surface.

"How long is this going to take?" Melvin asked over his shoulder.

"Do you have someplace else to be?" Rohan asked.

"No, but I'm working back here. I need to finish what I'm doing. It's not something I can start and then come back to later. It's why I took so long to answer the door. I was hoping you'd give up and go away."

Rohan nodded in understanding. "We're happy to talk while you work." He threw a glance at Bryce who suddenly paled. "Aren't we Detective Sutcliffe?"

If looks could kill, Rohan would have died on the spot, but then, to his credit, Bryce nodded. "Of course, Detective Coleridge. No sense keeping Melvin from his work."

"If that's the case," Melvin said, looking relieved, "come on through. I have Molly Matthews hooked up to the aspiration machine. It's in the process of draining her gas and fluids and it's really something I need to oversee. I'd already started it before you rang the doorbell."

Bryce turned a paler shade of gray and even Rohan took a breath and braced himself for what lay beyond. Melvin opened the door, apparently oblivious to the discomfort and lack of enthusiasm of the officers who followed in his wake.

"Here she is! Oh, good! It hasn't finished yet."

Rohan and Bryce stepped into the average-sized room where Melvin had entered ahead of them. The body of an elderly woman lay naked on the steel table. Rohan expected her skin to be bluish and purple, like it usually was in death, but was surprised to find she looked more alive than dead.

"I've already injected the formaldehyde," Melvin explained, taking note of Rohan's surprise. "It gives the body color and a more lifelike appearance. It plumps out the features and helps the body look less drawn. It's worked magic on Molly, don't you think?" he grinned.

Rohan nodded in agreement. Though he hadn't seen Molly before the process, he'd seen his fair share of dead bodies. He didn't dare look at Bryce. "You're good at your job, Melvin. For a moment there, I wasn't sure if Molly was still alive."

The man cackled in delight, as pleased as a

small child with a bagful of candy. "Detective, you are too wicked!" He shook his head and then turned back to the body.

A trocar had been inserted just under the ribs and helped drain Molly Matthews of her body fluids. The aspiration machine continued to hum in the background. Melvin squinted at the suction pump and tubing that led from the trocar to a large sink and nodded in satisfaction.

"Almost done," he murmured.

Bryce removed himself to the furthest part of the room and stood leaning with his back against a counter, his arms crossed over his chest. It looked like he was trying hard to breathe through his mouth. Rohan could understand why. The stench of formaldehyde and the indescribable smell of death permeated the air and even Rohan struggled with it. Breathing as shallowly as he could manage, he concentrated his attention on the funeral director.

"Do you work on your own, Melvin?" he asked.

"Yes, I do a lot of the time. I have a young girl who comes in a few hours a day to assist me during our busier weeks. Over winter, we always see a greater influx of bodies. The cold weather. It's hard on old bones."

Rohan moved closer. From the corner of his eye, he noticed Bryce also stepped forward—albeit reluctantly.

"Have you noticed anything unusual this winter?" Rohan asked, taking a notepad and pen out of his shirt pocket.

"Not that I can think of."

"Nothing strange about the bodies coming through?" Bryce added.

Melvin frowned and peered at him through his thick lenses. "Strange? In what way?"

"What about bodies with donated organs and tissues?" Rohan supplied, not wanting to lead the potential witness more than was necessary. "Have you noticed an increase in the number of them?"

"Now that you mention it, there have been a few more of those than normal. I hadn't really given it much thought, although I should have." He laughed. "It gets me out of here a little earlier if some of the organs are missing. Not as much formaldehyde required and the aspiration process is quicker, too."

"How many have you seen this winter?" Rohan asked.

Melvin paused a moment to think. "Maybe seven or eight a week. Yes, now that I think about it, I've probably had at least one a day for the past couple of months. And they've been generous donors, too," he added.

"Generous? What do you mean by that?" Rohan asked.

"The usual donor body that comes through has the standard surgical scar indicating the heart and lungs have been removed, but the more recent ones appeared to have been cleared of a whole lot more. The incisions have extended all the way through to the lower abdomen, as if everything inside has been removed. I can't think of another reason for making such a long incision."

It was exactly as Hannah Langdon had

described. Rohan made eye contact with Bryce and could tell his partner was thinking much the same thing.

"What about other areas of the body? Have you noticed anything unusual?" Rohan asked.

Melvin lifted a large bottle of fluid off a nearby shelf and proceeded to inject it into the body on the table. "I'm distributing the fluid between the thoracic and abdominal cavities," he explained, noticing Rohan's curiosity. "I saturate all the organs to eliminate any residual odors."

Rohan nodded and well understood the reasons why most people chose to go through life oblivious to what happened to them after they died. Melvin's work practices fell fairly and squarely into that category. Still, if Rohan wanted to ask questions, he had no choice but to listen to the undertaker's enthusiastic explanations. Keeping up his part by plastering an interested expression on his face, Rohan steered the conversation back to the investigation.

"How often do people donate other types of tissue, such as skin or ligaments and tendons?" he asked.

"Not often at all, Detective. It's a shame, really. So much more could be put to use. I don't think enough people turn their mind to how much good donating their organs can do. Of the small number who do, they usually restrict their donation to the standard organs: heart, kidneys, liver and lungs."

"So, have you seen any recent bodies with wounds that might indicate ligaments, tendons and the like could have been harvested?" Rohan asked, needing to make sure.

"No, I don't think so. Not in the last little while, anyway. It would have been six or eight months ago since I saw one that was missing skin." He turned back to the body on the table and removed the apparatus he'd used to insert the cavity fluid into Molly Matthews. A moment later, he pulled a container out of the cupboard that was filled with cotton wool. Calmly and efficiently, he began packing the woman's mouth and nose.

Rohan looked across at Bryce and indicated with a movement of his head that perhaps it was time to leave. Bryce's face flooded with relief. Rohan turned back to Melvin who was now stitching the mouth of Molly Matthews closed.

"We'll leave you to it, Melvin. We appreciate your time," Rohan said. Bryce lifted his hand in farewell and both men turned and headed toward the door. Rohan had just reached for the handle when the door opened. He almost collided with the young girl who stood on the other side.

"Oh, I'm so sorry!" she gasped. "I didn't realize you were there."

She looked like she was no more than eighteen or nineteen. Her skin was scarred with severe acne, but she had the bluest eyes Rohan had ever seen.

"It's fine. Don't worry about it. We were on our way out."

"Oh, Jane, you're here. That's great," Melvin said, looking up from Molly Matthews. "I got an early start on this one, but there are another four in the fridge. I'd appreciate it if you could get started right away."

"Of course," Jane replied.

Rohan stepped back to allow the girl he assumed was Forsyth's assistant, into the room. She threw Rohan and Bryce a look filled with curiosity.

"I take it these men aren't making funeral arrangements, Mr Forsyth, given that they're back here."

"You're right, Jane," Melvin replied, as he squirted a dob of peach-scented shampoo into Molly's wispy, white hair. "These men are detectives. They're making enquiries about the bodies with donated organs we've had come through the funeral home over the past few months."

Jane nodded, but Rohan noticed a new tension in her stance. "What did you tell them?" she asked, keeping her gaze on her boss.

"I told them we'd had a greater number than usual, but I haven't really noticed anything else out of the ordinary—and it's winter, after all."

Rohan watched Jane closely. She chewed on her lip and looked both scared and uncertain all at once. He wondered what had caused her curious reaction and instinctively directed his next question to her.

"What about you, Jane? Have you noticed anything unusual?"

For a second, she froze and then sighed quietly, almost looking relieved. "It's... It's really weird that you're here. Only yesterday I was working on a woman who bore signs that she'd donated some of her organs, but...there was more."

"What do you mean?" Rohan asked.

She drew in a deep breath. "The woman was missing a couple large areas of skin on her back and on the back of her legs. She also had wounds across both wrists and ankles. It was weird and awful and it stuck in my mind... It made me feel sick. I wasn't even sure I could come in today."

"Why didn't you say anything?" Melvin asked, looking stricken.

"You were on the phone when I finished up yesterday. I had an appointment in the city. I couldn't wait around." She turned back to Rohan and Bryce.

"I've only worked here a few months, but I've never seen anything like it. It was lucky the family requested that she be buried in a pantsuit. I don't know how I would have concealed the incisions if they'd wanted her dressed in shorts and a T-shirt."

"Is the body still here?" Bryce asked hopefully.

Melvin shook his head. "No, the funeral was scheduled first thing this morning."

"What do you think about the incisions, Melvin?" Rohan asked.

"It's more likely than not the wrist and ankle wounds were the result of ligament and tendon removal. The skin removal speaks for itself."

Rohan digested the information and couldn't help but compare the similarities with the body Hannah Langdon had spoken of earlier in the week. Another question occurred to him.

"Which hospital have these donor bodies come

from?" he asked the funeral director. "Do you keep a record of such things?"

"No, but there's no need," Melvin replied. "We're right down the street from the Sydney Harbour Hospital and it's the only hospital that services this area. Most people who live around here, and end up in there, come here if they don't make it out alive. I call it near-ology, Detective. Most families choose the funeral home closest to where they live. It's convenient and also a way of giving back to their community, you could say."

"What about the nursing homes? There are a few of them in this area," Rohan said.

"Yes, and we get our fair share from those establishments. In fact, they keep us even busier than the hospital, but you asked about donor bodies. Nursing homes don't go in for organ and tissue harvesting. They're neither qualified nor equipped to handle it. The only people who have even any chance of seeing their organs and tissue donated are those that die in a major hospital, and even then it doesn't always work out."

CHAPTER 8

Rohan and Bryce left the premises of the fifth and final funeral home on Rohan's list and climbed back into the squad car. They'd been at it all day and both of them were beyond fatigued. Rohan didn't want to step inside another embalming room for the rest of his life and he was sure Bryce felt the same. Both were convinced they'd never get the smell out of their clothes.

"So," Bryce said, turning to tug on his seatbelt, "what do you think?"

Rohan pursed his lips. "Most of the people we've spoken to agree they've seen an increase in the number of donor bodies and the majority of the bodies have come from the Sydney Harbour Hospital."

"Yeah, although given that the Sydney Harbour Hospital is the closest major medical facility to our funeral homes, it's not exactly surprising, is it?"

"It's a pity the hospital only supplies the funeral parlors with the most basic of information. It would be interesting to see if there's a pattern with regard to the doctors involved in the care of these people."

"We should call Deborah Healy."

Rohan quirked an eyebrow. "Who's Deborah Healy?"

"She's one hell of a good-looking woman, even though she must be close to fifty—and she runs a tight ship. I admire her and I wouldn't want her job for quids."

"Which is?" Rohan continued to stare at Bryce, waiting for his partner to get to the point.

"She's the general manager of the Sydney Harbour Hospital."

Rohan was filled with eagerness and anticipation. "I think we need to meet with Ms Healy and sit down for a little chat."

Bryce grinned. "You won't get any argument from me."

———

Rohan and Bryce climbed the flight of stairs that led to Deborah Healy's office. Rohan had called ahead to arrange an appointment. He'd half expected to be put off until the morning, given that the day was almost done, but the general manager had agreed to see them within the hour.

She'd enquired about the reason for their visit and Rohan had told her. Her immediate expression of shock and denial hadn't surprised him. Until the recent Doctor Leo Baker scandal, the Sydney Harbour Hospital had enjoyed an enviable reputation as being among the most prestigious hospitals in the country.

The executive suites were in an older part of the hospital and still showed signs of the grandness and style that had gone into the design of the building more than a century and a half ago. Original stained glass windows were surrounded by heavy wooden frames painted a forest green color. The late afternoon sunlight that shone through them, fell softly onto the polished wooden stairs beneath Rohan's feet.

They reached the landing at the top. Having been there before, Bryce gave directions and within a few moments Rohan was knocking on the closed door. It was opened almost immediately, and he was impressed by the general manager's punctuality. The middle-aged woman who greeted them was smartly dressed in a woollen suit of navy-blue, threaded with gold. A silk blouse in pale pink complemented the outfit.

"Good morning, I'm Detective Sergeant Coleridge and this is my partner, Detective Sergeant Sutcliffe. Are you Ms Healy?"

The woman chuckled. "Good heavens, no! I'm Veronica Blackwell, her receptionist. I'll let Ms Healy know you're here. Please, come in and take a seat."

Rohan and Bryce entered the room. The waiting area was small but tidy, with a dark leather sofa against one wall. A spread of magazines was artfully arranged across the glass top of a wooden coffee table.

"It looks just like it did the last time I was here," Bryce murmured. Rohan acknowledged his comment with a nod.

"Ms Healy will be with you in a moment," Veronica advised. "Can I get you something to drink? Coffee or tea?"

Rohan glanced at Bryce and answered for both of them. "No, thanks. We're fine."

The woman nodded and returned to her seat behind the counter. A moment later, a door to their left opened and a tall, slender woman wearing a tailored, olive-green suit and lemon-colored blouse strode into the waiting room. Without pause, she came straight to where they were sitting and extended her hand.

"Detective Coleridge, I'm Deborah Healy."

Rohan stood and shook the proffered hand. The general manager turned her attention to Bryce.

"Detective Sutcliffe, it's nice to see you again. I trust Chanel and your children are well?"

"Yes, thank you. They're fine."

"Doctor Sutcliffe is one of the finest on our team. We're very pleased she decided to return to work after the triplets were born, although I was a little surprised. It must take some doing, trying to juggle everything."

Bryce nodded in agreement. "Yes, it certainly does."

"Well, anyway, give my regards to your wife. Shall we?"

She turned on one four-inch, black leather heel and headed back the way she'd come. Rohan couldn't help but check out her shapely butt. She must have been edging fifty, but she was trim and toned and had a pair of attractive, stocking-encased legs that would put women half her age to shame.

They followed her into a corner office that overlooked the front entryway of the hospital, a floor below. The room was airy and bright. Sunshine poured through the tall windows that lined the wall behind her desk, flooding the room with natural light. Potted plants that were not only real, but flourishing stood along the window ledge. Rohan was relieved the place smelled nothing like a hospital. He'd had enough of the stench of cleaning fluid, formaldehyde and other undesirable odors to last him a lifetime.

"Please, take a seat."

Rohan turned. Three chairs stood opposite a large wooden desk. He was surprised to discover one of them was occupied. The general manager made the introductions.

"This is Doctor Alistair Wolfe. After you told me you were enquiring about our organ and tissue donation unit, I asked Doctor Wolfe to attend. He is the head of the Organ Donation for Transplantation Unit. I hope you don't mind?" She directed the question to both Rohan and Bryce, but it was Rohan who responded.

"No, of course not. I'm pleased you did. Doctor Wolfe is perhaps in a better position to answer our questions."

The doctor stood and the men greeted each other with handshakes. Rohan took the time to study him. He was one of those good-looking, athletic types and appeared to be in his mid-forties. Silver wings at his temples were in stark contrast to his otherwise dark hair, but they only enhanced his air of keen intelligence and authority.

Small crows' feet jostled for space around his eyes and faint smudges of fatigue left shadows beneath them, but his direct gaze was friendly and open. Something about the man seemed familiar and a memory niggled at the back of Rohan's mind, but it disappeared before he could cement it into a coherent thought.

Deborah took a seat behind her cluttered desk and drew her chair in close. Sitting tall, she folded her hands together in front of her and addressed them.

"So, Detectives, how can we help you?"

Rohan pulled his notebook out of his pocket. "Ms Healy, it's come to our attention that someone in this hospital might be carrying out the removal of some human organs and body tissue on deceased patients without consent."

To the credit of both hospital employees, they maintained their composures. The only evidence that they were affected by Rohan's announcement appeared in the form of a tightening of Doctor Wolfe's lips and a flush that spread slowly across the general manager's cheeks. She motioned for Rohan to continue.

"There are a number of factors that have led us to this conclusion. We've spent some time interviewing staff from various funeral homes in the vicinity of the hospital. As you can imagine, there are a lot. We chose to attend the businesses that were closest to you and we've uncovered some rather disturbing results."

As Rohan spoke, Deborah's expression grew more and more grave. When he finished, her gaze held the smallest hint of fear. Rohan understood her sense of foreboding. It had been less than three years since the fiasco with the murderous Doctor Baker. It had taken the hospital some time to recover from that bad press. He could sympathize with her dread of hearing yet another rogue doctor was on the loose in the Sydney Harbour Hospital. Clearing his throat, he spoke again.

"We also talked to staff at the Glebe Morgue. All of the people we spoke to agreed that they had noticed an increase in the number of bodies coming through their establishments who presented as organ donors."

The general manager held Rohan's gaze and appeared to regain a little of her equilibrium. "That's not entirely surprising, Detective. The hospital has spent considerable funds over the past few months on extensive organ donor advertising campaigns in both the print and electronic media. We've seen some very positive results. I'm sure Doctor Wolfe can provide you with the statistics we've been able to collect so far."

Alistair turned in his chair until he faced Rohan and Bryce. "We're very pleased with how it's all going. Organ donations are up by thirty percent and the campaign only kicked off at the beginning of June. Of course, we always see an increase in deaths over winter, particularly in the elderly and those who run out of skill on the icy roads. It's a tough time of the year for a lot of people. Even with the marvels of modern medicine, we can't always save them."

Rohan thought of his mother and her persistent cough and resolved to call her again and insist she attend upon another doctor. Her regular physician kept claiming it was no more than a bout of the flu, but Rohan and his father weren't entirely convinced by that reassurance.

"What's your role as the head of the Organ Donation for Transplantation Unit, Doctor Wolfe?" Bryce asked.

"The position is relatively new and one that's not without its challenges. I'm a surgeon first and foremost and I assist with many of the organ retrievals. This is done in conjunction with retrieval teams from the various other Sydney hospitals."

"How do you decide which retrieval team to call?" Bryce asked. "Is there a roster?"

Alistair shook his head. "It doesn't work like that. The hospitals involved in the organ transplantation program usually specialize in the transplantation of specific organs. For example, the Royal Prince Alfred Hospital specializes in kidney and liver transplants. Heart and lung transplants tend to be carried out across town at St Vincent's Hospital. Westmead does kidneys and pancreas. So if we get a donation of a kidney, the retrieval teams from RPA and Westmead are notified. If a heart is donated, the St Vincent's team will be called, and so on. Of course, if more than one organ is donated from the same individual, several teams might receive the call."

"It must involve quite a crowd in the operating room," Rohan commented.

The doctor smiled. "You have no idea."

"Whose job is it to approach the relatives of the dying patient and obtain the necessary consents?" Rohan asked.

"I'm head of the Unit," Alistair replied. "If I'm working when such an occasion arises, a staff member will page me and I meet with the relatives, explain the circumstances and the condition of their loved one, talk about the organ donation process and how much it can mean to someone on a transplant list—and then hopefully, obtain their consent."

"You're obviously a good communicator if the recent stats are anything to go by, Doctor Wolfe," Rohan said.

The doctor eyed Rohan somberly. "It's a difficult job and one I never look forward to, but I know how important it is to at least try and convince people to donate."

He leaned forward, as if to emphasize his point. "More than sixteen hundred Australians are on a transplant waiting list at any given time, Detective. You might not know it, but less than one percent of patients die in hospital in the specific circumstances where organ donation is even possible."

He drew in a quick breath. Determination and a steely resolve deepened the color of his brown eyes. "The numbers are against us. Demand far outstrips supply. It's the reason I work so hard to raise awareness and to increase the donor rate."

The general manager sat straighter and clasped her hands together in front of her. "Doctor Wolfe does his job with an admirable level of skill, sensitivity and compassion. The hospital receives countless letters thanking us and Doctor Wolfe for the manner in which he has dealt with them and the assistance he gives in helping grieving relatives make an extremely difficult decision. There's no doubt about it, the recipients of those organs owe him a great debt of gratitude."

Alistair looked both humbled and grateful at the general manager's words. Rohan was moved by his modesty and his dedication.

"I can't imagine how hard it is for you to do that kind of thing," he said. "It must take its toll."

The doctor grimaced. "Of course, both physically and mentally. I leave here most nights feeling drained, but I believe wholeheartedly in what I do. I took an oath to do all I could to ease the suffering of people and help sustain life. If that means approaching grieving relatives during their darkest hour in order to persuade them to give the gift of life to others, I'll do it over and over again. No question."

Rohan glanced at Bryce and he could tell his partner was just as moved by the doctor's passionate belief as he was. Rohan hadn't lied when he'd told Samantha he'd never given much thought to organ donation, but after the research he'd undertaken, and listening to Alistair Wolfe, he was struck with an urgent need to do whatever was necessary to register himself as a donor.

All of a sudden, the niggling feeling of familiarity he'd had upon first meeting Alistair came back to him in a rush and he realized its cause: The good doctor closely resembled Samantha. Rohan blinked, surprised it had taken him so long to make the connection. Surely, the two of them must be related? He turned to the doctor, wanting to have it confirmed.

"Are you any relation to Doctor Samantha Wolfe?"

The tension in the doctor's face eased and he smiled with genuine warmth. His voice conveyed his affection. "Yes, of course. She's my baby sister."

Rohan acknowledged the man's words with a slight smile. "When we were introduced, there was something about you that appeared familiar. Now I know why."

"You know Sam?"

"Yes."

"You've spoken to her in the course of your investigation," Alistair guessed.

"Yes, but I've known her for much longer than that. We met when she was in college."

Alistair's eyebrows rose high in surprise. "Wow, that long ago. She's never mentioned you."

"That doesn't surprise me. I was dating her roommate at the time. Things didn't end well."

Alistair nodded in understanding and Bryce cleared his throat. "Let's get back to the investigation."

"Of course," Rohan replied.

"What's the procedure when a patient whose relatives consent to donate their organs requires an autopsy?" Bryce asked. "I had it in my head that a coroner's case would have to arrive at the morgue intact, but I understand that's not necessarily the case?"

Alistair nodded. "That's correct, Detective Sutcliffe. It depends upon the circumstances of the individual case. Once we know a critically ill patient's relatives desire to donate the patient's organs, usually a senior ICU doctor will contact the coroner or one of his deputies to obtain his authorization. The matter will be discussed and things such as the likely cause of death, whether there are any suspicious circumstances and that kind of thing, will be taken into account prior to the coroner making his decision.

"If the coroner gives the go ahead to comply with all or part of the donor's request, then the doctors go to work and the retrieval process begins. If something is suspicious or unclear about cause of death and the coroner declines to authorize the donation, the deceased will be sent to the morgue with their organs intact."

Rohan listened. It was much as Samantha had described when she'd attended the police station. "How many donor requests end up going ahead with the authorization of the coroner?" he asked.

Alistair thought for a moment. "On average, perhaps one or two a week. The odds increase with a rise in the number of deaths, such as during a harsh winter. Sydney might not see snow, but that doesn't mean people here don't feel the cold and we know that even temperatures that don't fall below zero can have a fatal effect."

Rohan nodded. This information also fit with what Samantha had told him. "How often do you get patients who donate a substantial number of organs and tissues? Does it ever happen?"

"Yes, occasionally," Alistair replied. "When I approach a patient's relatives to discuss the possibility of organ donation, my aim is to have them consent to us taking anything we can use, but more often than not, they limit consent to the major organs: heart, lungs, liver and kidneys."

"What about skin and eye tissue? Or ligaments and tendons?" Bryce asked.

"If I've managed to convince a relative to give consent for everything, then that means everything. Unfortunately, like I said, it doesn't happen very often."

"How often is not very often?" Rohan asked.

Alistair shrugged and looked across at the general manager. "I don't know. Maybe once every three or four months."

Deborah Healy nodded. "That sounds about right."

"During our investigations, we've discovered that recently there has been substantial removal of organs and tissue from at least two bodies and the two we know of were patients of this hospital. Does this surprise you?"

Alistair nodded. "Yes, it does. Are you sure about your information?"

"Absolutely certain," Rohan replied.

"Well, I guess it's not impossible. It's certainly not the norm."

"If you're not around at the time a patient dies, who obtains the consent and who does the surgery?" Rohan asked.

"There's a roster. I have a whole team of very capable doctors who work with me."

"I see," Rohan said. "So a single doctor couldn't be in the situation where he could act upon something like this on his own?"

"We have certain protocols in place," Deborah interjected smoothly, her expression firm. "There is a strict procedure that is adhered to in every circumstance and we always treat our donor bodies with the utmost care and respect."

Rohan looked at Alistair. "Do you always follow protocol, Doctor Wolfe?"

The deliberate gibe didn't seem to ruffle the doctor's composure. "Of course, Detective. That's why we have them."

Rohan stared at him a moment longer. Satisfied with the doctor's response, he returned his attention to the general manager.

"Thank you for your time, Ms Healy and for arranging for Doctor Wolfe to be in attendance. It's been most enlightening and has saved us a good deal of time." Rohan reached across the desk and shook her hand before pushing away from his chair. Bryce followed suit.

Rohan turned to Alistair and again held out his hand. "Thank you for your cooperation, Doctor Wolfe."

"My pleasure. I hope I've been able to help. The very thought that someone might be interfering with patients without consent is abhorrent. If it's true and news of it gets out, it would set the entire organ donation movement back decades."

"Don't worry, at this point our work is confidential. I agree wholeheartedly with your concerns and it's why I'm determined to get to the bottom of it as soon as possible," Rohan replied and then turned back to the general manager. "I'll need a copy of the records of any patient who went through an organ donation retrieval process in the past three months, including details of treating doctors, retrieval teams, patient consents and so on. I appreciate it's a lot to ask, but we need to find out what, if anything's been happening."

"Of course," Deborah replied. "The hospital will fully cooperate. If someone's acting illegally, we need to identify them and remove them, without delay."

"And charge them," Bryce added.

"Yes, of course," the general manager agreed.

Rohan looked back at Alistair. "Give my best to your sister the next time you see her," he said.

Alistair nodded and threw him a quick smile. Rohan turned away and headed for the door.

———————

"What do you think?" Bryce asked as he and Rohan headed back to the squad car.

"I can see why Wolfe's the poster child for the hospital. He's old enough that people will trust him—charismatic and good-looking to boot. What more could they want?"

"I agree. If his data is to be believed, he's certainly turned things around as far as raising awareness of organ donation. I had no idea less than one percent of hospital deaths are eligible for donations."

"Yeah, it's made me realize I need to do something about putting myself on a register. Someone else might as well have the benefit of what's left after I'm gone."

Bryce nodded. "After Chanel and I talked about it I filled out the form."

"Alistair Wolfe is certainly devoted to the cause. We need more people like him." They continued across the car park. Rohan pulled the keys out of his pocket and tossed them to Bryce. "Here. You can drive. I thought I might pay a visit to Doctor Samantha Wolfe. The morgue's not far out of our way. I'll call ahead and check if she's there and if she is, I'll get you to drop me off. I'll take a cab back to the station."

"Do you want me to come with you?"

"No. This is personal."

Bryce threw him a sly look. "I heard you say you'd known her since college. If she takes after her brother in the looks department, I can see why you might want to spend a little more time with her."

"Fuck off, Sutcliffe. I'm not trying to get into her

pants. All I want to do is talk with her. About something that happened in the past."

"Yeah, yeah, yeah." Bryce grinned.

It was clear Bryce didn't believe him for a minute. Rohan bit down on another sharp retort and decided silence was his best defense. As Bryce pulled out of the parking lot, Rohan phoned the morgue and asked to speak with Sam.

"I'm afraid Doctor Wolfe's in the middle of an autopsy at the moment. May I take a message?"

"No, that's fine. I'll catch up with her a little later." He ended the call and slid the phone back in his pocket.

Bryce shot him a quick look. "I take it she's not at work."

"She's there. She just can't come to the phone at the moment. I'll go and wait there until she's available."

Ten minutes later, Bryce pulled up to the curb outside the Department of Forensic Medicine and Rohan climbed out. He leaned in through the open car window.

"Thanks, mate. I'll see you tomorrow. Until we get the paperwork from the hospital, there's not much more we can do."

"No problem. I might even try to get home early for a change."

"Yeah, just in time to help with dinner and all the bathing," Rohan joked.

Bryce grimaced. "Maybe I won't leave early. I'm sure there must be some filing I can do around the office... Or maybe I'll even put my hand up for a double shift."

Rohan laughed "See... Now you can understand why Chanel wanted to get back to work." He stepped away and threw Bryce a wave. A moment later, the squad car disappeared into the traffic.

———————

Sam stared down at the tiny body on the steel gurney and braced herself against a surge of emotion. She hadn't known the two-year-old who lay so still and cold on the table beside her, but she couldn't help feeling distressed and sad that an innocent young life had been cut short.

The child's parents claimed the baby was dead in his cot when they found him. The preliminary findings were Sudden Infant Death Syndrome, but after close examination of the little boy, it was obvious he hadn't died from natural causes.

Numerous bruises around his chest and neck area indicated he'd been held down with a fair degree of pressure. Tiny petechial hemorrhages in his eyes indicated suffocation. An X-ray identified several old fractures, now long healed, but the hospital notes that had come with him indicated no previous history of broken bones. Sam could only assume the parents had taken him elsewhere for treatment. She couldn't bear to think the poor baby might have had to heal all on his own without proper medical care.

Sighing quietly, she finished the autopsy and closed the incision. Anger and helplessness burned inside her at the thought of how the little boy had suffered. Some people didn't deserve to be parents. It was as simple as that.

Here she was, at thirty-four and getting more and more desperate for a baby and yet this little boy hadn't been given a chance. Abused and discarded like unwanted trash, he'd died a terrifying death. She couldn't imagine how it felt not to be able to breathe. It broke her heart that no one had been able to save him. The only thing she could hope for was that the parents would suffer in jail.

"Sam, I have a Detective Coleridge out in the waiting room. He's asked if he could see you."

Sam looked up and blinked, focusing on the young girl who manned the front desk. "I'm sorry, Angie, I was a million miles away. Could you repeat that?"

"Detective Coleridge is outside. He'd like to see you."

Sam's stomach did a flip-flop and her heart skipped a beat. The thought of seeing Rohan again, filled her with nerves. It wasn't because he was so attractive, or that he looked at her like her could read her innermost thoughts, it was just...

She shook her head. He might be good-looking, but that didn't excuse his despicable treatment of her friend. Sam didn't care that it had happened a decade ago. Children were a gift from God. No one had the right to abandon them or treat them with so little love and disrespect. The child on the gurney was a tragic example of that.

"Tell him I'm too busy, Angie. I have another PM to do after this one and it's already late."

"Of course, Sam. I'll let him know." She disappeared the way she'd come and Sam drew her attention back to the child. With the autopsy finished, all she had to do was return him to the fridge and complete the paperwork.

With gloved hands, she picked up the baby and carried him back to the refrigerator. She did her best not to look at him as she placed him back on the rack. He looked so tiny among the thirty or so other bodies that lined the shelves. With a sad sigh, she headed back to her workstation and collected her notes. Her report to the police would be heavy going. Turning away, she almost collided with Angie, who gave out a little yelp.

"Oh, Sam, I'm so sorry. I didn't realize you were coming this way."

"It's all right, Angie," Sam replied, brushing the girl's apology away. "I should have been watching where I was going. I wasn't expecting anyone to be behind me."

Angie's face flushed with embarrassment. She opened her mouth again, but Sam cut her off. "Angie, it's fine. Don't worry about it. Now, what can I do for you this time?"

"It's the detective. I told him you were too busy to see him, but he insists it won't take long. He says he's not leaving until he gets a few minutes of your time. What would you like me to do?"

Sam drew in a deep breath and eased it out slowly. She'd just carried out a PM on an abused baby. She didn't feel like talking to anyone, even if it was someone she knew. Very few people understood what it was like to deal with death, day after day. Some days were easier than others. This wasn't one of them.

The thought that Rohan had said he was prepared to wait until she was available, irritated her. He had no right to turn up at her place of work and demand to see her. He could have telephoned and left a message, like every other police officer she dealt with.

Maybe he had? She'd been in the autopsy room all morning and most of the afternoon. She'd only returned to her desk briefly during her lunch break and hadn't checked her messages. There was probably a handful of them sent by the receptionist via email, including a call from him. There was no way of knowing without returning to her office.

But to do so meant getting out of her scrubs and cleaning up, only to have to return and get dressed in more scrubs afterwards. She wasn't lying when she'd told Angie she still had another autopsy to do. It would be easier to simply agree to give Rohan the few minutes he wanted and then be done with it.

She sighed with resignation. "Send him in, Angie."

"Are you sure?"

"Yes. That way you won't have to put up with him annoying you out there for what's left of the day."

Angie giggled. "Oh, I don't mind. He's very easy on the eye. I could happily gaze at him all night."

Sam raised an eyebrow and Angie giggled again and turned away. A short time later, there was a brief knock on the door to the autopsy suite and Rohan strode in.

Dressed in a charcoal-gray suit and white business shirt, it wasn't hard to understand Angie's reaction. Rohan looked hot enough to set the pulse rate of any woman under ninety racing. Sam was no exception and the knowledge she was so susceptible did nothing to lighten her mood.

"I'm busy, Detective, and I don't appreciate you bullying my staff into allowing you in here when I simply don't have the time. You have five minutes. What do you want?"

If he was surprised at her abrupt tone, he didn't show it. Instead, he closed the door and came over to where she stood. Most of the other pathologists had left for the day. Save for Phillip, who worked on a body on the other side of the room, the area was empty.

"I wanted to talk to you," Rohan said, his tone low.

"What about?"

"Daphne."

Sam's breath caught in her throat and her pulse took off at a gallop. Was he finally willing to accept responsibility for the way he'd treated his former girlfriend and his unborn child? Sam didn't know whether she was relieved or disappointed.

"What about Daphne?" she asked, keeping her voice even.

"I've been thinking about what you said, what you accused me of. It's obvious Daphne was the one who told you. What she didn't tell you was that the baby wasn't mine."

Sam reeled back in shock and her heart pounded double time. In all the years since college, she hadn't once questioned Daphne's word. Had her former roommate lied when she'd sobbed all over her, crying about how Rohan had gotten her pregnant and then dumped her when he found out? The possibility she'd been misinformed was so enormous, it was too much for Sam to take in. She stared at Rohan, searching his face for the truth.

"Are you saying you weren't the father? That Daphne *cheated* on you?" she said, still aghast.

His face remained impassive. "Yes, that's exactly what I'm saying."

Sam let out a laugh that was tinged with panic. "No, I don't believe you. Daphne was in love with you! She thought you were the moon and the stars! There's no way she would have cheated on you! You're making it up, to justify why you left her. It can't be true. It can't be."

"Do I look like I'm lying?" he said quietly, his tone edged with steel.

Sam stared at him again and the panic inside her increased. If he *was* telling the truth that meant Daphne had deceived her all those years ago. The possibility filled Sam with horror.

She'd spent ten years simmering with anger over Rohan's appalling treatment. Years ago, she'd resolved if she ever crossed paths with Rohan Coleridge again, she'd give him a piece of her mind. He'd be left in no doubt about how she felt about men who walked away from their responsibilities. And yet, now she had to consider the possibility it had all been a lie.

Her first impulse was to speak with Daphne. She wanted to hear it from her old roommate if she'd lied to her and why. But even as that thought formed, Sam realized she'd already subconsciously accepted Rohan was telling the truth. It made so much sense.

It explained why he'd been so shocked when she'd attacked him about abandoning his unborn child. She should have known he was too decent and honorable to do such a despicable thing. A decade ago, they'd been such good friends... Had she wasted years burning with indignation for a liar, a woman who didn't deserve it?

"Why didn't you say something, that night at the station?" Sam asked, her voice cracking with emotion.

Rohan shook his head. "I was so stunned by your accusation, it took me awhile to comprehend. Never in my wildest dreams did I suspect you, or anyone else, thought I'd walked out on my unborn child. You knew me almost as well as Daphne. It cut me to the quick to realize you thought I was capable of such a thing."

"I... I..." Sam couldn't even complete the thought. Had there really been no justification for her actions? Despite their friendship, she'd never once asked him if it were true. She'd believed Daphne's story and that had been the end of it.

Over the months of Daphne's pregnancy, Sam had been a caring and considerate friend, all the time seething over what Rohan had done. She'd plotted ways to make him pay, to bring him to his knees, but by then he was long gone and she hadn't seen him again. Until now.

"You never knew she told me the baby was yours?" she croaked.

"Samantha, I swear I had no idea. When Daphne told me she was pregnant, I was shocked because she'd told me she was on the pill. Then she reminded me she'd been on antibiotics and it can sometimes interfere with the effectiveness of the pill. I guess I panicked a little because it wasn't in our plans, but I assured her I loved her and somehow, we'd work it out.

"A few days later, she was in the shower when a text came in on her phone. I picked it up. It was from some guy called Nathan and he was talking about the "fun" they'd had the last time he'd been in town. It was obvious they'd had sex.

"I confronted her. At first, she went on the offensive and accused me of invading her privacy by looking at her phone, but after awhile, she broke down and admitted she'd had a fling with some biker she knew from her hometown. That was when I asked her for a DNA test."

"And it came back negative."

"Yes."

Sam breathed in heavily and her shoulders slumped on a loud sigh. Once again, she couldn't help but think about all the wasted hours she'd spent hating Rohan Coleridge. She looked up at him and was relieved to find no trace of anger in his eyes. "I'm sorry," she whispered. "I said some terrible things."

He moved closer until she could see the flecks in his bright blue eyes. "It doesn't matter, as long as you understand now."

Sam shook her head back and forth, dismissing his words. "Of course it matters! Don't you see? For ten years, I've thought of you with anger and resentment and so many other awful things. We were good friends! I'd known you for a year and a half! I should have gone to you and demanded to hear your side of the story before taking Daphne's word. You called me a few times afterwards and I refused to answer or call you back. I was so angry at you for what you'd done. You must have wondered what had happened."

Rohan's expression filled with resignation. "I remember thinking it was just the way it was. You were Daphne's friend long before you were mine. When she and I broke up, I forced myself to accept that losing my friendship with you was collateral damage. It was hard to let it go, but I didn't think I had any choice. I wasn't going to make you choose between us."

Caught in a quick shift of emotion, Sam wanted to go to him and throw her arms around him and beg his forgiveness. But she was dressed in scrubs that were stained from the blood of a dead baby and he looked like he'd stepped off the set of a fashion shoot.

"I'm sorry," she said again and hoped he could see how much she meant it.

"And I'm sorry, too. I should have tried harder to

speak with you, to assure you I valued our friendship, despite the fact Daphne and I had gone our separate ways."

"I can't believe how much time I wasted hating you."

"There's no point in looking back, filled with regrets. Let's put it behind us and look to the future." Rohan's voice filled with hope. "It's not too late to pick up where we left off. If I remember rightly, you used to be a mean chess player. You certainly gave me a run for my money, more often than not. How about we get together this weekend? Are you free on Saturday night?"

Though Rohan's tone was light and friendly, a sudden rush of nerves tightened Sam's throat. They'd always been friends, but did she want more than that now? Did *he*?

Daphne was no longer the elephant in the room. They could be anything they wanted to each other...if they wanted. Was she brave enough to find out if his feelings ran any deeper? Did she want to become involved?

The questions raced around inside her head until she was almost dizzy. Aware that Rohan was waiting for her answer, she opened her mouth and surprised herself by saying, "Your place or mine?"

CHAPTER 9

I watch my mother's health deteriorate. Every time I see her, she's weaker. If only I could find her a kidney! I'd happily donate one of mine, if it would do her any good. We're not a match. We never will be. It tears me up inside.

All the organs and tissue I've harvested and I can't find a kidney for my mom. It doesn't seem fair. It isn't fair! And yet, I must continue on. It brings me comfort knowing how many lives I've saved by doing what I do.

And then there is the added benefit of knowing no matter what happens, my wife and children will want for nothing. My actions might be illegal, but for me, the good far outweighs the bad. If I'm caught, I will surrender with dignity and courage, but I will not be sorry for what I've done. I will beg forgiveness from no one...

Rohan stood outside Samantha's apartment block with a bouquet of aromatic oriental lilies and tried hard to summon the courage to go inside. Over his lunch break he'd telephoned his parents to enquire about his mother's ongoing battle with her health. His father had assured him they had an appointment scheduled for the next day with another doctor. Rohan hoped that after another course of antibiotics, his mother's cough would go away.

He heard the sound of his mother coughing in the background. It sounded like she was hacking up a lung. When she finally had enough breath to speak on the phone, they spent most of the time discussing the fact that he was in his thirties and still hadn't found a wife. It was a topic his mom never tired of. It didn't help matters that he was the oldest child and as such, was expected to lead the way.

Unlike Rohan, all of his seven siblings were under thirty. His mom accepted that some of them were still finishing college and others were putting their efforts into pursuing their various careers. But Rohan had made detective at the age of twenty-four and five years ago, he'd been promoted to detective sergeant. What more did he want? She couldn't seem to figure out why he continued to put so much time and effort into his career when there were other, more important things to focus on—like finding a girl and settling down.

It wasn't that Rohan was against commitment. He believed in marriage, like many other people did. But he also believed that it was a lifelong promise and not one to take lightly when the going got tough. During the rare times his parents disagreed, he learned that married life wasn't always sunshine and roses, but no matter how bad things got, they worked through their differences and stuck by each other.

Now, he stood outside the building of a girl he'd never thought of in a romantic way. And yet, here he was, wiping sweaty palms on his jeans, trying to slow his heart rate and scrounge up the courage to knock on her front door. He was filled with anticipation at the possibility there might be something more between them. The only stumbling block was not knowing how she felt.

Ten years earlier, they'd shared a lot of fun, laughter and good times, but he'd been Daphne's boyfriend and that had always stood between them. He couldn't help but wonder how it would be now that such a barrier had disappeared.

Would she find him attractive? Would she still laugh at his jokes? A decade was a long time. A lot of things had changed.

Samantha hadn't had a steady boyfriend during the time he'd known her in college, but that didn't mean there wasn't a significant other in her life right now. He wondered what he'd do if the door was opened by her husband. She hadn't said anything about a partner, but their recent conversations hadn't exactly been conducive to sharing personal information. If she was already married...

In sudden panic, he stashed the flowers in a

nearby hedge and turned on his heel. He'd barely taken four steps when he heard her call his name.

"Rohan! Where are you going? I'm here, on the second floor. Hang on a minute. I'll come down."

With no other choice, Rohan thrust his hands in the pockets of his jeans and headed back to the foyer of the apartment building. Made of red brick, the three-storey structure was reminiscent of the apartment blocks built in the early seventies, but it appeared to be well maintained and the surrounding garden beds were newly planted and freshly mulched. A pair of large wattle trees stood either side of the entry and were heavy with golden flowers. Their sweet scent filled the air.

"There you are!" Samantha announced and Rohan turned to greet her. He gave her an awkward hug and then quickly stepped away.

"I thought you'd gotten lost," she said, smiling.

Her shiny hair was loose and wavy and fell in soft curls around her face. Like him, she wore Levis and a sweater to ward off the late winter chill. He couldn't help but notice how the fabric molded to her breasts and how the pale pink color complemented the olive tones of her skin. She smiled again and his belly somersaulted.

"Not quite. I... I couldn't remember the number of your apartment," he quickly improvised. I was going to call you and then I realized I didn't have your number."

A tiny frown marred the smooth skin of her forehead. "I gave you my contact details that night at the station."

"Yes, but they're in the file at work. I didn't put

your number into my phone. I'm sorry, I didn't even think—"

"It's fine," she interrupted him. "I'll give it to you now." She waited for him to pull his phone out of his pocket and then rattled off the numbers.

When he'd finished entering her into his contacts, he put the phone away and then offered her a smile. "Now I don't have any excuse."

"Come on," she said, taking him by the hand and leading him inside. "I have beer and pizza."

He groaned in exaggerated delight and tried to ignore how good it felt to have his hand in hers. "What more could any man want?"

Sam took a couple of plates from the cupboard and carried them over to the table. She collected two beers from the fridge and handed one to Rohan. Having him seated at her small kitchen table was a little surreal. They'd shared plenty of meals before, but that had been a decade ago, when he was someone else's boyfriend. It was different now. Not only were they older and wiser, he was no longer attached. At least, she assumed he was single. She hadn't even asked.

Her heart had been racing from the moment she'd spotted him from her living room window. She wasn't sure why he looked like he was heading in the opposite direction, but she wasn't prepared to let him leave. Though she'd surprised herself by agreeing to catch up for a game of chess, the moment she had, she was all aflutter and couldn't help but think about what spending time together might mean. For so long, he'd been the enemy; the asshole who'd left his pregnant girlfriend high and dry. Even now, knowing the truth, it was a little difficult for her to accept him as the good guy.

She'd gone home the very night Rohan told her about Daphne's deception and spent an hour on the Internet. Surfing several social media sites, Sam had finally located her old roommate. A quick search through the White pages online and she had an address and phone number.

She'd dialed the number before her courage ran out and prayed Daphne would answer. Her luck had held and Sam asked the one question that had burning inside her brain from the moment Rohan told her: *Why had she lied?*

Daphne didn't even pretend to misunderstand. She apologized for her immature behavior and said she'd done it out of spite. She knew Sam thought highly of Daphne's boyfriend and that Rohan admired Sam. When it was obvious Rohan was going to end the relationship, Daphne couldn't help but seek revenge.

She was angry and upset and wanted to tarnish his good-guy image and what better way than accuse him of abandoning his unborn child?

Sam had shaken her head back and forth in wordless horror and disbelief. She couldn't imagine being so cruel to someone who hadn't done anything wrong and she felt even worse when she thought of how she'd maligned Rohan's character—even if it were only in her mind. She was relieved he'd finally clarified the truth.

Sam had always prided herself on being observant and an astute judge of character. Her ability to notice things held her in good stead in her job and had helped her solve difficult questions about puzzling causes of death. To have that confidence shaken by not one mistake, but two, was hard to take. She was only grateful Rohan accepted her apology and was prepared to renew their friendship.

At the thought that it might turn into something more, her insides turned to mush. Nerves fought for space inside her stomach. She had to remember the reason they'd met again was connected to a potential police matter that could very well turn into a full-blown investigation. She wasn't even sure if she should be meeting with him like this. What if she became a witness? Would a personal relationship with the lead detective jeopardize the case?

She shook her head and told herself not to be so silly. As far as she knew, the police were a long way from making an arrest, if there was even an arrest in the works. The whole thing with the cadavers missing organs could be nothing more than a coincidence. Surely there was no case to jeopardize... Besides, she and Rohan didn't have a close relationship. He was someone she'd known in her past. No big deal. She was making way too much of it.

"Are you going to stare out the window all night, or sit down and eat? This pizza is incredible, by the way. Maybe even the best I've ever eaten."

Rohan's words broke into her thoughts. He smiled in her direction and she blinked and forced herself to smile back. He was an old friend. They were enjoying a casual night of beer and pizza, and maybe afterwards, they'd have a game of chess.

She hadn't played for years, but there was a time when they'd both enjoyed it and had been competitively matched. She wondered if he'd found someone else to help him hone his skills in the time they'd been apart and realized it was none of her business. Feeling a tiny twinge of jealousy—toward no one in particular—she took a seat, sat her beer on the table and reached across for a slice of super supreme.

"So, do you live here on your own?" he asked around a mouthful of pizza.

"Yes. I moved here a couple years ago. Before that, I worked at the morgue in Westmead. I had a condo in Parramatta."

His smile widened and she wondered why. "What's so funny about Parramatta?"

"Nothing," he hurried to reassure her. "I used to live in Penrith. We were practically neighbors."

She laughed. "Well, if you ignore the thirty-minute commute in between." She took a sip from her beer. "Where do you live now?"

"Believe it or not, I don't live very far from here. I have a house in Cremorne."

She raised her eyebrows, impressed. "Wow! A whole house? I didn't realize the police service paid so well."

"Well, the privilege of owning it takes a hefty bite out of my pay each week, but it's worth it. I'm not on the water, but if I stand on tiptoes on my balcony, I can catch a glimpse of the harbor."

"Nice," she said and smiled.

He stared back at her with such intensity, Sam's heart kicked into gear with a slow and heavy thump. Butterflies swarmed in her stomach and she couldn't think of a single thing to say. It was like the world had frozen in that moment and there was no one but the two of them. The pizza, the kitchen, the murmur of traffic outside—it all disappeared into nothingness.

The tension continued to climb until she couldn't take it anymore. It was too soon. They'd been friends and then they weren't. Now they were... She didn't know what they were now. She blinked and averted her gaze and the spell was broken.

"Would you like another beer?" she asked, in an effort to break the uncomfortable silence.

"Yes, thanks. That would be great."

She pushed away from the table and moved over to the fridge. Feeling nervous and edgy and out of her depth, she cast around for something else to say.

"Why did you transfer from Westmead to the city?" Rohan asked, saving her from having to initiate more conversation.

"I'd lived out west for several years. I loved

working at the Westmead Morgue. I'm not sure if you noticed, but that part of town is very orientated toward families. There are lots of houses with large backyards and kids playing in the parks. I guess I kind of felt I didn't belong. The city seemed to be a better option for a single, thirty-something woman and it means I'm closer to my mom. She lives in Lindfield."

He digested her answer and seemed satisfied with her response. "Fair enough. And you're right about the western suburbs. It was the same out in Penrith. I felt strange not having to rush out the door to do the school run or to leave early in order to take a sick child to the medical center. I think I was one of a very few at work who was unattached."

"You were in love with Daphne. It must have taken some time to get over her. She treated you shabbily."

He snorted. "That's an understatement. We'd been together a year and a half and then she decided to have a fling with an old high school flame. And a biker at that." He shook his head as if still unable to believe it and Sam could see the irony. Bikers were renowned for living on the wrong side of the law.

And Rohan was a detective.

"Well, after hearing about her dishonesty and what she did, I'm sure you're better off without her."

"I agree wholeheartedly." He twisted the top off his second beer and held the bottle up in the manner of a toast. "Here's to exes and accepting that sometimes things have a way of working out for the best."

Sam smiled and clinked her bottle against his. "To exes." They both drank from their bottles and then simultaneously sighed in satisfaction. Catching his eye, Sam burst into laughter and Rohan joined her.

It felt good to laugh and relax and forget about the complexities that filled her life, even for a moment. Her mother was dying of kidney failure; her brother was embroiled in... She didn't even know what. She was thirty-four and didn't have a significant other by her side. Nor was there one in sight. It was enough to turn anyone to drink.

"I met your brother this week."

Rohan's quiet statement registered in Sam's brain a couple of seconds after he uttered the words and her heart skipped a beat. *Rohan had spoken to Alistair?* That couldn't be good. Forcing a nonchalant tone, she asked, "Really? Where did you come across him?"

"At the hospital. My partner and I set up a meeting with the general manager and she asked Alistair to attend. Initially I didn't realize he was your brother but then I finally put it together. He's obviously quite a bit older, but he looks a lot like you."

"Yes, he does," she managed. "Why... Why were you meeting with the general manager? Have you discovered something else? Why did my brother attend?"

Rohan looked at her. "It's an ongoing investigation. I can't really talk about it. Let's just say I think you and your friend's suspicions that something isn't quite right with the donation process is spot on."

And just like that, Sam's joy of the previous moment disintegrated. Dread weighed heavy in her belly. It was clear Rohan had discovered more evidence to support her and Hannah's concerns. Rohan had gone so far as to meet with the general manager of the Sydney Harbour Hospital. A request had been made for Alistair to attend. The possibilities circled around and around in her head and none of them were good.

Then, she took a moment to think about it. Alistair was the head of the Organ Donation for Transplantation Unit. It made sense that the police would want to speak with him and tap into his extensive knowledge of how the organ donation process worked. Perhaps that's all it was.

Feeling slightly better, she took another bite of her pizza and followed it with a mouthful of beer. Her gaze traveled over the white T-shirt that stretched across Rohan's broad shoulders and hugged his chest.

He'd arrived in a light Nike sweater, but had discarded that upon walking inside. Though the night was cool, it held more than the promise of spring and the temperature in the kitchen was pleasant. He'd always been fit, with a tall, athletic physique. Even when he'd been around in her apartment in his capacity as Daphne's boyfriend, Sam had always been aware of his physical appeal. After all, she was a normal young woman and she certainly wasn't blind.

But a decade ago she'd never allowed her thoughts to wander in that direction. She had a strict moral compass as far as poaching someone else's partner was concerned and though she could appreciate how effortlessly handsome he was, she'd never given in to a single naughty fantasy.

But now he was in her kitchen and there wasn't a girlfriend in sight. At least, not that she knew of. As if reading her mind, Rohan asked the question she was dying to ask.

"So, Samantha, are you seeing anyone?"

Heat crept up her neck. She kept her eyes averted and shook her head. "No, I'm not. How about you?" The words were out before she could stop them, but all of a sudden, she didn't care.

The truth was, attraction for him had been steadily building way down deep inside and she needed to know, for the sake of her own self-preservation, if there was a possibility of something more happening between them.

"Nope. There have been girls on and off over the years, but no one serious."

"Why not?" she asked. "You're good-looking, you have a steady job and you're certainly of age. Why haven't you found the right one?" Sam's heart thudded at her audacity, but her gaze remained fixed on his. The answer had become more important than she imagined.

"I could ask the same thing of you," he murmured, staring right back at her.

Once again, the air around them grew charged and the blood pulsed through Sam's veins. Rohan leaned forward across the small table until his face was inches from hers. Her breath quickened and the butterflies in her stomach took off in a frenzy of flight, but she couldn't move away. A moment later, his lips brushed hers, soft, slippery and tasting of beer and pizza.

Tentatively, she returned the kiss and his hand came up to cup her cheek. Gently holding her head in place, he slowly explored her mouth. When at last he pulled away, their breathing was unsteady. Rohan stared at her. Filled with desire, his eyes had darkened to cobalt. Sam was powerless to look away.

The kiss had been like nothing she'd imagined or experienced before. Though she'd dated in college and one relationship had lasted nearly six months, she'd never had the time or inclination to spend hours in the college bars, flirting and drinking like many of her friends had. She looked back now and realized her college days had been fairly boring. She'd go to class, study hard, enjoy the occasional social outing and then do the same things over again.

"I probably should be sorry for doing that," Rohan said, his voice husky, "but I can't bring myself to apologize. I didn't come over here with the intention of seducing you, but you are just too damned hard to resist. The whole time I knew you, I was with Daphne and I never really noticed you."

She was stung by his insinuation. "Gee, thanks."

"No, I don't mean it like that," he hurried to reassure her. "Of course I *noticed* you. You're beautiful. No man could overlook that. But I was in love with Daphne and she was in love with me. At least I thought she was," he added with a grimace.

He reached out and took her hands. She resisted, but he merely tightened his hold. "I can tell that you're mad and I didn't mean to make you feel like that. This is coming out all wrong."

He drew in a deep breath and blew it out. "What I meant was I never noticed you in a sexual, *available* way. I was involved with another girl. Something in my head shut down the normal kind of response I might otherwise have had if we'd both been single." He shook his head and sighed. "Is any of this making sense?"

Sam squeezed his hands. "I know what you mean. I was having similar thoughts only a little while ago. I used to see you come and go with Daphne and sometimes you and I would play a game of chess. Even though I was aware of your good looks and easy charm, they didn't get me all hot and bothered because it was like you said, my brain acknowledged you were with someone else. The time we spent together was fun and relaxed and carefree because there wasn't the added pressure of sexual attraction. It can put a strain on things, especially if it isn't reciprocated."

Rohan nodded in agreement. "I was like a brother."

"Yes! That's exactly how it was!"

His gaze shifted to her mouth, to her breasts and then returned to her face. Her heart skipped a beat at the heat in his eyes. "I don't feel like a brother anymore," he growled.

"I... I see that," Sam stammered, trying to catch her breath.

"I want to kiss you again."

"I'd... I'd like that."

Desire flared brighter in his eyes. As if needing no further encouragement, he pushed back his chair and took her by the hand and drew her up close until she was pressed against him. His head came down and he captured her lips in a kiss that seared her brain and flustered her wits.

While the first kiss had been sweet and tentative, this one was anything but. Rohan's lips moved over hers like a man starving. Everywhere they touched, heat followed. She wound her arms around his neck and pulled him even closer and sighed with relief when he cupped her bottom and held her against his erection.

The hardness of it strained against her belly and sent tingles of desire racing to her core. She couldn't remember the last time she'd felt like this. She didn't know if she'd *ever* felt like this. The few times she'd had sex with her one-and-only, long-term boyfriend, they'd come together, more often than not, late at night after quite a few drinks.

It was always her boyfriend who initiated it. She'd merely gone along for the ride. While she'd found the encounters pleasant, her world hadn't shifted off its axis. Not like it was with Rohan—and they'd only kissed. She couldn't help but wonder how extraordinary it would feel to make love with him.

"You taste so good," he groaned against her lips and Sam opened her mouth and tangled her tongue with his. Emboldened by his desire, she slid her hands down his arms, across his back and finished at his butt. It was taut under her fingers. She cupped his cheeks the way he was cupping hers and pressed him closer against her core. Liquid heat flared to life and the blood rushed through her veins.

His hands went to the hem of her sweater and he dragged it up and over her head. A moment later, he unclasped her white bra and dropped it to the floor. He stared at her with such need, she felt like she'd explode.

Slowly, he lifted his hand and ran his fingers over one of her breasts. Her nipple puckered in response and she gasped from the heat of his touch.

"You're so beautiful, Samantha," he murmured huskily. "I can't believe I never looked at you like this before."

"*Shh,*" she whispered, pressing a finger to his lips. "Let's not talk about the past. We're here now—single, consenting adults. There's nothing standing in our way."

He bent his head and kissed her soundly on the mouth. "You're right and I intend to make the most of it. I want to feel you naked," he growled. "Will you make love with me?"

She stared at him and her breath came fast. Her body screamed out for her to say yes. She thought about her brother and the investigation, but just as quickly, pushed those thoughts away.

She didn't want to think about the complications. Right now, all she wanted to do was feel.

Running her hands across his chest, she reveled in the feel of his muscles. Moving lower, she snagged the end of his T-shirt and tugged it out of his jeans. He stared at her as if he didn't dare breathe. She eased the shirt upwards, exposing his taut flesh inch by inch. Her fingers skimmed over the flatness of his belly and he sucked in a breath.

Slowly, the T-shirt and her fingers crept higher until they skimmed across his nipples. She flicked at the hard brown nubs with her nails and was rewarded with a groan.

"You're killing me, Samantha!"

"Good things come to those who wait. Don't you know that?" she smiled, feeling all-powerful and in control. It was intoxicating. At last, taking pity on him, she pulled the shirt over his head and discarded it.

Her breath caught at the sight of his male beauty. His broad chest was almost hairless and rippled with definition. Even in late winter, he sported a pale golden tan. She could stare at him for hours.

As if impatient, he stood on one foot and pulled off each shoe before tugging at his belt and loosening the clasp on his jeans. A moment later, he stepped out of them and stood before her, clad only in his underwear.

The snug pair of briefs hugged his hips and stretched taut over his erection. Sam stared at the bulge in fascination, wondering how it would feel.

She wanted to see him naked and to press herself against all that hard, warm male flesh.

He must have seen the need in her eyes because he slowly drew her forward with his hands firm on her hips. Pulling her close, he rubbed against her and her knees went weak with need. She could feel the long hard length of him pressing into her belly.

"I want you, Samantha."

She stared up at him and nodded. "I want you, too."

His hands went to the clasp of her jeans and he slid them down her hips. She toed off her shoes and then grabbed the bottom of her Levis and pulled them the rest of the way off. Clad only in their underwear, they stood and stared at each other, their breath coming fast.

Then Rohan reached out for her hand and drew her slowly out of the kitchen. With her heart pounding in anticipation, Sam followed him down the hall.

He paused at the spare room that was set up as an office and then continued on. Past the bathroom, he halted outside her open bedroom door. Turning, he took her in his arms and kissed her tenderly on the mouth. "Are you sure about this?"

She gazed at him. She was unsure about a lot of things, but making love with Rohan wasn't one of them. They might not have seen each other for a decade, but she felt like she'd come home to someone warm and familiar; someone she cared about.

"I'm sure," she whispered and meant it.

"Do you have any condoms?" he asked and she blushed to the roots of her hair.

"No, I'm sorry. There hasn't been any need... "Besides, I take oral contraception to help with my periods. They've always been heavy and I get cramping and... She dropped her gaze to the floor, beyond embarrassed. "Too much information, right?"

With gentle fingers, he tilted her chin until she was forced to meet his gaze. "Hey, I see and hear a whole lot of things in my job that most men wouldn't be able to stomach and I have three sisters. Talking about periods and cramping won't send me running for the hills. And as for being without a supply of condoms, that's nothing to be ashamed about. I like that you're unprepared. It means you're not into bringing men home with you too often and that makes me feel special." He winked. "Lucky for us, I have one in my wallet."

"If you're worried about disease, I assure you I have regular check ups and being in the police force, I assume you do, too."

He nodded. "Of course, but it isn't only STD's I'm concerned about."

His words took a moment to register inside Sam's brain, but when they did, she tensed. Anger stirred inside her. "Thank you very much, Rohan Coleridge," she snapped.

He frowned in confusion and shook his head. "What did I say?"

She was filled with disbelief. "Really? You're really going to pretend you don't know how much you just insulted me? There's only one other thing that concerns a man when he's about to have sex without a condom and we both know what it is."

She jammed her hands on her hips and her anger found its head. "Admit it! You think I'm lying when I tell you I'm on the pill! It's the only reason why you still feel the need to use a condom."

"No! It has nothing to do with you, Samantha! You have it all wrong! Daphne's the one who screwed with me. When I questioned her about how she could be pregnant, she gave me the story about the antibiotics messing with her on the pill, but later, she told me she'd stopped taking them. Apparently, the pill was making her fat. At least, that's what she thought."

He laughed without humor. "Too bad she didn't think to tell me she'd stopped using contraception. I would have made sure we used condoms and I'd have known right away the baby couldn't have been mine. I wouldn't have gone through all those sleepless nights, wondering how the hell I was going to support a wife and child because don't get me wrong, I would have married her."

He dragged in a ragged breath and tiredly ran a hand through his hair. "I guess I learned from that moment on not to trust sole responsibility for contraception to the woman. It's nothing personal."

Sam shook her head in disbelief. "Nothing personal! How else am I supposed to take it? Here we are, with barely any clothes on, about to engage in wild, spontaneous sex and you're insisting on a condom when I've already told you I'm on the pill. How is that not personal?"

His gaze pleaded with hers. "You're misunderstanding me, Samantha. My reluctance to trust a woman to take care of contraception relates to *all* women, not just you."

"And that's supposed to make me feel better? What the hell planet are you on?" she shouted.

Hurt and confusion filled his eyes. "I think it's time I left," he said, his voice thick with tension. "Let's just say, I'm no longer in the mood."

She took a step toward him. "Rohan—"

Without another word, he stalked away from her and disappeared into the kitchen. Clad once again in his T-shirt and jeans and carrying his shoes in his hand, he opened the front door. It closed with a click that sounded so final the hollowness of it reverberated all the way through Sam's heart.

Chapter 10

Dear Diary,

It seemed like such a good idea, a win for everyone. Now, I'm not so sure. The pressure to supply more and more tissue is consuming me. I was under the impression Biologistics was in this business for much the same reasons I was: to increase the supply and availability of viable human tissue and give a greater number of people a better chance at life.

But it seems I've been led astray, or perhaps I just didn't want to see. For Biologistics, it's all about quotas and money and I am powerless against their contagious greed.

With no government restrictions, Charles Shillingworth and his company are free to take whatever they can get. The quotas get higher and higher. Where will it all end?

And then I look at the money in my account and I just want more and more. The truth is, I'm as bad as Charles Shillingworth. The money and the promise of more has corrupted my soul.

I've cleared Richard's gambling debts and paid off the next year's school fees in advance. The money is everything I thought it would be, but I'm frightened of its hold. Of their hold.

I've stepped into a yawning abyss and I have no way to get out. God, help me! What have I done?

"What the hell do you mean, you need more money? I already told you I'm cutting back on my activities," Alistair growled at Richard, already regretting his decision to meet with the deputy coroner after the man left a message on Alistair's cell phone. It had been filled with desperation and none-too-subtle threats.

They sat, hidden in a booth in the back of yet another secluded bar in the city. Alistair clenched his jaw in an effort to keep his anger in check. Over the past few months, he'd not only cleared Richard's sixty-thousand-dollar gambling debt, but he'd given the deputy coroner a fifteen percent cut of the earnings he received from Biologistics.

Even before Alistair decided to reduce his extracurricular undertakings, only a small percentage of the tissues he delivered overseas came from bodies that passed through the Glebe Morgue. He'd been willing to give his friend a respectable share of the booty in return for his cooperation and silence, but he was damned if he'd increase the percentage or be intimidated by the man's threats.

"I did some research on the Internet," Richard said in a whining tone that grated on Alistair's ears. "The supply of human tissue is big business overseas. There are companies in the US who pay a fortune for that kind of thing. I've done a few sums. All I'm saying is that fifteen percent isn't enough."

"You stupid idiot! Do you have any idea the risk involved in doing what I'm doing? If I get caught, I'm facing serious jail time, not to mention the end of my career. You're the one who begged me to keep going, cried on my shoulder about how you couldn't afford for me to stop. Now you're sitting back, keeping your hands clean and raking in the cash. You can't have it both ways, Richard. Fifteen percent is fair payment for your services."

"Don't tell me I'm sitting back doing nothing! I've been copping some flak from the State Coroner. That sister of yours has been causing trouble. Apparently, she mentioned her concerns about a missing consent form to the coroner and yours truly was closely questioned."

Dread filled Alistair's gut, but he refused to show any sign of weakness. "Just so you know, my sister didn't stop with your boss. She and a friend of hers, who works in a funeral parlor, went to the police."

"The police! Fuck! Why the hell didn't you tell me?" Richard wailed.

Alistair shrugged. "Why would you be concerned? I'm the one knee deep in all of this."

"You're right. The retrievals happened well

before the bodies arrived at the morgue. I can claim I didn't have a clue you were acting outside the terms of the consent." He stared hard at Alistair, gaining confidence. "Or should I say, without *any* consent."

Alistair gritted his teeth and accepted the gibe. It was true, after all. In order to keep up with the endless demand from Biologistics, he'd started forging the signatures on the consent forms. Sometimes, he hadn't bothered with a consent form at all. He tried to limit those to the bodies who were sent directly to the funeral homes, but every now and then, he slipped up—like with the one Sam had discovered.

Anger, tinged with a little desperation, coursed through Alistair's veins. All he was trying to do was save a bunch of people's lives. Otherwise, the organs and tissues would go to waste. What harm was there in that? In rescuing them for someone else? He couldn't understand why the law wasn't with him on this and, despite their potential involvement, he wasn't prepared to stop.

For one, he needed the money. He'd splashed out on some big-ticket items over the past couple of weeks. The bright red Ferrari 488 GTB that now sat in his garage had cost more than half a million dollars. It was extravagant, but he hadn't been able to control himself. Once he knew he had a bank account with a balance of seven figures, it had done his head in and he'd lost his common sense.

He'd told his wife he was minding the car for a

friend who'd gone overseas for several months. The man hadn't wanted to leave it unattended in the garage beneath his building. Nancy didn't argue with him over his explanation, although she'd walked away with an expression of doubt on her face.

He didn't know what he was going to do when the months passed and the Ferrari wasn't returned. He'd deal with that headache when he had to. Right now, he had more pressing matters requiring his attention.

"Give me an extra ten percent and I'll head your sister off at the pass."

Richard's statement jerked Alistair's thoughts back to the present. He stared at the deputy coroner in disbelief. "Didn't you hear what I said, Richard? Sam's filed a report with the police. This has gone way beyond what you can control in your little domain. Deborah Healy and I have already met with two detectives. They asked a lot of questions and requested the records of any patient who'd died and donated organs since June. If they're on the ball, they'll discover the rates of organ and tissue donation have skyrocketed over that time."

Richard shrugged, looking unconcerned. "It'll be easy enough to pass that off as a result of a successful advertising campaign. You have the backing of the State Government. The police won't be able to argue with that."

"True, and if they leave it at that, we'll be safe. What I'm worried about is if the police get a hint that the organ retrievals weren't done in accordance with the terms of the consent or done without any consent."

"There's no reason to suspect they'll even consider it," Richard replied nonchalantly and Alistair wished he could feel so blasé.

"You're getting way too anxious about this, Alistair. Trust me, the people who work in the funeral parlors won't know one way or the other what was taken and what wasn't. Short of exhuming bodies, the police will never know, either. It's only the morgue staff who have access to those kinds of records."

Alistair threw Richard a hard stare and responded. "*Exactly*. That's the reason I wanted to stop harvesting additional tissues from the bodies destined for autopsy. If I recall correctly, *you* were the one who begged me not to exclude them from my work."

Richard scoffed. "It didn't take much effort on my part to convince you."

"And *you* were supposed to make sure you conducted the autopsies. Your staff, and most certainly not my sister, should never have come anywhere near those bodies. We had an agreement and you fucked up."

"It wasn't my fault I came down with a stomach virus! I wasn't the one who called your sister in! Staffing was responsible for that! I couldn't get myself off the floor of the bathroom. I was in no position to carry out a post mortem."

"You should have told me that when I called you to authorize the pre-autopsy donation."

"You called me the night before. How the hell

was I to know I'd be face down in a toilet bowl by the time the body arrived at the morgue. That bug lasted more than twenty-four hours! I've never felt so sick in my life!"

Alistair gritted his teeth against the hopelessness of it. There was no arguing with Richard and it hardly mattered, anyway—even if the man wasn't telling the truth. Sam had done the autopsy in Richard's absence and had been concerned enough to report her findings to the police. Alistair had no doubt that the detectives he'd met in the general manager's office were smart enough to work it out. Most of the organ retrievals had been carried out by Alistair and those that had been transported to the morgue for autopsy had been authorized by Richard.

Alistair could only hope that the detectives didn't pursue it any further. If they examined the autopsy records and compared them to the consents...

"Speak with my sister," he said, urgency gripping him inside. "You need to make sure she's well off the scent. If the police come asking questions, wanting to compare the bodies in the state they arrived at the morgue to the signed consent forms, they'll notice the anomalies and then both of us are in a world of hurt."

Richard gave him a narrow-eyed stare. "You, at least. Let's not forget who started this."

Alistair leaned across the small table and pushed his face up close to his friend's. Fear filled the other man's eyes, replacing the earlier defiance.

Good. Alistair needed him scared. "Make no mistake, mate. We're in this together. If I go down, you'll go down with me. I promise."

They eyed each other for a full minute before Richard lowered his gaze. He put more space between him and Alistair, and sat back.

"All right. I'll talk to Samantha, try and distract her from her idea that something's wrong. I'm not sure how I'll manage it. She's as sharp as a tack. But I'll think of something."

Alistair smiled, relieved. "Good. I also want you to get hold of the morgue records from the donor bodies autopsied over the winter months. It seems that's the focus of the police investigation."

Richard frowned. "What am I supposed to do? They're all stored in a secure computer database."

"I don't know. I'm sure you'll think of something. A convenient computer virus that just happens to wipe out a heap of files. Make sure it's not only the donor body files, though. That would be plain stupid. Do it right and hopefully, neither of us has anything to worry about."

Richard nodded and then picked up his glass of beer and held it up to propose a toast. "Here's to increasing the rate of organ and tissue donation at the illustrious Sydney Harbour Hospital and here's to its even more distinguished boss of the organ donation and transplantation team."

Alistair could tell the man was mostly being facetious, but he clinked his glass to Richard's all the same. As was often said, it was better to keep your friends close and your enemies even closer.

He intended to keep Richard very firmly in his sights.

———————

Rohan turned the page and read the words scrawled across the next document. Why were doctors allowed to get away with such indecipherable handwriting? It made his job that much harder when he had to guess nearly every other word. Not having a medical background or being familiar with medical terminology didn't help.

He'd received the records he'd requested from the general manager and had been plowing his way through them for more than three hours. The copies he'd made of all the hospital notes that related to every patient who'd died and donated their organs since June were piled on every available surface. The squad room was quiet, empty of almost everyone except Bryce and him. Rohan let out a heavy sigh and glanced over at his partner who was similarly engaged.

"Find anything yet?" Bryce asked, turning his head in Rohan's direction.

"No, but I've learned more about the myriad of illnesses and disease that attack the elderly and ultimately cause their death than I'll ever need to know. It makes you look forward to getting old; that's for sure."

Bryce grinned and leaned back in his chair, stretching his arms above his head. "You've got that right. I wouldn't want to be old and frail, for quids."

"Except, if we don't grow old and frail, it means we've died before our time. That's not such a comforting scenario, either."

Bryce shook his head. "There's no way we can win! Man, sometimes life sucks!" He opened his mouth on a huge yawn and then settled back into his seat.

"One thing I have noticed is that a lot of these patients or their relatives were seen by Doctor Alistair Wolfe. We'll have to get Hannah Langdon's records and see what matches up. It will be interesting to see if the patients she identified as having unusually excessive evidence of organ and tissue donation were among his patients."

"He *is* the head of the Unit and nobody can question his devotion to the cause. It's not surprising to find his name on so many of the files."

"Still, it's worth making note of," Rohan replied. "I've also been going through the consent forms obtained prior to the retrievals. All the ones I've seen so far have been limited to one or two of the major organs and I'm almost through the pile. I haven't seen any that gave consent for skin and eye tissue, and yet, according to Hannah and the girl at Forsyth's funeral home, there were at least two bodies that came from the Sydney Harbour Hospital with those removed."

"Yeah," Bryce nodded, his expression thoughtful. "I haven't come across a consent for that kind of thing, either." He returned his attention to the remaining files in front of him.

Rohan did the same. A moment later, he frowned. The file of Ronald Miller was missing the consent altogether. He must have overlooked it.

Starting at the front, Rohan slowly went through the file again and came up empty. It wasn't there. *Could it have been misplaced? Incorrectly filed?* It wasn't beyond the realm of possibility. He could only imagine the amount of paperwork generated every day in a busy hospital.

"This is a little strange," Bryce murmured, eerily echoing Rohan's thoughts.

"What is?"

"I've been through this file three times. I can't find the consent form."

Rohan's heart thumped hard against the walls of his chest. *Coincidence?* Surely two of the hospital files couldn't have fallen victim to sloppy administrative staff?

"What's the name of the patient?"

"Cassandra Jackson."

Rohan suddenly recalled the night at the station when Samantha had told him one of the donor bodies she'd autopsied had arrived at the morgue without a consent form in the hospital notes. He hadn't asked her for a name or if the deceased had been a patient at the Sydney Harbour Hospital, but that information could be obtained easily enough. Under other circumstances...

At the thought of again having to come face to face with her, his gut twisted with nerves. He hadn't spoken to her since the night at her apartment. Every time he thought of that moment when everything went so off course, he cringed.

Okay, he knew this much: She'd overreacted to a throwaway statement. He hadn't meant to insult her. Not for an instant did he believe she was deceiving him about being on the pill and, at the time, he'd been unable to see how she'd made such a leap. He was just being cautious. Like he'd told her, it wasn't personal.

Later, after he'd had a chance to cool down, he'd replayed their conversation in his head and could see how she'd misunderstood, but their argument had made one thing even clearer: She didn't know him at all.

It hurt that she thought he believed she was capable of such dishonesty when that couldn't be further from the truth. She was the most honest, honorable, selfless woman he knew. How else would she be able to devote her time examining corpses in order to find answers for relatives of the deceased? Most people, for all their good intentions, would turn and run a mile. But not Samantha.

In the short time he'd known her he'd discovered she was unique and special and sweet and wonderful. And he couldn't get past the feeling that he'd stuffed things up big time. She was always in his thoughts and he had no desire to erase her from his mind or his heart, but damage had been done. There didn't seem to be a way out.

All he could do was apologize and hope that she'd give him another chance. Now that he'd begun to get to know her properly and had kissed her, there was no way he could walk away. She touched him deep inside like no other woman had and he was determined to make her see they were good together, in every possible way. Years ago they'd had a strong friendship based on mutual interests and respect. It was time to convince her he was worthy of that connection again, and so much more.

CHAPTER 11

Sam put the last suture in place and straightened her back. A muscle in her shoulder complained. She'd been bent over the gurney for way too long and now she was paying for it. She'd give anything for a back massage. If only she had the time...

Night after night, driving home from work, she vowed to leave a little earlier the next time so she could visit a massage therapist in the city, but over and over it happened like tonight: She'd end up taking the exit that took her over the Harbour Bridge and arrive home with the kinks still in her tired muscles and the knots still in her back.

Placing her tools in the stainless steel tray beside the gurney, she returned the body to the fridge. Tugging off her protective clothing, she dropped the pile into the laundry bin and headed into the showers. At close to five, the day was as good as done. With September now upon them, the days were getting longer. She smiled at the thought of enjoying a few rays of afternoon sunshine and finding new flowers blooming in the garden beds that lined the pathway to her building.

On spring days like this, she missed the large backyard she'd had as a child. During those early years, she spent hours in the garden with her sisters and her mom. Even Alistair would come out and help sometimes and they'd gather around and listen while their mother told them stories about when she was young: how she'd worked in the garden with her own mother and how she was taught what each plant was and where it would grow best.

Sam's smile turned sad. It had been a long time since her mother had been well enough to do anything other than enjoy a little fresh air and sunshine in her beautiful garden. She was far too sick to get down on her hands and knees and weed and plant and water like she wanted to.

Sam and her siblings now contributed to the cost of a gardener and once a week, a man came in to trim the hedges, weed the garden beds and water the plants. It didn't make up for the fact Enid Wolfe couldn't do it herself, but Sam knew it gave her mother pleasure to know the property was being cared for and treated with love.

Scrubbing away the effects of the day, Sam rinsed off and then stepped out of the shower. Drying herself, she slipped on the clothes she'd worn to work and then ran a brush through her damp hair. It curled around her face and she impatiently tucked it back behind her ears. It irritated her that the gesture reminded her of how Rohan had run his fingers through her hair.

She was grateful he'd left when he had. She might have done something embarrassing—like apologizing and begging him to stay—and as much as time had taken most of the heat from the memory of his words, she was still convinced her anger had been justified. It saddened her to think she'd lost his friendship—and what could have been a whole lot more—for a second time. The look he'd thrown her before he left her apartment told her it was unlikely he'd ever set foot in her building again.

With a sigh, she returned to her office. Taking a seat before her computer, she began to enter her findings for the autopsies she'd conducted throughout the day. The phone at her elbow rang, momentarily startling her. She assumed, this late in the day, most of the people she dealt with would have packed up and gone home. Picking up the receiver, she answered the call.

"Doctor Wolfe."

"Sam, it's Angie. Sorry to bother you, but you have a visitor in the waiting room. It's that detective again. The cute one. Are you available to see him?"

Sam's heart skipped a beat at the mention of Rohan. She hadn't expected him to seek her out. In fact, she hadn't expected to hear from him ever again.

"Sam?"

She blinked and cleared her frantic thoughts. "Um... It's fine, Angie. Tell him I'll be out in a minute."

"No problem. I'm about to finish for the day

and I think most of the other staff are gone. Are you going to be all right with him here on your own?"

"Yes, of course, I'll be fine. The detective's a...a friend of mine."

"In that case, I'll see you in the morning."

"Thanks, Angie. Have a good night."

Sam hung up the receiver and did her best to slow the racing of her heart. Rohan was outside, waiting for her. A part of her wanted to run and hide. How could she face him at work? The last time they'd shared company, they hadn't worn many clothes and knowing how that evening had ended so disastrously...

She drew in another deep breath and eased it out between dry lips. She'd told Angie she'd see Rohan. He was waiting for her. Everyone else had gone home. She couldn't leave him out there forever. Besides, even if she felt like running, she was the last staff member in the building and needed to set the alarm in the main foyer—right beside the waiting room.

"For goodness sake, Samantha, get it together!" she chided herself out loud. She was being silly hiding in her office like a school girl. The sooner she met with him and got it over with, the better.

He was obviously here on police business. Why else would he come and see her at work? That reminded her of the last time he'd been there and how their conversation had centered on the two of them and their shared past. A fresh wave of nerves assailed her, but she forced herself out of her chair. Leaning over, she saved the work on her computer and logged out. It would have to wait until tomorrow.

She collected her handbag from the closet in the corner of her office, and slung it over her shoulder, tossed back her hair and headed out the door.

She saw him before he saw her. He stood just inside the entryway, with his hands jammed into the pockets of his suit pants. His tie was slightly askew and his hair was rumpled. He looked like a tired professional who'd had a hard day. She wondered what, in particular, had caused his fatigue.

Though her rubber-soled shoes made no sound on the tiled floor, his head snapped around seconds after she stepped into the reception area. His gaze zeroed in on her. Tension held her immobile and her heart felt like it might leap right out of her chest, but she drew in a few surreptitious breaths and willed herself to appear outwardly calm.

"Rohan. What are you doing here?" She gave an inward sigh of relief. Even to her ears, she sounded cool and composed.

"It's about the investigation."

She looked at him steadily and tried to ignore her disappointment. "What about it?"

"The autopsy you told me about at the station—the one where you couldn't find the consent form. What was the deceased person's name?"

Sam cast around in her memory and then came up with it. "Natalie Piccoli."

"Are you sure?"

"Yes."

"I've been over all of the donor files that came from the Sydney Harbour Hospital. Natalie Piccoli's notes weren't among them."

"Perhaps her records were sent here by mistake, along with the report for the coroner?"

"Is that possible?"

"Of course. It happens more often than you think. Administrative staff often assume the coroner's office needs access to everything in the file. The truth is, anything of relevance in the hospital notes is included in the report prepared for the coroner."

"Could you get me a printout of all autopsies conducted in this morgue since June—the ones where the deceased has donated some, or all, of their organs?"

"Yes. It might take a little while and I don't have time right now, but I'll get on it in the morning."

"Thank you. I'd appreciate that. By the way, where did Natalie Piccoli come from?"

"You mean, which hospital treated her?"

"Yes."

Sam took a moment to think, but in reality, it was an excuse to buy time and gather her thoughts. She thought of her brother and prayed silently he had nothing to do with it—whatever "it" was.

"Do you want to check your file?" Rohan asked, interrupting her thoughts.

"No. The patient had been treated at the Sydney Harbour Hospital. The organ retrieval was carried out there and then the deceased was sent here for a post mortem."

Rohan appeared to digest her information and then asked the question she'd dreaded.

"Who was the treating doctor?"

She closed her eyes briefly and then opened them again. She kept her gaze steady on his. "Doctor Alistair Wolfe."

"Your brother."

Sam nodded and forced herself to hold his stare.

"Was he in charge of the organ retrieval, too?"

"Yes."

"I see." His words sounded so final, like it was confirming something even bigger that he knew and she didn't. She did her best to control her panic.

"It's not unusual," she said quickly. "My brother's head of the Unit. He's present for a good number of these things. Besides, it's not like he's a one man show. The theater would be full of people: retrieval teams from various other hospitals, nursing staff and the like.

"In fact, the more I think about it, the more I'm sure that the fact some of us have noticed a higher incidence in organ and tissue removal over the past couple of months is nothing more than a coincidence, or the result of an extremely effective donor awareness campaign. Unless you're thinking whole teams of professionals could be involved in a conspiracy." She laughed, hoping to convince him how ludicrous the very thought of such a thing was, but it came out sounding flat.

"I understand what you're saying," he replied firmly, his expression somber, "but I'm not sure I believe it's only coincidence. The file you mentioned isn't the only one missing a consent form."

Her mouth fell open in surprise and a fresh wave of panic tightened like a band around her chest. Her thoughts flew once again to Alistair and she didn't know why. He was a passionate campaigner for organ and tissue donation, but she'd never believe him capable of something as heinous as removing a person's organs without their consent. And yet, it appeared someone on his team could be doing just that.

She shook her head in silent denial, hoping and praying it wasn't true. "I... I don't know what you want me to say."

"There's no need for you to worry. It's my job to find out what's happening and who's responsible. To some extent, I understand why a doctor, devoted to saving lives, might feel the need to remove whatever can be used by others from a patient on the brink of death. Your brother explained how frustrating it is for him to send healthy tissues to the grave. I can see how it would be so, especially now knowing how much good an unlimited consent for organ and tissue donation can do."

"It doesn't make it right, though," Sam whispered.

"Or legal. And that's why I'll do what I have to in order to get to the bottom of it."

She looked at him and tried hard to keep the

hot sting of tears at bay. No matter how much she tried to convince herself otherwise, something deep inside her told her Alistair was involved.

He might not be the doctor removing the additional tissues, but as head of the Unit and participating in so many of the retrievals, it stood to reason he knew something about it. She could only hope and pray his knowledge wouldn't send him to prison.

Swallowing a sigh, she drew in a deep breath and squared her shoulders. Crossing her arms over her chest, she addressed Rohan again. "Will that be all?"

"At the meeting I had with your brother and the general manager, he confirmed what you said: that in order to harvest organs from a deceased who requires an autopsy, the authorization of the coroner or one of his deputies must be obtained. Do you remember telling me that?"

"Yes. It's standard procedure. The coroner gets the final say when cause of death is yet to be determined."

"Who was the coroner who authorized the retrieval of Natalie Piccoli's organs?"

"Deputy Coroner Richard Davis."

"Did you mention to him that the consent form was missing?"

Sam thought back. "No. He was off sick at the time I conducted the autopsy, but I raised it with the State Coroner because I was concerned our procedures might need to be reviewed. I assumed the paperwork had been mislaid somewhere between here and the hospital. In that case, it's impossible to know who's at fault. It could have been lost on the hospital ward, during the transfer to the hospital morgue, or while the body was being transported here. I wanted to make sure it hadn't happened on our end and if it had, that it didn't happen again."

Rohan pulled a notebook and pen out of his pocket and scribbled in it. When he'd finished, he closed the notebook and returned it and the pen to his pocket.

"Are we done?" Sam asked.

He stared at her. The silence between them lengthened. She wanted to look away, but the intensity of his expression held her enthralled. His eyes darkened with emotion and he opened his mouth to speak.

"I... I needed to see you."

She licked dry lips and forced herself to respond. "And you have."

He shook his head, dismissing her words. "Not only about the investigation. It's been too long. I... I can't stop thinking about you and...about what happened. I'm sorry. I wanted to explain about what I said... I didn't mean it the way you thought. The words came out all wrong. It never occurred to me you were trying to deceive me. What I said was stupid and I upset you. I didn't mean to. God, upsetting you was the last thing I wanted to do."

Sam listened to him stumbling over his words and could see how genuinely sorry he was. Her heart softened. Their disagreement and subsequent misunderstanding wasn't entirely his fault. She'd been quick to jump to conclusions and she should have given him a little more time to explain—or at least been prepared to listen when he tried.

"It's fine, Rohan. You're not the only one to blame. I'm sorry, too. I pride myself on my honesty. Lying about something as important as birth control is something I'd never contemplate. I guess I was a little taken aback that you thought me capable of it, especially right when we were about to..."

Heat scorched her face and she turned her head away. It was one thing to be into it in the heat of the moment, but to discuss it in the cold light of day...

He stepped closer and palmed her cheek with his hand. The tender expression on his face snatched her breath. She stared at him and her heart beat faster as he bent his head and grazed her mouth with his.

"*Shh*," he murmured against her lips. "Let's not talk anymore."

Blood pulsed through her body and need struck, hot and urgent. Her mouth parted on an indrawn breath and his eyes flared with desire. Her arms went around his neck and she clung to him, loving the strength and solidity of him. His lips moved over hers with increasing urgency and she gave back all she had.

The kiss, fiery in its intensity, went on forever. Their tongues danced and tangled. He tasted of coffee and breath mints. His mouth felt divine. A myriad of exciting thoughts raced through her head while a saner part of her mind warned her to slow things down. She was at work, and although she and Rohan were alone in the offices, this wasn't the best time or place.

"Rohan!" she gasped, pushing against him. "I... I think we should stop." He lifted his head, looking dazed, and stared at her with eyes that were filled with desire. And then he blinked and refocused and slowly moved away.

He drew in a deep breath, eased it out and then breathed deeply again. Sam understood how he felt. Her heart was pounding as fast as if she'd just sprinted a marathon.

"I'm sorry," she said and watched him tense. "Not about the kiss," she hurried to reassure him, "but I'm at work. I can't be making out with a hot guy in the foyer of my building."

His face and body relaxed and he offered her a slow and sexy smile. "You think I'm hot?"

She blushed, but nodded. "Damn right," she grinned.

With two long steps, he closed the distance between them and scooped her up in his arms. He swung her around and she laughed, clinging to his shoulders. When he set her down, he did it slowly and slid her all the way down his length. Her body clenched at the feel of his hard cock pressing into her stomach.

Desire rekindled as quickly as it had been doused and she reached up and dragged his head back down to hers. Kissing him thoroughly, she once again pulled away and stared up at him. "How about we try this again: Your place or mine?"

He stared at her with such heat in his gaze, her toes curled up inside her shoes. "Mine."

————————

Sam followed Rohan's unmarked police car through the streets of Sydney. Evening peak hour was in full swing and the traffic was heavy in both directions. They crawled across the Harbour Bridge and then turned left toward an exit that would take them to the affluent, lower North Shore suburb of Cremorne.

Less than three miles from the city, it was an old, well established area with many large and expensive homes. There were also a number of high-rise apartments, with prices for a modest unit starting at a little less than a million. Rohan had done well for himself by securing a house with such an impressive zip code and she couldn't help but admire him for it.

It wasn't the only thing she admired about him...

She blushed anew at the thought of their heated kisses and knowing she was on her way to his house for the sole purpose of sleeping with him shocked her. Though far from inexperienced, she'd never acted with such brazenness in her life. She couldn't deny it felt naughty... But it also felt right and undeniably good.

A surge of excitement rushed through her. Somehow, she knew instinctively that Rohan would be an amazing lover. If his kisses were anything to go by, she was in for a magical time.

And she wanted to touch him too, and give him pleasure and familiarize herself with every bump and hollow... She squirmed with impatience.

Keeping his squad car in sight, she wove in and out of the traffic. It had thinned since she'd taken the exit, but it was still heavy enough that she was forced to drive at a slower pace than the speed limit allowed. She chafed at the delay, but there was nothing she could do. Perhaps she should use the enforced time in her car to think through her rash decision to sleep with Rohan... Or maybe not.

Up ahead, his indicator light came on and she breathed a sigh of relief. Following him around the right-hand turn, it wasn't long before he swung into a cobbled driveway that led to what was once a grand old house. Rohan cut his lights and climbed out of his car. Sam pulled in behind him and did the same. Clutching her handbag to her chest, she walked toward him and fought off a wave of nerves.

The house beckoned to her with all its old-world charm. Though it was in darkness, there was enough light from the street for her to see the two-storey, old red-brick façade. Manicured hedges, four feet high, bordered the pavement and added to the appeal. Now that she was here and the reality of what she was about to do was upon her, she was filled with indecision.

"Stop looking so scared, Samantha," Rohan chided with a smile. "It's not like I'm going to jump you in the driveway. Come in and have a drink. Enjoy the view from the balcony. We'll see how you feel after that."

Sam drew in a deep breath and nodded, relieved that, despite what had gone on in her workplace, he hadn't assumed she was a sure thing. If anything, Rohan Coleridge was polite and respectful. Other attributes she admired.

"Thank you, that sounds lovely. I'm sorry; I'm a little nervous. I don't usually follow men home for the purposes of having wild, passionate sex."

He chuckled, then drew closer and cradled her face in his hands. "I know. It's one of the many things that makes you so special." With that, he pressed a soft kiss against her lips, lingering only long enough to leave her wanting more. When he pulled away, her legs were unsteady and her lungs clamored for air.

Giving her no time to respond, Rohan turned on his heel and began to walk up the driveway toward the house. Cremorne was perched among some very steep hills and by the time Sam reached the wide front porch, she was once again breathing heavily.

Reaching out for one of the pale columns that held up the red-tiled roof, she fought to catch her breath. Rohan inserted a key in the front door and pushed it open with his shoulder. Stepping back, he indicated she could enter.

The house was just as Sam imagined and remained true to its earliest roots. The walls were painted in federation colors and the rooms were furnished in the same style and period, to match. Polished floorboards gleamed in the soft light that spilled out from a freestanding lamp.

The front room had been styled as a sitting

room and a fireplace stood against the far wall. It was dark and cold, but Sam could see it had recently been used and she could imagine how comfortable and cozy the room would be with the fire blazing.

"Are you cold?" Rohan asked, as if reading her thoughts.

"No, I'm fine. The weather's really warmed up the past couple of weeks."

"Yes, it won't be long and we'll be into summer and everyone will be complaining about the heat."

She smiled and he smiled back and once again, the air grew charged.

"I love how your hair does that," Rohan murmured, reaching out to touch the riotous waves.

"What?" Sam asked with a catch in her breath. His nearness was a hazard to her equilibrium.

"Curls madly after it dries," he said and twisted a lock around his finger.

"I washed it in the shower at work."

He nodded and continued to work his fingers through her hair, massaging her scalp as he did so. It felt so good, she couldn't hold back a groan.

"Is that good?" he asked, maintaining the pressure on her head.

"*Mm*, more than good. It feels fantastic."

"Sit down," he ordered and led her to a couch with fabric upholstery lavishly embellished with large gold flowers. He picked up a silk-covered pillow and handed it to her.

"Lie down and relax. Let me iron out some of

your kinks." Gently he pressed her into the couch.

Kicking off her shoes, she succumbed to his urgings and lay down on her stomach with her head on the pillow. Rohan sat on the couch beside her and his hands went to her shoulders.

With slow, firm, repetitive movements, he massaged the tight muscles in her neck. Her upper back was also given some attention. She groaned into the pillow at the exquisite feel of his strong hands pressing into her flesh. It felt so good she didn't want it to end and was pleased when he moved lower.

Tugging the ends of her blouse out of the waistband of her skirt, he slid his hands under the fabric until he was touching her skin. He continued to work at the tight knots in her muscles, working his way up from the base of her spine, across her neck and back down again. He traced the bumps of her vertebrae and spanned the side of her ribs. His fingers skimmed over the soft swell of her breasts and she couldn't hold back a gasp.

Warmth tingled everywhere that he touched, and her nipples grew hard with need. She yearned for him to touch her fully and to stoke the fire kindled low in her belly. His hands reached down to cup the cheeks of her butt and his fingers worked over the soft muscle. She flexed and tightened beneath his touch and heard his low, satisfied chuckle.

"Do you like that?" he murmured.

"*Mm*," she said, her voice muffled against the pillow.

He moved on the couch and a moment later,

his hands went around her foot. Kneading first one, and then the other, then moved onto her calves and slowly inched his way up. By the time he reached the sensitive skin of her inner thighs, she could barely remain still.

Her heart beat fast and hard against her ribs and she wasn't sure how much more of his attentions she could take. When his fingers skimmed the lace of her panties, she gasped, rolled over and surged upright. Her gaze found his and her mouth parted when she recognized the raw desire in his eyes. She was sure it was reflected in her own.

"I want to touch you, Samantha."

His voice was rough with need and she felt it all the way to her core. Liquid heat consumed her and all of a sudden she needed him like she'd never needed any man before. With her heart pounding in anticipation, she shuffled over on her knees to where he sat. Her gaze burned into his. She hitched up her short skirt and straddled him, positioning herself in his lap.

Her hand grazed the top of his suit pants and she heard him catch his breath. His cock lay thick and hard beneath the fabric and once again, she was filled with fiery need. Tightening her fingers around his erection, she pulsed her hand around his shaft. He watched her with eyes hooded with desire. His breath came faster and faster. She pulled at his belt and loosened it, all the while keeping her gaze on his. Her fingers found the button of his trousers and slid the zipper down.

She reached inside, beneath his underwear, for

his thick, hard, throbbing cock. Tightening her hand around it, she stroked him once again.

"Christ, it feels so good." He groaned and then put his hand over hers. "Don't stop. Whatever you do, don't stop."

Emboldened, Sam bent her head and licked the head of his cock. His skin was warm and silky beneath her tongue. With her hand still tight around his shaft, she opened her mouth and took him all the way inside. He sighed in relief and stretched out on the couch, giving her better access.

Over and over again, she licked the sides of his cock and sucked him deep into her mouth. His breathing became more and more frantic.

"I'm going to come if you keep that up," he murmured and gently pulled away. "Before that happens, I want to pleasure you like you've pleasured me."

With that, he stood and gathered her in his arms and carried her down the hall until they came to a bedroom. Tucked against his chest, she barely had time to register the king-sized bed that filled most of the modest room before he lay her down on its softness.

He took a step back and pulled off his shoes. His suit jacket and tie quickly followed. Unbuttoning his shirt, he tugged it off and then shucked his pants off over his hips. She watched him, breathless with anticipation. When at last he came back to her, naked apart from his underwear, she sighed in relief.

Gathering her close, he nuzzled the side of her neck. "You have way too many clothes on."

She pulled away and quickly dispensed with her blouse and skirt. Her hands went to the clasp of her bra, but Rohan stilled them.

"Let me," he murmured huskily. Sliding his hands beneath the lacy fabric, he kneaded each breast. His head came down and his mouth opened hot and wet over her nipple. She arched into him, wanting and needing so much more. Plunging her hands into his hair, she held his head in place.

"You taste so sweet," he mumbled, sucking her nipple deeper into his mouth. A rush of heat flooded through her and she moved against him.

As if sensing her impatience, Rohan reached around her back and released the clasp of her bra. Her breasts sprang free. He slid the garment off her shoulders and tossed it in the direction of the floor. Burying his face between her breasts, he breathed in deeply.

"You smell like jasmine, or maybe honeysuckle, or vanilla. Maybe cinnamon. Whatever it is, it smells good." He groaned and his mouth found her other nipple.

Licking and sucking, he used his mouth and tongue until she was wild with need. Just when she didn't think she could take another minute of his sensual attack, he moved lower and pressed more kisses against her soft skin.

His tongue found her belly button and dipped in and around the small nub. She lay back against the pillows and enjoyed his attentions. Moving lower still, he kissed his way across her flat stomach and came to a halt at her underwear. Without hesitation, he slipped his fingers beneath the lace and covered her mound with his hand.

Her hips came off the mattress and she stifled another gasp. His fingers explored her soft folds. Slick with desire, they swelled and throbbed beneath his touch. When his hand dipped lower and his fingers slipped inside her, she couldn't hold back a groan.

"Do you like that?" he asked, his eyes glittering with desire.

"Yes!" she gasped and surged up against his hand.

"Patience, Samantha. All in good time." When he shifted and his tongue replaced his fingers, she thought she'd die. She was about to combust from the inside out; burn up in a fire pit of need. In and out, his tongue slid over her, driving her wild.

Just when she didn't think she could stand the onslaught another minute, he lifted his head and gazed at her. "You're so beautiful," he murmured, his voice rough with desire.

Sam half sat up and reached for him and he climbed back up her body. Taking a moment to shuck off his underwear, he lay full-length upon her and pressed her against the sheets. Her breasts were crushed against his muscular chest and his cock lay thick and hard and pulsing against her stomach. She ached to feel him inside her and in a harsh whisper, told him so.

Needing no further encouragement, Rohan surged upward and reached over and pulled open the drawer of his nightstand. Grabbing a condom, he sheathed his erection and then returned to her side. Bracing his weight on his hands, with his knee, he spread wide her thighs and then settled himself between them. She stared up at him, filled with yearning and anticipation.

He prodded her entrance with his cock and she lifted her hips to meet him. He inched in a little further and once again, she offered him wordless encouragement. He reached for her hands and threaded his fingers through hers and as his fingers tightened, he thrust all the way inside.

She gasped at the feel of him and at the pull of her inner muscles as they struggled to accommodate him. He slowly withdrew, but not quite all the way and then plunged into her all over again. Over and over, he slid in and out and the pressure inside her grew. She clung to his shoulders and dug her nails into his back and held on tight.

With a cry, she reached the pinnacle and went free-falling over the other side. For a long time afterwards, her muscles clenched and unclenched around his cock. Slowly, she returned to earth and her breathing became more normal. Rohan gazed down at her, his expression a mix of satisfaction and wonder.

"Was that good for you?" he asked.

"More than good," she breathed. "It was amazing."

He smiled and leaned down to press a lingering kiss on her lips. With his forehead on hers, he moved again and it wasn't long before she felt him tense in her arms and shudder as he found his release. He collapsed against her and his breath came harsh in her ear. Gradually, it quietened and he lifted his weight off her.

"You're right," he whispered. "It was amazing."

CHAPTER 12

Dear Diary,

Please, God, somebody stop me! The Devil has wrested control of my soul. I started out with such noble intentions, but I no longer recognize who I am.

I wanted to help people, to help the lame walk again, to help the blind to see. But all that drives me now is the money. I'm consumed by it every second, every minute, every hour of the day.

The more packages of human tissue that depart for distant shores, the more dollars land in my bank account and I'm addicted to their impact. I have enough money for a hundred lifetimes. But even that is not enough. Greed has taken hold of me and will not let me go.

Dear God, where will it all end...?

———

Rohan sifted through the files that covered every available surface of his desk and had even spilled over to Bryce's. He'd received the files he'd requested from Samantha and had examined each and every one of them closely. There was one thing for certain: None of the people he'd interviewed had exaggerated about the sudden rise in the number of organ donations over the winter months.

From the beginning of June to the end of August, there had been ninety-three deaths at the Sydney Harbour Hospital that had resulted in organ donations. Fifty-nine of them were female. There were a range of ages, but the majority of the deceased were over the age of seventy-five. There was no doubt about it. Winter was harsh on the elderly.

His mother was no exception.

Rohan had spoken to her only that morning and was relieved that she sounded much better. The cough had almost disappeared and she talked about going out for lunch. The health crisis seemed to be over and he was glad. It was hard enough working a difficult investigation without worrying over his mom's well being.

His thoughts drifted to Samantha and her mom who was so much sicker than his. She'd confided in him the night they'd made love that her mother was in desperate need of a kidney. It saddened him to think the woman could die before a donor was located and he understood Samantha's frustration and fear. He sure as hell wasn't ready to lose a parent and he knew Sam's mother was all she had left.

She'd told him about her father and how he'd died when she was barely twelve months old. With no memories of the man who'd helped create her, she was forced to rely on photos and stories shared by Alistair and her older sisters to gain any sense of him at all. The thought that she might also lose her mother prematurely was a lot for her to bear. She refused to even contemplate the possibility, preferring to concentrate on the present and make the most of her time with her mom.

Many people would have succumbed to despair. Samantha knew better than most the odds of finding a match weren't in her mom's favor. Rohan admired her positive attitude. It wasn't the only thing he admired. He was only just discovering what wonders existed beneath her surface even though a decade earlier they'd considered themselves good friends.

The affable girl he'd had fun hanging out with every now and then had given him no indication of the passionate, cheeky, loving woman she'd become. He only hoped their very new and fragile relationship could stand the test of time and the inevitable pressures it would come under.

With a sigh, he flicked through the notes he'd made during the course of his examination of the records. Out of the ninety-three donor cases, thirty-six of them had been sent to the Glebe Morgue for autopsies. All but seven of those thirty-six cases had the death certificate signed by Alistair Wolfe.

On the surface, it wasn't entirely unexpected. The doctor was the head of the team, but when Rohan looked closer and discovered that out of the thirty-one cases bearing Alistair's Wolfe's signature, every one of them had the organ donation authorization given by Richard Davis, a cold ball of suspicion settled deep in his stomach and refused to go away.

The next step was to ascertain whether the organ retrievals had occurred in accordance with each patient's consent. That duty was at the heart of the investigation. Of itself, a surge in organ donations wasn't cause for concern. In fact, he was sure there were many people ecstatic over the figures. They showed that the various private and government initiatives to increase public awareness had been a huge success.

Those campaigns might very well be the true reason, but Rohan's gut was telling him there was more to it. Besides, both Hannah and Samantha had come forward because they'd felt something wasn't right and they were in a good position to know. For his sake and for Samantha's, he hoped everything was aboveboard. The alternative was unthinkable. If it turned out the organ retrievals hadn't been carried out in accordance with donors' wishes, it would mean the doctors involved in the retrieval process, and maybe even the deputy state coroner, were responsible for something unspeakable.

The thought was beyond abhorrent and Rohan refused to waste another moment in speculation.

First, he'd compare the consent forms they had with the reality of what had been removed and go from there. As for the missing consent forms... He'd deal with them later. With a firm course of action, he reached for the phone and dialed the Max Grace Funeral Home. His call was picked up on the fourth ring.

"Is that Hannah Langdon?" he asked when it was answered by a young female.

"Yes, it is. May I help you?"

"It's Detective Coleridge. You attended the station with Samantha Wolfe and spoke to me about your concerns regarding deceased persons showing signs of beyond the usual organ donation."

"Yes, of course. I remember you."

"Good. I was wondering if you could help me. I've obtained the records of everyone who died since the beginning of June who consented to donate their organs. In order to know if the organs were lawfully obtained, I need to compare the terms of the consent forms with the state of the bodies. Are you able to provide me with a list of names of the deceased you've had through your office and the evidence you witnessed of the removal of tissues?"

"I'm sorry, Detective. I won't be able to help you."

Rohan frowned. "Why not?"

"We don't keep those kinds of records. I noticed the unusual number of bodies coming in with signs that they'd been organ donors, but I didn't make a note of who it was or what was missing. And even if I did, it would only be a guess. I don't reopen the incisions. I can only speculate about what might have been removed."

Rohan's shoulders slumped with disappointment, but he wasn't willing to concede defeat at that point. "What about some of the other funeral homes? Would they keep those kinds of records?"

"I wouldn't think so," she replied doubtfully. "There's no need. We prepare the body for its final burial and at all times, we treat it with courtesy and respect. It's not necessary for us to open the body—and keeping notes concerning who donated what just seems wrong. I think most embalmers would feel that way."

Rohan bit back a sigh. Thanking her for her time, he ended the call. Flipping through the police file, he located the phone numbers of three of the other funeral parlors and called them one by one. After the third call, he hung up the phone, defeated. It was just as Hannah had predicted. No one kept records of who had donated organs and tissues and what had been taken. His only hope was to compare the consents with the autopsy reports of the thirty-six coronial cases that had been examined in the Glebe Morgue.

Tugging his cell phone out of his pocket, he speed-dialed Samantha and couldn't help but smile when she picked up right away.

"Hey, you," she said and he could hear the laughter in her voice. He hated that his request was going to sour her mood.

"Hi, how are you?" he asked. "How's your day so far?"

"Not too bad. Busy. You know how it is."

"Yeah, I sure do."

"What time will you finish?"

"I'm not sure. I'm hoping to get out of here by six. How about you?"

"If I'm lucky, I'll get out of here by then. Do you have any plans?" she asked.

"That depends," he teased.

"On what?" she replied and the laughter was back.

"On whether you're up for another night of passion."

"Rohan!" she gasped. "I'm at work! Someone might hear you!"

"What, do you have me on speaker?"

"No, of course not." Her tone lowered. "But, you know..."

"No, I don't. Please, enlighten me."

"Rohan!" she protested and he could almost feel her embarrassment. It endeared her to him even more.

"Okay! Okay! I'll behave; I promise." He laughed.

"Good. Now, was there a reason for your call, or did you just want to say hello?"

Just like that, his mood sobered. "Actually, it is partially work-related. I have a question: When you record details of an autopsy, do you make a note of all of the organs present and those that are missing?"

"Yes," she answered warily, as if she wasn't quite sure where this was headed. "The reports should be in the files I've given you."

Rohan frowned. He'd been through each and every file more than twice. He hadn't seen any such reports. "They don't seem to be there."

"They might still be waiting to be filed. We've had some of our administration staff down sick on and off this winter. It doesn't take long for paperwork to pile up."

Rohan nodded, accepting her explanation. "No problem, but I need to get hold of the autopsy findings on the thirty-six people who went through your facility over the winter months. I need to compare what was found during the post mortem to the actual consent forms."

Samantha was quiet on the other end of the phone and Rohan could understand her reticence. She was a smart woman. She had to know it was almost certain her brother was involved. The question was, whether the good doctor was merely doing his job to a high degree of dedication, or whether something illegal had occurred.

"I'll get on it," she murmured.

Sam sat beside her mom and did her best to keep her mind off the fact they were once again in the Dialysis Unit of the Sydney Harbour Hospital. Each hemodialysis session lasted about four hours and Sam sat with her mother to keep her company whenever she could.

It was difficult to sit there week after week and

pretend she wasn't affected by the sight of her beautiful mom getting weaker and frailer each time. The cloud of thick, wavy black hair she used to sport had thinned and faded to a salt-and-pepper gray. Her once-healthy skin now held a sickly pallor and the lively personality was more often than not buried beneath the burden of her chronic illness.

Sam wished for the thousandth time that either she or one of her siblings had tested positive as a compatible donor, but it hadn't worked out that way. Enid Wolfe had given birth to four children and despite the fact any one of them would have willingly offered her a kidney, not one of them had been a match. After years of suffering with kidney disease, Enid's kidney function was totally compromised and she was now forced to rely on dialysis to keep her alive.

It had been nearly six years since her kidney function had deteriorated to the extent dialysis was necessary. The longer it went on, the more likely it was her kidneys would call it quits altogether. Sam knew as well as anyone that when that day came, her mom's life would be as good as over.

Squeezing her eyes shut, she made a conscious effort to block out that depressing thought. Her mom was the only parent she'd ever known. She couldn't imagine life without her. She didn't *want* to imagine life without her.

There was still so much they had to share. Sam hadn't given up hope of getting married, having children, celebrating birthdays, christenings;

graduations. All the bits and pieces of everyday life that many people, including Sam, used to take for granted. She'd assumed her mom would be around to see Sam live them and yet there was a real chance she wouldn't.

Dammit, it wasn't fair!

"How have you been, Sammie?"

Sam forced her lips into a smile and replied in a light tone. "Good, Mom. Busy at work. The usual." She tried not to think of Rohan and his investigation.

"How's Alistair? I haven't seen him for a week and he hasn't called for ages."

"I think he's okay. I haven't seen him for a while, either. He's really busy, too."

"You all work too hard. Ava and Jessie are the same. They sit with me when they can, but I know they both have clients waiting while they're here keeping me company. Jessie's phone never stops ringing. She has it switched to silent, of course, but I still hear it vibrate."

She grinned and Sam grinned back, pleased to see her mom was in good spirits. It was hard enough for Sam to contemplate what would happen if a donor kidney wasn't found in time. She couldn't imagine how much harder it must be for her mom.

"I'll call Alistair and let him know that you're here. He might be able to get away for a little while, and come down and say hello."

"Is he at work today?"

"I'm not sure, but it's worth a try. He spends most of his waking hours here." Sam pulled out her phone and dialed his number. The call went through to his mailbox and she left a brief message.

Enid shook her head. "Like I said, he works too hard. He has a wife and two children who need some of his time, too. He forgets that." She turned to look at Sam. "How are you doing on that front? Are there any possibilities on the horizon? Have you met anyone special on that dating site?"

Heat swept across Sam's cheeks. "Mom! I can't believe Alistair told you! I'm going to kill him!"

"Don't be too hard on him, Sammie. He wasn't making fun of you and he didn't mean to breach your confidence. I think he thought it would cheer me up, knowing you were doing something about finding a husband. You're thirty-four, honey. Your body's clock is ticking. I hate to remind you, but time's running out if you want to have a family."

Sam rolled her eyes. "What about Ava and Jessie? They're a year older than me and they haven't managed to produce a grandchild."

"Yes, and I give the same talk to them," her mother smiled. "But at least they have boyfriends. That's a start."

Sam sighed. It wasn't like she hadn't heard it all before. "It's not just kids I want, Mom. I want the whole package—the perfect fantasy. A husband I adore and who thinks just as highly of me. A kid or two. The big backyard and the white picket fence."

She reached over and took her mother's hand. "I want what you and Dad had. I know I was too young to know him. Hell, I don't even remember him, but I've heard so many stories about him from you and Alistair as well as a few from Ava and Jessie. I've watched the family movies over and over again. They were taken before I was born and yet I can't help feeling the love and respect that you had for each other and I yearn to have the same. I don't want to settle for anything less."

Enid squeezed Sam's hand. The faint pressure brought tears to Sam's eyes. Her mom had been a strong and vibrant woman until the onset of this insidious disease.

"And so you shouldn't, Sammie. Hold out for your prince charming. It's a long time married to the wrong man. A lot of my friends have lived to regret their hasty decisions."

Sam nodded. She also had friends who'd married way too young. Many were her age and already on their second time around. She didn't want to be one of those women. She had too much respect for the institution of marriage and all that it represented to commit herself to someone for life without thinking it through from all angles.

"Would you like a drink of water, Mom?" she asked and received a grateful nod.

"That would be lovely, Sammie. Thank you."

Sam stood and filled a glass with water from a jug that stood near the armchair where her mom reclined. She handed it to her mother and waited for her to drink.

"Thank you, honey," her mom said when she finished and handed her back the glass. "I was a little thirsty. That water tasted good."

"You let me know if you want some more, Mom," Sam murmured.

"I will, darling. I will." Sam returned to her seat.

"You didn't answer my question."

"What question was that, Mom?"

"I asked if you'd met anyone special on that dating site. I mean, it's a little unconventional and it certainly isn't the way we did things when I was young, but if that's how people meet each other these days, then I guess it's all right."

Sam laughed. She bent down and picked up her handbag from where she'd stowed it under her chair and pulled out her iPad. Logging onto the dating website, she turned the screen around so that her mother could see it.

"Take a look at some of the people who set up profiles on these sites. Read their bios. Some of them are bound to give you a laugh."

Her mother reached for the iPad and began to scroll through the pages. Every now and then, she'd let out a chuckle. Once or twice, she laughed.

"Oh, this one is downright desperate!" She smiled. "Why on earth would anyone go out with someone like that?"

Sam grinned. "I guess you have to give them points for trying. You never know... They say there's someone out there for everyone, don't they?"

Her mom's attention remained on the screen and she didn't answer. A few moments later, she said, "That's a nice photo of you, Sammie."

Sam blushed. Her mom had obviously found Sam's profile page. Knowing that her mom wouldn't stop at the photo, heat crept further across her face. She pulled out her phone and busied herself by pretending to read through emails.

Her mom eventually broke the silence. "It reads well, Sammie, although I didn't know you like watching black and white movies. Still, your bio's appealing and you look fabulous in that photo. If I were a man looking for love, I'd snap you up right away!"

Sam burst out laughing and her mom joined her. It felt so good to share such a simple thing with the woman she loved more than anyone else in the world. She thought of Rohan and wished for a moment he were there. He'd spoken to her about his parents and siblings and she could tell from the love and quiet pride in his voice how much they meant to him.

Family was important to him. It was just another thing she liked about him. He was a man with many admirable qualities, not the least being the way he made her feel. On impulse, she opened her mouth and found herself talking about him.

"It's funny you say that, Mom. I'm thinking about taking that profile down."

"Why, Sammie? It's lovely and I've reconciled to the fact young people do things differently these days. I guess with all this technology at your fingertips, you might as well put it to good use. You won't be the only person to find the love of their life on the Internet."

"Well, actually, I think I might have found him the good old-fashioned way."

"What do you mean?"

"My prince charming."

The surprise that flooded her mother's beloved face was almost comical. "Samantha Grace Wolfe! How could you have kept something so momentous from me! We've been sitting here for at least three hours and you haven't breathed a word! Shame on you!"

Sam laughed and her mom joined in. "I want to hear all the details," Enid begged.

Now that she'd opened that Pandora's box, Sam wasn't sure what to say. Since she'd spent the night at Rohan's house they'd barely seen each other. He was busy with the investigation and she was also doing long hours at work. Between the two of them, they'd only had time to make the occasional phone call and most of those had been late at night.

Sam thought of the call they'd shared the night before and blushed. It wasn't exactly phone sex, but it had sure sent the heat rushing through her veins. Her mother's eyes narrowed and a smile played around her lips.

"Sammie... Talk to me," she said sternly, mock warning in her voice.

Sam took a deep breath and exhaled. "His name is Rohan Coleridge. He's a detective, stationed in the city."

Her mother's eyebrow rose in surprise. "A detective? How did you meet?"

"I've known him since I was in college. He used to date my roommate."

"Oh, wow! That's interesting! All that time and you never thought about hooking up."

"It was...complicated."

"And now it's not?"

She shrugged. "Something like that. Let's just say, we sorted out our differences."

"Well, I'm glad, Sammie. Is he nice?"

"Yes, Mom. He's very nice."

"When do I get to meet him?"

"Mom! We've only just started going out! We're not exactly up to the 'meeting the parents' stage."

"But you've known him for a decade."

"Yes, but... As I said, back then it was complicated."

"Are his parents still alive?"

"Yes, they live at Cronulla. His mom's been sick with a prolonged bout of the flu, but otherwise I understand they're reasonably healthy."

"That's good. Does he have any siblings?"

"Yes, a lot. Four brothers and three sisters. I'm not sure where they all live, but Rohan's the only one in Sydney."

"*Mm*, I'm glad he has family. Family's important. Life can throw you curve balls when you least expect it. Having family around is one of the things that can see you through to the other side. Nobody knows you like your family and you can't rely on anyone like you can on them."

"If you're close," Sam added.

Her mother frowned. "Is he not close to his family?"

"I'm not sure, Mom. I guess so. He speaks about them with fondness. That's how I know he cares."

"You said he's a detective. That's a very

challenging job. Long hours and very little gratitude from those they serve and protect. I think life's tougher on police officers than most."

"Yes, more often than not, it's a thankless job. You couldn't pay me enough to be one."

Enid smiled. "And this is coming from you—a person who spends their days examining corpses."

"Mom! I love my job! It's very intriguing and rewarding and—"

"Hey, I'm glad you feel that way," her mom said holding up her hands in a sign of surrender. "All I meant was, some people would find your job as undesirable as you find that of a police officer."

"You're right. We're all different. I guess that's what makes things interesting."

A comfortable silence fell between them. Sam returned to her emails.

"So, is he good-looking, this detective of yours?"

Sam blushed. "He's not *mine*, Mom! We're dating; taking it slowly; seeing where it might lead." She paused and then added, "But yes, he's definitely been blessed in the looks department. He reminds me of pictures I've seen of Dad. Blond and blue-eyed with a broad chest and shoulders."

Enid's expression turned serious. "Do you think that might be why you're attracted to him? Because he looks like your dad?"

Sam contemplated the question. Until now, she hadn't given it any thought. "I don't think so."

"It's not good to go looking for a substitute father figure, especially one you never knew. Nobody can live up to the ideals of a ghost."

Sam was shaking her head even before her mom had finished. "No, Rohan's definitely not that. He has coloring like Dad's, but that's where the similarities end."

"How old is he?"

"The same age as me."

Her mother nodded and her expression relaxed. "Good. I'm glad he's young. If you'd told me his was fifty, I'd have been concerned."

Sam smiled and reassured her mother once again. "I'm okay about growing up without a father, Mom. I am. Some people would be bitter and twisted about the fact they never knew their dad, but I'm not one of them and I'm not looking for someone to replace him." She shrugged and then continued. "Dad was a heavy smoker. He died of lung cancer years before his time. It happens. I'm a doctor. I understand these things."

A sad smile tugged at Sam's lips. "I'm not saying I haven't wished that things were different or that I don't hate that he died so young, but I'm not hung up about it and I'm not going around trolling for men who remind me of him. Okay?"

She looked up at her mom and her throat tightened when she saw the tears that filled her mother's eyes.

"Okay," Enid whispered in a choked voice.

Sam fished around inside her bra for a tissue and handed it over. "Don't cry, Mom."

Enid accepted the tissue gratefully and dabbed at the moisture in her eyes.

Sam grimaced. "I'm supposed to be here cheering you up and keeping your mind off things and here I am, making you cry. What kind of dialysis buddy am I?"

Her mom reached over and patted her hand. "You're the best dialysis buddy anyone could hope for."

Sam laughed. "Don't let Ava or Jessie hear you say that, or even Alistair! They'll never sit with you again!"

Her mom's eyes twinkled with mischief. "How do you know I don't tell them the very same thing when they sit in that chair?"

"Mom!" Sam gasped in mock outrage. "You've wounded me to the quick!" Despite her attempt to keep a stern expression on her face, her laughter spilled over.

Enid chuckled, unperturbed. "I'm sure you'll get over it, Sammie. Maybe your detective can help."

The sly look in her mother's eyes sent heat once again rushing to Sam's face, but she closed her mouth and refused to reply. A nurse appeared before them.

"All finished, Enid. Give me a moment and I'll get you unhooked and then you'll be free to go."

"Finished already? Wow, the time went so quickly! How about that, Sammie? Maybe you really *are* the best dialysis buddy!" Her mom winked and Sam couldn't help but grin. She was filled with gratitude that once again, her mother had been able to maintain her sense of humor. Until a donor kidney was found, the dialysis sessions would remain a regular part of her mother's life.

The need to attend upon the clinic three times

a week had severely curtailed her mother's activities. Once upon a time, before the word dialysis was part of her everyday vocabulary, Enid Wolfe had been a very active woman. In her younger years, she'd raised four children on her own with only a nurse's wage. In later years, she'd been involved in so many different charity projects, Sam used to wonder how her mom managed to spend any time at home.

Since she'd been told she could no longer survive without dialysis, Sam couldn't help but wonder if sometimes it got her mother down. Pleased that she'd been able to take her mother's mind off her troubles, even for a little while, Sam leaned over and pressed a kiss against her mother's soft cheek.

"I love you, Mom."

"I love you, too, Sammie. You're a good daughter and I appreciate you taking the time out of your busy day to spend some time with me. I wasn't lying when I said the time's gone by more quickly today. I enjoyed our chat and I'm so pleased to hear you've found someone special. I can't wait to meet him."

"You will, Mom. I promise. Soon. I just don't want to rush things."

"I understand, honey and thank you again for sitting with me."

"It's fine, Mom. I love spending time with you. Besides, walking from work up to the hospital gets me out in the sunshine. Most days, it's only during my commute that I even know what the weather's like!" She grinned and her mom grinned back.

A rush of tenderness and gratitude flooded through her. Neither of them knew how many more hours they had left to spend together. Sam intended to make every one of them memorable.

"I have to get back to work, Mom, but I'll make sure the nurse has arranged for the patient transport to take you back home," she promised.

"All right, honey. I'll see you soon."

Sam leaned over and kissed her mom again. Collecting her handbag from beneath her chair, she turned and quietly left the room.

CHAPTER 13

"Are you at work? I need to see you."

Sam heard the urgency in Rohan's voice and her heart skipped a beat. The last time he'd turned up at her work they'd ended the night in his bed. The fact that they hadn't found time to repeat the experience was at the forefront of her mind and she couldn't help but think it was also in his.

"Yes, I'm here until six."

"Good. I'll be there in an hour."

Sam ended the mid-afternoon call and tossed her cell phone back down on her desk. She was doing her best to catch up on the endless paperwork that crowded her desk. Autopsy findings, lab results, blood work and a whole host of other data had to be entered into their system and then forwarded to the relevant police commands around the state. It was a never-ending, but necessary aspect of her work and the part that she least enjoyed. She'd been at it almost an hour and still had a pile to go, but at the thought of Rohan's imminent arrival, her spirits lifted.

If she stayed focused for the next hour, she'd come close to getting to the bottom of the most urgent of the paperwork. If she came in early in the morning, she could finish off the rest. Decision made, she bent to the task at hand.

"Sam, how are you doing?"

She looked up and spied Richard leaning on the doorframe to her office. She threw him a distracted wave. "Hi, Richard. I'm fine. Trying to get up to date on the paperwork. You know how it is."

He nodded and moved further into the room. "Back in my day, we had to type it all up on manual typewriters. You guys have it easy! A couple of strokes on the keyboard and the computer does the rest."

Sam chuckled. "Yeah, right!"

"True story!" Richard protested in mock distress.

"Next you'll be telling me how hard it was to conduct a post mortem without electricity. Don't worry, Richard, I've heard it all before."

"Now, Sam. Be fair. How old do you think I am? I've never once said I worked in the days before electricity."

He grinned and her lips tilted in response. "Is there something I can do for you, boss? I'm kind of busy here entering information into my computer," she said cheekily.

"Anything in particular?"

"Just trying to catch up on last week's cases. I have a ton of pathology reports that need to be entered, along with the notes I've made about the PM's I did yesterday and today."

Richard nodded. "I was speaking to the coroner the other day. He told me you mentioned a donor body that came through without a consent form."

"Yes, I meant to tell you about it, but it happened on the weekend you were sick. I ran into the coroner first thing Monday morning. I wanted him to know so that he could speak to our transportation staff. We can't pinpoint exactly where the form was mislaid, but we can make sure our guys had nothing to do with losing it and if they did, they need to smarten up their act. Lost paperwork can have serious implications. We can all do without the hassle."

"Is that all there was to it?"

Sam frowned at the sharpness of Richard's tone but nodded and continued to enter data into her computer. Her boss remained where he was. After a moment, she glanced up at him again. "Is there anything in particular you needed to speak with me about?"

"No, I just wanted to touch base and see how you were doing. You haven't noticed anything else that's strange, have you?"

"No. In fact, I haven't caught a single donor body for a while, other than when I filled in while you were sick that time. My brother might have been right. He assured me the extra numbers were probably the result of the higher toll winter has on people. Now that the weather's warmed up, we certainly have fewer bodies coming through."

"I think I said something to you along those lines when you first raised it with me ages ago." Richard's smile was followed by a friendly wink.

"Okay, okay. No need to rub it in," she laughed good-naturedly. "It was strange, that's all and when I did the PM on that woman who had no consent form in her paperwork, I kind of freaked out."

"Nothing wrong with that. Our line of work freaks a lot of people out."

She grimaced. "You know what I mean."

"Of course. You were being thorough, Sam. It's an admirable trait. Don't be too harsh on yourself. There's no harm done."

"I guess not. Still, I feel a little silly that I mentioned it to the police."

Richard frowned, as she expected him to. "The police? Why would you go to the police?"

Sam shrugged, uncomfortable. "A friend of mine who works as an embalmer at the Max Grace Funeral Home suggested it. She'd also noticed a few weird things."

Richard's expression grew stern. "You should have come to me, Sam, before you went to the police. I could have spared you and the department a whole lot of embarrassment. I hope this doesn't get out."

Sam ducked her head, feeling his disapproval. It was true. She should have gone to Richard first, before jumping to such wild conclusions.

"What did they say?"

She looked up. "Who?"

"The police?"

"Oh, we met with a detective and he promised to look into it. I'm not sure what's up with it now." She opened her mouth to tell him that the detective in question was on his way to the morgue, but something held her back. Rohan hadn't told her why he was paying her a visit. It might be purely personal and there was no way she was going to share that with her boss.

"From now on, I'd appreciate it if any requests made by the police come through me. Are we clear?"

Sam caught the hard edge in his gaze and was a little taken aback. She was a senior pathologist, well versed in dealing with the law enforcement. Still, she nodded in response. "No problem, boss. Will do."

"Good. Now, I have to leave for an outside appointment. I won't be back today. I'll see you in the morning." With that, he hurried from the room.

Pushing the visit from her mind, Sam returned her attention to the reports in front of her. It hardly seemed like any time at all before Angie buzzed to let her know Detective Coleridge had arrived.

Butterflies swarmed in Sam's stomach and she did her best to slow her breathing down. *Would she end this night like she had the last time he'd arrived at her place of work?* Anticipation surged through her. She couldn't wait to find out.

Assuring Angie she'd come out to the reception area in a few minutes, Sam took her handbag and hurried to the staff restrooms, pleased she'd already taken the time to shower and change out of her scrubs. Scrabbling inside her handbag for a lipstick, she quickly applied a couple of coats and then refreshed her eyeliner and mascara. Peering at her reflection critically, she at last deemed herself presentable. Dumping the makeup back into her handbag, she turned around and left.

———————

Rohan heard the sharp click of heels on the tiled floor and turned in time to see Samantha open a door and stride into the waiting room. She wore a tailored dress in a smart purple-and-white checkerboard pattern that ended above her knee. It was made from some kind of stretchy fabric that clung to her in all the right places. A pair of four-inch, black heels complemented the outfit.

She smiled and he noticed her lips were freshly glossed in a bright red color. It looked good against her dark hair and olive skin. He found himself smiling back, wanting to take her in his arms and kiss her senseless. Aware of the receptionist seated behind the counter a few yards away, he played it safe.

"Doctor Wolfe, thank you for taking the time to see me."

Surprise lit the corners of her eyes at his formal manner, but she responded in kind. "What can I do for you, Detective Coleridge?"

"I was wondering if there was somewhere we could talk in private?"

Her eyes flared with heat and his groin

immediately reacted. He cursed under his breath but was relieved that behind his suit pants his erection would remain concealed to all but a very astute observer.

"Of course. I'll take you through to my office."

She turned and opened the door she'd just come through. He followed, enjoying the gentle sway of her hips as she led the way. Memories of holding her naked against him, loving her through the night, bombarded him and it was all he could do not to groan.

She pulled up outside a doorway that had a faux bronze nameplate with her name on it and he swallowed a sigh of relief. At least he wouldn't be forced to keep up the pretense of being almost-strangers much longer. As soon as they were in the privacy of her office…

She opened the door and he closed it behind them. A second later, he grabbed her and pushed her back against the wooden panel. When his lips found her mouth, he kissed her like he'd wanted to from the moment she'd greeted him and was gratified when she melted against him. Her arms went around his neck and she clung to him as if her life depended upon it. He knew how she felt.

"Christ, it's been so long since I tasted you." He groaned and kissed her over and over again. Her lipstick was smudged all over her mouth, but he didn't care. He was like a drug addict being offered a line of coke and he couldn't inhale quickly enough. It scared him to think how important she'd become to him in such a short time, but there was nothing he could do, or wanted to do, to curb that.

He pressed himself against her, leaving her in no doubt about the state he was in. She groaned softly and he caught the sound of it in his mouth. With his body pinning her to the door, he reached out and cupped her breast... Squeezed it. His thumb skimmed over her nipple. She gasped and angled her head so that she could access his mouth more easily and continued to kiss him.

A lifetime later, he pulled back his head and tried hard to slow his breathing down. His heart pounded and his cock throbbed, but he was also aware they were in her office. Though the walls were solid and the door was closed, it wasn't like he could take her spread-eagled across her desk. *Or could he...?*

As if reading his mind, Sam shook her head. "No."

He grinned. "No? Are you sure?" He captured her mouth again and kissed her until they were both gasping for breath once again. This time, Sam pulled away.

"Yes, I'm... I'm sure."

He winked. "In that case, how have you been? It feels like forever since I last saw you."

She blushed a little—which he found endearing—but nodded. "Yes, for me, too."

"As much as I'd like to collect you and drive hell for leather to my place, I'm actually here on official business."

"Oh?" she asked, moving away from him and straightening her dress. She took a seat behind her desk and pulled a tissue from her bra and daubed around her mouth.

"Yes, it's about that information I asked for—the autopsy findings of each of the bodies that donated organs over the winter months."

"Yes, of course. Sorry, I've been so busy I haven't had time to gather all that. When do you need it?"

"As soon as possible. The more I delve into this investigation, the more I suspect the terms of the consent won't gel with what's been found during the autopsy."

Sam frowned. "You mean, you think there might have been tissue harvested illegally?"

"Yes, that's exactly what I mean."

She stared at him. "That's a big call. Do you have any proof?"

"Not yet. Call it gut instinct." He grimaced. "I might be wrong. Hell, I'd be more than happy to be proven wrong. The thought that a doctor could be on the loose, doing something like that is appalling. Unfortunately, there's only one way to find out."

Sam chewed on her lip and Rohan could see the worry and indecision on her face. In all likelihood, she was thinking about her brother. He could understand her concern. If something were amiss, there was a very strong possibility her brother was involved.

"What is it, Samantha?" he asked gently.

"My boss—Richard Davis. He was in here just before you arrived. He gave me a not-too-subtle dressing down about going to the police before coming to see him. He instructed me to send any future police requests through him. I should tell him you're here."

Rohan nodded. "By all means, let him know. I don't want to get you into trouble. I'm happy to speak with him about it. It's not like he's going to refuse."

Sam looked relieved and then another frown marred the smooth skin of her brow. "The only thing is—Richard's already left for the day."

"Damn. I really need them as soon as possible. The sooner I can compare the paperwork, the sooner I'll know what we're dealing with—if anything."

Samantha sighed. "Perhaps I could call him and let him know you're here. He should be happy to give permission over the phone."

She reached for the phone and dialed a number. From where he stood, Rohan could hear the sound of a voicemail message and then Sam spoke.

"Hi, Richard, it's Sam. Sorry to annoy you, but I have a detective here right now requesting copies of paperwork associated with the donor bodies we spoke about earlier. Can you please give me a call?"

She hung up the phone and waited. A few moments later, she began to tap her nails on the desk. Rohan reached out and covered her hand with his.

"Relax, I'm sure he'll call back. In the meantime, I can think of any number of ways we can keep ourselves occupied."

"What did you have in mind?" she murmured

suggestively and his cock once again sprang to life.

He reached down and cupped her cheek and then stroked her bottom lip with the pad of his thumb. Heat flared in her eyes and his body tightened almost painfully. If they didn't get out of there soon he'd bend her over the desk, work be damned. From the expression on her face, he could tell she was equally affected.

The phone at her elbow rang and both of them jumped. Sam pulled away from him and reached over to answer it. Rohan moved to lean against the door.

"Hi, Richard, thanks for calling me back," he heard her say. She listened to what was being said on the other end of the phone and then replied.

"Yes, that's right. The autopsy reports on the donor bodies." Once again, she fell silent and listened and then responded again.

"Yes, he's here now. Okay, I'll get them printed out. Thanks, Richard. I'll see you tomorrow." She hung up the phone and looked at Rohan.

"Richard's given me the go ahead." She dragged her keyboard toward her. "It shouldn't take me long. Do you have a list of names? It will be easier to search that way."

"Yes." Rohan pushed away from the door and handed her the folded sheets of paper he took from his pocket. Sam glanced at them and then began typing. A few moments later, she frowned.

"That's funny," she murmured and then began typing again. Her frown deepened. "This is really weird."

Rohan moved closer and stood behind her,

leaning over her shoulder. He peered at the screen. "What is it?"

"I've tried the first three names on your list and I keep coming up with a message that tells me the file doesn't exist. It doesn't make sense. Of course it exists! A file is created within the hour of a body being received. We have very strict procedures. With so many cadavers coming through here each day, it's important a record is created for each one as soon as possible."

She turned in her seat to face him. "Are you sure your list is correct?"

"I'm certain. The names were taken directly from the files I received from the Sydney Harbour Hospital."

Samantha's brow creased again. "I don't get it. How could the database not have their records?" She shook her head. "I'll try Natalie Piccoli. I know for sure her name's in here. I was the one who entered it."

Turning back to face the screen, she typed in the woman's name. Peering over her shoulder, Rohan saw she came up with the same result. The name wasn't known to the database.

A sense of foreboding slid through Rohan's veins and his jaw tightened. From the fear and confusion that now clouded Samantha's eyes, he could tell that she felt it, too. Something was very, very wrong.

Richard swung into the driveway of his comfortable bachelor pad. Small and compact, but boasting sensational water views, it was the place he called home. With the extra money he received from Alistair, he might even upgrade to something bigger. That is, if he could keep his gambling under control and if the money kept pouring in.

After climbing out of his tidy Active 5 Hybrid BMW, he leaned back in through the open door and retrieved his phone from the car kit. He thought of the call he'd taken from Sam and couldn't help but smile. It was lucky Alistair had thought of deleting those records or they'd both be in all sorts of strife. Now, he didn't have a thing to worry about.

Sam would no doubt be confused about the missing computer files, but she'd never suspect foul play. Like Alistair had suggested, Richard had made sure he deleted a lot more files than those that mattered. With computer viruses and Trojans and God knows what else attacking C-drives every day, it should be easy enough to blame an anonymous hacker for wreaking havoc over their system.

A satisfied grin stretched his lips wide. Yes, all in all, it had been a productive day and one that he'd make sure Alistair compensated him for, over and above his usual cut. It was only fair, after all.

CHAPTER 14

Sam stared up at Rohan and her heart thumped double time. Her mouth was so dry, she could hardly swallow, let alone talk. Time after time, she'd entered names into the Glebe Morgue database and each time it had come up empty.

The records she searched for had disappeared.

She didn't want to jump to wild conclusions, but dread settled heavily in her stomach. With every name she'd entered that yielded the same result, her apprehension increased. She could see the suspicion on Rohan's face.

"Where are they?" His quiet words spoke volumes, as much as his grim expression. His jaw was clenched. Tension filled the air. Sam wanted to turn back to her keyboard and keep searching, but she knew it would do no good. The records had simply vanished. She didn't even want to think about how or why.

She cleared her throat and answered him. "I... I don't know. I can't find them."

"What do you mean, you can't find them? You just finished telling me about the strict procedures you have in place to ensure accurate record keeping. They must be in there somewhere."

With increasing dread, she shook her head. "They've gone. They must have been deleted. I'm not sure how it could have happened, but it has. The records aren't there."

Rohan stared at her with narrowed eyes. "That's convenient. Are there any others missing, or just the ones I need?"

His voice was full of accusation and her heart filled with dread. Fear clutched at her insides. "Surely you don't think I had anything to do with it?"

His gaze remained hard. "You tell me. I called two days ago to request the information. You had plenty of time to erase evidence."

She shook her head with increasing force. "You're kidding me, right? You think I had something to do with this? That I'd impede a criminal investigation? You must be insane!"

He stared at her in silence for a long moment and then his body slumped on a heavy sigh. "Christ, Samantha. Don't look at me like that! What am I supposed to think? I asked you for information. You told me you've been too busy to deal with it. When I turn up here looking for it, it's suddenly gone!"

He threw his arms up in the air, his voice taut with frustration. Sam did her best to hold on to her temper. With a deep breath, she looked him squarely in the eye.

"I had nothing to do with making those files disappear. I don't know how you expect me to prove it to you. As far as I'm concerned, I shouldn't need to prove it to you at all. Surely, after all we've been through, you've learned you can trust my word."

His gaze held hers, intense with conflicting emotions. Eventually, he looked away and blew out another sigh.

"I believe you, okay? Given that your brother seems to have a lot to do with my investigation, there would be plenty who wouldn't—but they don't know you like I do. You're good and honorable and trustworthy. If you say you didn't have anything to do with this, I believe you."

Once again, his gaze met hers and she could see he was telling the truth. A little of the tension eased from her shoulders.

"What about the hard copies you told me are normally in the files? You said something about a backlog of filing."

"Yes, of course, I'll go and check the box right now. Even if I can't find them, I'm sure everything gets backed up to another server. The only problem right now is that I don't have access to it."

"Let's check the filing and see what that turns up. Then we'll have another think about it."

"I'm sure they'll be there." She made the statement as confidently as she could manage, but couldn't help the doubt that flowed through her veins. Hoping for both their sakes that the paper reports hadn't disappeared, she sighed when he pulled her upright and into his arms. Planting a kiss on her mouth, he squeezed her tightly before quickly releasing her, as if he sensed they were on unsteady ground.

"Do you need help?" he asked quietly. "If not, I'll wait for you here."

———

Rohan came awake with a start, for a moment, disorientated. Unfamiliar striped curtains were drawn against a wide bay window, blocking out most of the morning sunlight. The room was tastefully furnished with matching white wooden furniture. Even the soft pillows and other decorative things matched. It looked like something out of a home decorator's magazine.

He turned to gaze at the woman who lay beside him, her eyes still closed. Even in sleep, she was beautiful. He couldn't believe that, despite all the time he'd spent around her while he'd been dating Daphne, he hadn't once noticed how extraordinary she was.

Despite the initial consternation over the vanishing files the previous afternoon, to his relief, Samantha had managed to locate the paper files and had provided him with copies. It had been a mutual decision to spend the evening together and they'd found plenty to keep them occupied. Exploring each other until there wasn't an inch of skin on her body that Rohan hadn't tasted, she'd been almost as thorough with him. Afterwards, they'd shared a bottle of wine out on her balcony and enjoyed the balmy spring night, listening to the hum of the traffic and the occasional croak of a frog.

They'd talked some more about their families and he learned she had two older sisters who were identical twins. Ava and Jessie Wolfe were a year older than Samantha and were both professionals who appeared to be making an impact in their chosen careers. Along with their oldest brother, there was no doubt they were a family of high achievers. Rohan couldn't help but be impressed, particularly knowing they'd grown up without a father. Samantha's mother must be a remarkable woman. He couldn't wait to meet her.

Easing out of bed, so as not to wake Samantha, he padded into the bathroom and showered and dressed. Heading into the living room, he found his briefcase and tugged out the pile of papers she'd given him the day before. Taking a seat at the modest kitchen table, he began to scan the autopsy reports, making notes as he went.

The corresponding consent forms were back at the station and without them, it wasn't possible to form an accurate picture, but the more he read, the more he was convinced something untoward was happening. He couldn't remember seeing any consent form that allowed the doctors to remove anything beyond the usual, yet there were several autopsy reports that documented nearly every useable organ and considerable amounts of tissue had been removed.

Most of the reports had been prepared by

Richard Davis. A handful of them had been prepared by other pathologists. Only a few of the earlier reports had been prepared by Samantha.

In order to speed the process when he returned to his office, Rohan put the reports in alphabetical order by surname and then placed them in his briefcase. He'd just stood, with the intention of setting about making coffee, when he spied Samantha standing in the doorway.

"Good morning," he said with a smile, loving her sexy I-just-climbed-out-of-bed look.

She pushed the hair out of her eyes and smiled back at him. "Why are you up so early? It's not even seven."

"I woke up and couldn't get back to sleep. I didn't want to wake you, so I came out here."

Her gaze dropped to his briefcase where it still sat open on the table. "You were working."

"Yes." He saw the questions in her eyes, but headed her off. Until he knew for sure, he wasn't prepared to speculate any further. "I was just about to make coffee. Would you like some?"

"Thanks, it sounds great. Do you know how to start the machine?"

He glanced over at the espresso machine that sat on her counter near the sink. "I'm sure I can figure it out. I'm pretty handy that way."

"Oh, yes, you're handy all right. I'll vouch for that."

Her provocative smile reached all the way to her beautiful brown eyes and he felt its impact deep in his gut. Before he could respond, she turned away. Her short robe lifted and he caught a glimpse of naked skin. Instantly hard, he ditched the coffee and followed her down the hall. She glanced at him over her shoulder, batted her eyelashes and continued to saunter toward the bedroom. Lust and anticipation heated his blood.

He caught her just inside the door and drew her up against him. Spreading the front of her robe wide open, he palmed her breasts, loving the feel of them in his hands. He rubbed his thumbs across her nipples and was gratified with her gasp of need. His cock throbbed.

They'd spent hours the evening before learning each other's bodies, but one look at the invitation in her eyes and Rohan couldn't get enough. Sliding his hands beneath the short robe, he cupped her naked bottom and pressed her against his cock. She threaded her arms around his neck and pressed her lips to his.

She kissed him with a passion that sent his blood pulsing through his veins and left him craving far more. His hands moved over her naked skin, her back, her bottom; her hips. She moved against him, urging him on, and all the while her sweet mouth tortured his.

Unable to bear the torment a moment longer, he bent and swung her up into his arms and cradled her against his chest. Striding to the bed, he lowered her to the mattress and followed her down. She shrugged off her robe and reached for his shirt.

"You have way too many clothes on, Detective."

He murmured his agreement against her lips,

content to let her undress him. To his relief, she made short work of removing his clothing and soon they were once again skin to skin. Almost simultaneously, they sighed in satisfaction.

"*Mm*, that feels so good," she purred.

"I could get used to this."

She looked up at him a little uncertainly. "Really?"

He kissed her soundly on the lips. "Really. I like you, Samantha. I like you a lot. I'd like to spend a lot more time with you. I want to know everything about you. What do you think?"

She lowered her lashes and hid her gaze from his. He felt a momentary alarm until she looked back up at him and smiled. "I think that's a great idea. I... I like you, too."

Relief surged through him and he tightened his arms around her. "I'm glad. I think we've found something very special. I'd like to give us time to find out."

She stared at him, her eyes huge and serious in her face. "I'd like that, too."

He bent his head and captured her lips and kissed her with every emotion that burned way down deep inside. She moved beneath him, holding his head in place and kissing him back. Hard and hot and ready, his cock pressed insistently against her belly. Tearing his mouth away from hers, he kissed his way to her breasts and then suckled one of her nipples.

She groaned and her hips came off the mattress, silently urging him on. Sheathing himself with a condom from her newly purchased supply, he positioned himself between her legs. His cock probed her slick entrance and without hesitation, plunged inside. Her arms tightened around his shoulders and she moved underneath him in a rhythm that drove them both toward the crest.

"Rohan!" she gasped a little while later and her inner muscles tightened around his cock, flooding him with heat. A moment later, he reached his own climax and came with a triumphant shout. When he was able to move again, he shifted his weight and lay down beside her, trying to slow his breathing.

"I'd have thought, after all the loving last night, you'd be keeping your distance," he teased.

She turned her head and looked at him. "Are you complaining?"

"Hell, no. You can love me any time you want."

Snuggling up against his chest, she breathed in deeply and then exhaled on a quiet sigh. A moment later, she gasped.

"Oh, my goodness! Is that the time? I'm going to be late for work!" With that, she bolted upright and dashed, naked, to the shower. Rohan chuckled and slowly climbed out of bed. He threw his clothes on for the second time and headed to the kitchen to prepare the promised coffee.

Hours later at his desk in the squad room, Rohan stacked his hands behind his head and blew out his breath on a heavy sigh. He'd been over the reports at least three times. The evidence was there for all to see.

No matter how he looked at it, one thing was certain: Between June and August thirty-one people had organs and tissue illegally removed—and those were only the ones they knew about. Short of exhumation, there was no way of determining how many others there were. The only records available for comparison were for those people who'd required an autopsy and were processed at the Glebe Morgue.

Rohan thought about the other fifty-seven patients who'd died over winter who had undergone organ removal at the Sydney Harbour Hospital before being sent directly to the funeral homes. He couldn't help but wonder how many of them had also suffered illegal organ and tissue removal. It angered him to concede that it was impossible to know. Even if the police went so far as to obtain exhumation orders from the court, that could only confirm suspicions in the ones who'd been buried. The cremated victims were lost to them forever.

One name kept coming up over and over again: *Doctor Alistair Wolfe*. In every single instance where the consent didn't match the actual organ removal, or there simply wasn't a consent form on file, Doctor Wolfe had led the surgical removal team and had signed off on the death certificate. Rohan derived no satisfaction when his suspicions were confirmed.

Now, he looked across at Bryce, whose expression was just as grim. "What have you found?" Rohan asked, dreading the answer.

"Doctor Alistair Wolfe's name dominates the list of organ retrievals. He's the only consistent staff member across the ninety-three cases. He has to be the one. There's no other explanation."

Rohan's gut tensed. Knowing Bryce shared his suspicions didn't make things any easier. If only their prime suspect wasn't related to the woman he cared for most. *Why the hell did life have to be so complicated, throw so many curve balls?* Reluctant to dump Samantha's brother firmly in the spotlight just yet, Rohan hedged his answer.

"It certainly appears that way, but we need hard evidence. All we have right now is proof that he was present during all of the suspicious retrievals. It doesn't prove that he was the one who removed the organs without consent. For all we know, he might have operated within the terms of the consent and then left the room. Anything could have happened after that."

"What about the ones where the consent form's missing? There are several of them. Don't you think that's suspicious?"

"Of course, but until we speak with the next of kin and confirm they did or didn't give consent we can't know for sure; it's anybody's guess if and where the consent forms were mislaid. The surgeons could blame the porters who transported the bodies to the hospital morgue. The hospital could argue the forms were lost during the transportation to the Glebe Morgue. We have to be careful not to muddy the waters. A good defense lawyer could tear our case to pieces. We need to concentrate on the relatives and ask them what they gave consent for—if anything," he added grimly.

"We need to understand the organ removal procedure, from start to finish," Bryce added. "We need to know what happens from the time the consent is given and the patient is wheeled into the operating room with everything intact, to when they come out...less."

"We'll have to interview all the theater staff who were present during each organ retrieval, in particular the nursing staff. They often work in the background, unseen and unacknowledged by the surgeons. It's possible some of them saw or know something that will confirm our suspicions."

Bryce nodded and Rohan added, "I'll call Deborah Healy and set up another meeting—this time without Doctor Alistair Wolfe. We need to make sure he's unaware we're onto him. If he's involved, I don't want him alerted too early. That could give him the opportunity to cover his tracks."

"Do you think he'd approach the staff with a view to changing their stories?"

"Who knows? Don't forget, we don't know anything for certain at this stage."

"My gut is telling me Wolfe's our man."

Pain and dread clenched Rohan's gut tight at the thought of Samantha and her family. For a moment, he thought he might be sick. Swallowing back bile, he grimaced. "So is mine."

"There's something else," Bryce said, his expression grave.

"What?"

"Based on the consent forms we've examined, we know that ninety-three people who were patients at the Sydney Harbour Hospital donated various organs and tissue since the beginning of winter. That's a hell of a lot of transplants."

Rohan stared at him and his heart began to pound. "You're right and if we accept that the autopsy records and statements made by the various funeral parlor staff members are closer to the true number of transplants, it's even greater."

He sucked in a deep breath and tried to get control over the adrenaline that surged through him. He pushed back his chair and began to pace. "Deborah Healy told us several hospital transplant teams can be present at a retrieval, depending on the organs involved. We need to interview the staff at the other hospitals with transplant units so that we can compare the transplant rates over the past few months with the number of organs we know have been harvested. Let's hope to God they match."

Bryce stared at him grimly. "And if they don't?"

Rohan slowly shook his head back and forth while icy dread poured into his gut. "Then this is far bigger than any of us ever imagined."

———

Sam removed the last of the organs from the male body stretched out on the gurney and carried the steel tray to a nearby bench so she could begin her examination. She was relieved Edmund Rolf appeared to have all of his organs intact. She looked across at Phillip where he worked quickly on the body of an elderly woman who lay on the adjacent table. "You seem like you're in a hurry, Phillip. What are you up to this afternoon?"

Phillip glanced up and gave her a quick grin. "It's my daughter's graduation from college. It's not on until seven, but it's being held in the Grand Ballroom at the Hilton Hotel in the city. If I don't get out of here on time, I won't get home, shower, change and get back in here again before it starts. Zoe will never forgive me if we walk in late."

"I can't believe Zoe's graduating! It seems like only yesterday she was starting her first year of college. Where has the time gone?"

"You're telling me!" Phillip laughed. "It feels like yesterday we were bringing her home squalling from the hospital."

"Two kids down and two to go, right? The way time's flying by, you'll have them all off your hands in no time."

"Yep, we're halfway there. Maree and I are counting down the years until the younger two are off our hands. Afterwards, we want to buy a caravan and travel around Australia."

Sam lifted Edmund Rolf's heart out of the tray and examined it closely. Several blood clots and narrowed arteries told an all too familiar tale. She put the heart into the bowl of the scales and weighed it. "Where are you planning to go?"

"Alice Springs, for starters. We've always wanted to see Uluru at dusk."

"Sounds good," Sam said, feeling a little wistful. She'd spent so many years working hard to further her career, she'd hardly been anywhere.

"Yes, it does, doesn't it?" he said, smiling.

Glancing at her colleague again, she nodded toward the body. "Are you nearly finished?"

"I just need to suture her up and she's pretty much good to go."

"I'll do it, if you like. Go and clean up and get out of here. It will give you a head start on the traffic."

Phillip smiled in surprise. "Really?"

"Yes. After this PM I'm done. It's no trouble to finish yours."

"Thanks, Sam. I really appreciate it."

"No problem. That's what friends are for."

Phillip blew her a kiss. "You betcha." He threw her a wave and headed for the exit, peeling off his mask and gloves as he went.

"Give my congratulations to Zoe and tell Maree I said hi," she called out.

"I will, and thanks again, Sam. I'll catch you tomorrow."

The door closed behind him and Sam returned to the job at hand. Quickly and efficiently, she finished weighing the rest of the organs and then returned them to the open chest cavity. Her findings would show Edmund Rolf had died from a massive heart attack. She was sure it wouldn't come as a surprise to his family.

Overweight by at least one hundred pounds

and with his lungs showing clear signs that, in life, he'd been a heavy smoker, death by heart attack was not only common, it had been predictable. In this case, the pathology confirmed it.

Closing the abdomen and chest with small, neat sutures, Sam restored the body to the way she'd found it and then wheeled the gurney back to the fridge. After depositing Edmund Rolf onto the shelf, she went back into the autopsy suite and finished with Phillip's lady.

It was nearing five o'clock by the time she cleaned up and deposited her scrubs in the laundry bin provided for that purpose. An ache in her lower back told her it was well and truly time to take a break. Heading to the showers, she stripped off and washed away the effects of the day.

She heard her phone beep over the sound of the water and hurriedly turned off the faucets. Drying quickly, she dug in her handbag and checked the screen. *Rohan.* He'd texted to say hi and to ask if she had any plans for dinner.

She smiled and excitement coursed through her. She was tired after a long day on her feet, but at the thought of spending the evening with him, her fatigue fell away. Naked except for the towel tied hastily around her, she sent off a reply.

No plans 4 dinner. Would love 2 catch up.

She stopped short of ending it with a "love Sam" even though she wanted to. It was still early in their relationship. Neither of them had taken the next step of introducing the other to their respective families, even though they'd talked about it. The more time she spent with him, the more certain she was that she was falling in love with him... But she didn't want to preempt things by using the word prematurely.

He was snowed under with his investigation. An investigation that involved her and Alistair. It would be best to wait for that to be resolved and have his undivided attention before making any rash statements. Her phone beeped again and she checked it.

Beer and pizza at my place? I owe u remember?

Sounds good, she typed.

Seven ok?

Seven's perfect.

———————

Rohan read the message on the screen of his phone and smiled. Knowing he was having Samantha over for dinner was the only good thing that had happened to him that day. He and Bryce had met with the relatives of the deceased patients whose files had been missing consent forms.

Unwilling to be premature in raising the alarm that something was amiss, they'd been purposefully vague about their reasons for needing the information and had chosen their words with care. It gave Rohan no joy to discover that all of the people they spoke to denied giving permission for any organs and tissues to be removed. It was no surprise those files were missing the consent form. There had never been one to start with.

A check with the other transplant units had also brought to light a strange and disturbing reality. Of all the organ and tissue harvesting that had been conducted at the Sydney Harbour Hospital over the winter months, not one single tissue sample had been received by any of them.

There was plenty of evidence the donated organs had been delivered to the places that put them to good use, but the additional tissue had simply disappeared. Skin tissue, eye tissue, ligaments and tendons—none of it could be traced to an Australian destination, no matter how hard they looked.

When he'd conferred with Bryce in the squad room afterwards, they'd both drawn the most obvious conclusion: The perpetrator was involved in trafficking the human tissue overseas. It was the only explanation that made sense. The question now was this: How had it all been orchestrated?

"We need to bring the boss up to date," Rohan said. "Given the likelihood this stuff is heading to international destinations, this will no doubt end up being outside our jurisdiction. Holt will need to call in the Australian Federal Police."

Bryce compressed his lips into a thin line, his expression grim. "Yep."

"But we have to pin down the person or persons responsible."

"I'm still liking Wolfe for it," Bryce said.

Rohan stared at him for a long moment and

then finally replied. "Me, too, but we need proof. Hopefully we'll get what we need after we speak to the theater staff in the morning. I've met with the general manager. She's agreed to arrange for everyone who was rostered on duty over the times in question to meet with us, one by one, in an interview room at the hospital."

"That will more than likely involve most of the staff. We're talking three months' worth of surgeries."

"Yep. We're going to be busy."

"What have you told the GM?"

"The bare essentials, but she's not stupid. She knows something bad is going down. I feel sorry for her, especially given the rot that went on a few years ago with Doctor Leo Baker."

"Yeah, wait until Chanel finds out. She's going to freak."

"Like a lot of people, I'm guessing. Staff and patients and families alike."

Bryce shook his head and blew his breath out on a sigh. "The hospital might never recover from another blow like this. It was hard enough to shake off the negative publicity last time."

Rohan shrugged. "Well, they could start by keeping a closer eye on their employees. If there were better procedures in place, checks and balances, this wouldn't have happened. Unless there's a whole team of theater staff involved, it must be someone operating on his own, or at the most, with one or two others. My money's on the former. There was only one name that showed up on every file—and we both know who that was."

"I wouldn't want to be related to Alistair Wolfe, that's for sure. Life for his family's never going to be the same again."

Rohan squeezed his eyes shut as tightly as they'd go and gritted his teeth. He counted a full ten seconds before opening them again.

Bryce stared at him in concern. "Are you all right?"

Rohan thought of spending the next few hours with Alistair Wolfe's sister, pretending that all was well and his shoulders slumped. "Never been better."

Rohan pulled up outside his Cremorne house a little after seven and spied Samantha's green Honda parked parallel to the curb. He smiled, despite the pain and anxiety that weighed heavily in his gut. He should have simply texted her back and called their evening off, but after all the crap that had gone down that day, he couldn't bring himself to do it.

It was selfish and totally unfair, but he wanted to have one last magical night with her before everything went to hell. If his suspicions proved correct, this time tomorrow, her brother could find himself behind bars and Rohan would be responsible for putting him there.

Forcing the depressing thoughts from his mind, he collected his briefcase, and the pan-fried, super supreme pizza—with extra cheese—from the passenger seat and headed toward the house.

Samantha was sitting on the front steps, dressed in a pair of denim cut-offs and a snug, gray T-shirt. Her hair was loose and hung in thick waves around her face. In the falling light, she smiled and he could tell she was pleased to see him.

"Hi, stranger," she murmured with a flick of her hair. "Nice of you to finally join me."

Her gentle rebuke had no malice and Rohan found himself smiling back. Despite the burden he carried on his shoulders, he was determined to make the most of their night.

Although they hadn't seen each other since the night he'd stayed with her, they'd been texting and phoning each other as much as their busy schedules allowed. He was falling for her fast. She was smart and beautiful and funny. It saddened him to think that after tonight, she might never want to see him again.

"Sorry I'm late," he said, "but I come with pizza."

"No beer?"

"In the fridge. I stocked up a few nights ago."

She grinned. "You must have known I was coming."

"Hoped, more like it. It's good to see you."

She stood and with the added advantage of the second step, was almost at eye level with him. Wrapping her arms around his neck, she pressed a soft kiss against his mouth.

Heat rushed to his groin and he burned with need. With his hands full, he had no way of holding her, but kissed her back like he was starved for the taste of her. And he was. It felt like forever since he'd held her in his arms.

When at last they drew apart, both of them were breathing fast. He smiled at her. "If that was the appetizer, I can't wait for the main course."

She punched him lightly in the arm and then followed him up to the front door. Taking the pizza from him, she waited while he inserted his key. Once inside, he tossed his briefcase on the couch and headed down the hall toward the kitchen, switching on lights as he went. Samantha trailed behind him with the pizza.

"This smells really good," she said.

"I ordered your favorite."

"You spoil me," she teased as they arrived in the kitchen.

"Nowhere near as much as you deserve." Her cheeks blushed a becoming shade of pink and he could tell she was pleased with his comment.

She went up to him and pressed a light kiss upon his cheek. "You're so sweet, Rohan Coleridge. I'm never going to let you go."

He smiled but couldn't help dreading what would happen tomorrow, and how that would affect them. "How's your mom?" he asked in an attempt to distract himself from the awful reality the morning was likely to bring.

"She's all right," Samantha replied, pulling out a chair and seating herself at the table. She opened the pizza box and took out a slice.

Rohan breathed in the warm, spicy aroma and his belly grumbled. He'd been so busy at work, he hadn't had time to break for lunch. The pizza smelled great. Twisting the tops off two bottles of beer, he headed back to the table.

"Thanks," she murmured when he offered her a drink. "Here's cheers." She clinked her bottle to his and smiled.

"What are we toasting to?" he asked, keeping his tone light.

"To you and me and the future," she declared in a dramatic voice and then burst out laughing.

Rohan followed suit, but the pizza in his mouth suddenly tasted like cardboard. He chewed and forced himself to swallow it and hoped she didn't notice his sudden loss of appetite. He should have known better.

Her expression grew wary. "What's the matter?"

"What do you mean?" he asked, buying time.

"When I toasted our future, you looked like you'd swallowed a toad. I... I thought we were on the same page here. I thought... I thought we both felt the same way. I know we haven't been dating very long, but..."

Her voice drifted off and all of a sudden, she looked terribly vulnerable and uncertain. Rohan hated that he'd made her feel that way.

"I..." *What good would it do to declare his love when in less than twenty-four hours, he could very well be leading her brother to a cell?* He was almost certain Alistair was behind the illegal trafficking of human tissue, and tomorrow he intended to prove it. Samantha wasn't stupid. She'd guess the moment she heard about it that he'd known right here, right now, what was going to happen.

He cursed silently and wished for the hundredth time that life wasn't so complicated. He looked at her sitting there eating a slice of pizza, and then, he no longer cared about tomorrow. There was only now. He was seated across from the woman he loved and nothing else mattered.

Pushing the pizza box aside, he reached for her hands and slowly drew her to her feet. Confusion and uncertainty warred on her face. She resisted him at first, but he coaxed her upright with gentleness and determination. At last she stood and stared at him with an expression filled with distrust.

"What are you doing, Rohan?"

"I'm not so good with words. It seems like every time I open my mouth around you, I get it wrong, but I want to try and tell you how much you mean to me. My life was a dull vacuum of work and sleep, with very little in between. I lived in a world that was made up of shades of gray. And then I met you."

He shook his head in disbelief. "All of a sudden, every corner of my universe exploded with bright, bold colors. Everywhere I looked, there was excitement, fun and laughter. Until that moment, I hadn't even realized how dull and boring my life had become. You've given me that, Samantha. You've given me a brighter life."

The distrust in her eyes gradually gave way to confusion and he wished in desperation that he could say the words he really wanted to say. The best thing to do would be to walk away from her, at least until after what transpired tomorrow was done. Then she could decide if he was worth the effort, worth her love, or if her loyalty to her brother would win out.

"What are you trying to say, Rohan?"

He cursed beneath his breath. She wasn't going to make this easy. He drew in a deep breath, intent on satisfying her with another vague promise.

"I love you, Samantha." The words fell out of his mouth and there was no way he could take them back. The confusion on her face was replaced with shock—and then wonder filled her eyes.

"You... You *love* me?" she whispered.

He nodded and died a thousand deaths. It should have been the most wonderful moment of his life, but all he felt was apprehension. His anxiety compounded when she threw herself against him and slung her arms around his neck. She kissed him on the mouth, the nose, the ears, the eyes. It was like she couldn't get enough. All the while, she was laughing and almost crying and telling him how much she loved him, too.

There was no tomorrow. Only now. With a heavy heart, he determined then and there to forget, at least for this night, the pitfalls that lay ahead. Scooping her up in his arms, he walked down the hall to his bedroom and vowed to give her the most wonderful night of her life.

CHAPTER 15

Rohan strode through the automatic front entry doors to the Sydney Harbour Hospital, his heavy thoughts centered on what lay ahead. Bryce kept pace with him, his expression similarly grim. They were on their way to interview the theater staff.

Rohan had left Samantha still asleep in bed, explaining in a note that he had an early start and would talk to her when he could. The guilt of walking away from her without breathing a word still weighed heavily on his mind, but there was nothing he could do about it—then, or now.

"Will Deborah Healy be present?" Bryce asked.

"No. I wanted to interview each staff member in private. They're more likely to be upfront with us that way."

"Yeah, let's hope we get what we need."

Rohan didn't reply and they walked the rest of the way in silence. Two levels up, they found the empty clinic rooms they'd been promised. The makeshift interview rooms had been furnished simply, with a desk and two chairs. A large blank legal pad and a pen and a jug of water and two glasses had also been provided.

"I have a list of the names of all of the staff who were rostered on in the operating room over the relevant time period," Rohan said. "I've divided it in half." He pulled a piece of paper from his pocket and used the desk to lean on. Tearing the paper down the middle, he handed one half to Bryce. "Here's your half."

"No problem." Bryce stepped out into the corridor and looked around. "Where are they?"

"There's a room a little further down the hall. The GM assured me the staff would be waiting there."

Bryce nodded. "Let's do it."

He strode in the direction of the waiting room. Rohan drew in a deep breath. Squaring his shoulders, he looked at the first name on his list. Swallowing a sigh, and setting his jaw, he followed.

Sam tucked her handbag beneath her desk and then leaned forward to switch on her computer. Despite the fact she was at work on a Saturday after agreeing to switch a shift with a colleague, and no doubt had a full list of autopsies ahead of her, she couldn't keep the smile off her face.

Last night, after Rohan told her he loved her they'd had the most magical night of her life. For the first time ever, she felt like they were truly making love. The tenderness with which he'd treated her, the love she felt in his every touch—it was like nothing she'd ever known and she knew the memory of it would stay with her for the rest of her life.

She was in love and was loved in return! How wonderful was that? Life didn't get any sweeter. She wanted to shout her happiness from the rooftops and tell anyone who stood still long enough to hear. At the thought of telling her mom, she giggled and blushed like a teenager. Her mom would be ecstatic. Planning the details of her daughter's wedding was an experience Enid hadn't been sure she'd ever live to see.

Sam smiled a little ruefully at the way her imagination had run away with itself. Rohan had only just made his declaration of love. It was a far cry from a proposal. She had no idea how he felt about marriage, about kids—about anything. She had a lot to discover; they had a lot to work through, but knowing they could do it together, with love and respect, was all she needed to know.

A brief knock on her half-open office door snagged her attention and she looked up in time to see Richard enter the room. She frowned momentarily, but then smiled in greeting. "What are you doing here? I didn't realize you were on call this weekend."

Richard didn't respond. Sam took in his appearance and her smile slowly faded. He was pale and trembling, and it looked as if he were trying not to break down. Concern surged through her and fear clutched at her heart.

"What is it, Richard? What's wrong?"

"Oh, Sam! You haven't heard?"

"Heard what?"

"Dreadful. Just dreadful. I can't believe it."

"Believe what, Richard?" Panic edged her voice. "What happened?"

A sob escaped Richard's lips and Sam lost her patience. Her tone was sharper than she intended when she pressed, "For goodness sake, Richard! Tell me what happened!"

Her words had the desired effect. He stopped mid-sob and blinked. "Oh, Sam! It's… It's Phillip!"

Icy dread took residence in Sam's belly. Her heart took off at a gallop and she had to concentrate to hear over the sound of her blood as it rushed through her ears.

"What about Phillip?" she said, amazed that she could sound so calm when inside she was a frenzy of panic.

"He-he was in an accident. On his way home yesterday. Nobody really knows what happened. There was no other vehicle involved. The police are still examining the scene, trying to work out how his vehicle collided with a tree."

Sam sucked in a breath and worked hard to control her breathing. Just because Phillip had been in an accident didn't mean he was seriously injured. Almost immediately, she corrected her thought process. Of course he was injured. Richard wouldn't be a sniveling mess if their colleague had walked away unscathed. She forced herself to ask the question.

"How... How is he?"

Richard shook his head, as if he were struggling to form the words. "He's... Sam... He's dead."

Another bout of sobbing overwhelmed him, but she barely noticed. The noise in her ears escalated until it blocked out everything else. *Phillip was dead.* He'd been killed in a car accident. She'd never joke with him, laugh with him, argue with him again.

He was dead. His wife had lost her husband. His daughters had lost their dad. On the night of Zoe's graduation.

Another thought struck Sam and she gasped aloud from the pain. *It was all her fault!* She'd sent him home early. She was the reason he'd been in his vehicle at that infinitesimal point in time. If he'd left at his usual time, he might have made it. He might even now be making coffee and moaning about the day ahead. There was no disputing it: She was the reason he was dead.

"Where is he?" she asked in a voice so dull and lifeless she hardly recognized it.

Richard hiccupped on another sob. "He's here. In the fridge."

Sam drew in a breath, but it came out as a howl of pain. She collapsed onto her desk. With her head on her arms, she sobbed so hard she didn't know if she'd ever be able to stop. Phillip was dead and it was all her fault. The thought kept going round and round in her mind.

Fresh pain overwhelmed her and she howled out her agony again. It wasn't fair. A few minutes ago, she'd been on top of the world, her every molecule bursting with happiness. Now it felt like a cement block had taken up residence in her chest. Every breath was snatched through lungs so tight, she felt like she might suffocate. The very next breath might be her last and right at that moment, she'd welcome the relief.

"Sam? Are you all right? Sam?"

It was Richard. His tone was tentative, scared—as if he wasn't sure how to approach her, or even *if*. She dragged in a deep breath and made a mammoth effort to pull herself together. She lifted her head. Her eyes were hot and swollen. No doubt she looked a mess. From the reaction on Richard's face when he looked at her, it wasn't far from the truth.

"Why is he here?" she rasped. "Is there some question about how he died?"

Richard fidgeted and looked away. Sam frowned. "What is it? Tell me what's wrong? Why does Phillip require an autopsy?"

"His insurance company wants to rule out suicide. They also want to know if there were drugs or alcohol involved. Apparently if they can prove contributory negligence it reduces their liability."

Sam shook her head, aghast. "Suicide? Drugs? You have to be kidding! We're talking about Phillip! He was the cleanest-living man I knew! And as for suicide—the reason he left early was to attend his daughter's college graduation! He was so proud of her. We talked about how he had plans to travel with his wife once their kids were off their hands. His plans weren't those of a man on the brink of ending his life!"

"You and I know him, Sam. It's different for outsiders. All they know is he's a client with a hefty life insurance policy and that life has just come to a very sudden and perhaps suspicious end."

Sam stared at the blank computer screen in front of her and tried to calm her scattered thoughts. Shock still rendered her largely immobile, but she couldn't sit at her desk all day, reliving her last hours with her friend. She'd go absolutely stark raving mad if she did. Phillip was gone and there was no bringing him back. Death was final. She knew that better than most.

"Who's doing the PM?" she asked, her voice still dull.

"I-I'm not sure. I haven't yet spoken to the coroner."

"If it's all right with him, I'll do it."

"Sam, I don't think that's a good idea. You're upset. You and Phillip were friends. I think—"

"I want to do it, Richard. I want to do it for Phillip. It's the least I can do. Please," she begged.

He frowned in indecision and moved from one foot to the other. At last, he sighed. "I'll speak to the coroner. He'll make the final decision."

She nodded. "Thank you."

"I'm not promising he'll agree..."

"It's okay. I understand. Just do what you can."

He stared at her a moment longer and then quietly took his leave. Sam held her head in her hands and tried to come to terms with the fact her friend and colleague was dead.

She wasn't sure how long she sat at her desk, but the next thing she knew Richard appeared before her again and told her she had permission to conduct the autopsy on Phillip Bond. Having cried herself out long ago, Sam merely nodded.

Richard disappeared from her field of vision and she took a moment to firm up her resolve. It would be her final farewell, a way she could say good-bye. Phillip had hated the thought of ending up in the Glebe Morgue. The least she could do was make it as quick and painless as possible—for both of them.

Pushing away from her desk, Sam stood and made her way to the change rooms. Peeling off her clothes, she dressed in scrubs and headed over to the fridge. Bracing herself for what was to come, she located Phillip, lying in a blue plastic body bag on one of the shelves. She wheeled him to the autopsy suite, all the while speaking to him in low tones. It helped her to think he could hear her and he was aware of this final act of friendship.

She removed the body bag and let out a little gasp because he lay as cold and lifeless as all the other bodies she dealt with every day. Forcing her brain into work mode, she prepared to conduct the PM.

Picking up a scalpel, she moved closer to the body. Her gaze drifted over him and she frowned. A recent incision had been made from the top of his sternum to his groin. She stared at it in disbelief, refusing to accept what it meant.

No! It couldn't be! Phillip wasn't an organ

donor! He hated the very thought of it and so did his wife. Maree would *never* have given her consent. Sam recalled the conversation she'd had with him when he'd told her how strongly he and his wife were against it. They had their reasons and that was fine. Sam couldn't even imagine what could have changed Maree's mind.

With a growing sense of dread, she reopened the incision and parted Phillip's chest. With gloved fingers, she felt inside. She located his heart and sagged with relief and then explored a little more. His lungs were missing. Liver, kidneys and pancreas were also gone.

A keening wail reverberated in her head and it was a long moment before she realized the sound was coming from her mouth. Clenching her jaw, she snatched quick breaths and did her best to get her panic under control. She pulled off her gloves and searched in the paperwork for the name of the doctor who had obtained the consent.

Alistair's name was printed in large, bold black letters right below the indecipherable signature of the next of kin. Sam stared at the form in shock and horror. Something was terribly, horribly wrong. She needed to find out what and who and how or she'd never have a moment's peace again. She owed that to Phillip.

Leaving Phillip on the table, she peeled off her mask and gloves and headed out of the autopsy suite. She rushed back to her office and dug out her phone from her handbag. Dialing her brother's number, she prayed he'd answer.

"Sam! How are you? Why are you calling me so

early? I've barely finished my morning coffee."

He sounded so cheery, so normal. It was the antithesis to how she felt. If her growing suspicions were correct, she'd never feel normal again.

"Alistair, I'm calling about Phillip! I'm here with him, in the morgue."

His tone immediately sobered. "Hell, I'm sorry, sis. He came in late yesterday afternoon. I should have called you, but I didn't realize for a while that it was him. He was…a little messed up. There was blood everywhere."

"Who signed the consent?" she demanded.

"The consent?"

"Yes!" she shouted impatiently. "The organ donation consent! Which of Phillip's relatives signed it?"

"Um… I'm not sure."

"You were the one who witnessed the signature, Alistair. I assume you remember which family member you convinced to sign it."

She was met with silence. Her breath continued to come fast. The silence stretched and all at once, she had the most terrible sense of foreboding. It was so awful, it snatched her breath and tightened her chest with fear. Adrenaline flooded her bloodstream and she could barely hear over the sound of it rushing through her ears.

"Oh, God! You didn't obtain a consent, did you? You've forged a signature to make it appear that way." Her tone turned deadly and her white-hot anger morphed into burning ice. "I'm right, aren't I?"

"Of course I didn't!" Alistair blustered, but all of

a sudden she knew with certainty that he wasn't telling the truth.

"Phillip was absolutely against organ donation and so was his wife," she exclaimed. "We argued over it more than once. He was adamant. He'd cut open enough people over the course of his career, he didn't want that for himself. But now he's here, lying in the morgue, with most of his major organs gone. There's no way you'll convince me his next of kin overrode his wishes and signed that damned consent form."

"What do you want me to say, Sam?" Alistair shouted, anger and irritation in his voice. "He came in unconscious, dead but for the life support. His next of kin gave the consent."

"Who?" she fired at him again, her hands clenched into fists.

"I don't know! His wife, I guess. I do this shit every day, Sam. Do you have any idea how many grieving relatives I speak to, trying to convince them to do the right thing? I can't remember all of them."

"The right thing?" she managed, her voice strangled with disbelief. "For who? For you and me, maybe, but we believe in the benefits of organ donation. Many people don't! Their rights need to be respected! It's not up to you to decide, no matter how much you might think it is!"

"Do you know how many transplants would occur in this country if I didn't?" he yelled. "I'm the reason so many people have been given another chance at life. I might not be able to give Mom my kidney, but I'm going to die trying to find her one."

Sam gasped and doubled over as pain wracked her from head to toe. She wasn't sure, but she thought her brother might have just admitted to fudging records to achieve his goal. There was no way she'd ever believe the consent had come from Maree.

"You *knew* Phillip didn't want to be an organ donor!" she sobbed. "We talked about it on my birthday, remember? You knew it and yet, you still went ahead! Please, Alistair," she sobbed harder. "Please tell me you didn't forge Maree's signature?"

It was a long moment later before he finally deigned to reply. "Wake up, Samantha. The world isn't always such a nice place. We all do what we have to. It's just the way it is."

CHAPTER 16

Rohan looked at the nurse who sat across from him and prepared to pose the questions that he'd put to all the staff members he'd interviewed before her. The answers were beginning to sound monotonously the same. So far, he didn't have anything of substance that pointed toward Doctor Alistair Wolfe's guilt and the knowledge irritated him to hell. This nurse was the third last one on his list. He could only hope she'd offer him something useful. Clearing his throat, he asked the woman the standard opening questions: name; address, date of birth and then moved on.

"Would you please tell me about the procedure from the time consent for organ donation is obtained to when a patient is taken off life support."

The nurse recalled for Rohan the timeline, like the other staff members had done. He scribbled a few notes and then asked the next question. "Is there any time during the organ retrieval process when a doctor is left alone with the patient?"

"No. The operating room is a hive of activity. Depending upon the type of organs being harvested, there can be up to four or five retrieval teams involved. That's a lot of people. The room is most definitely crowded."

Rohan nodded. The information supplied by the nurse was consistent with all the others. "I assume that as each retrieval team takes possession of their organ or organs, they leave the room. Time's of the essence here, right?"

"Right."

"So at some point, after the donated organs have been removed, there are very few people in the room. Perhaps the lead surgeon and a theater nurse?"

"Yes, that's correct."

"Who sutures the wounds closed?"

"Usually the surgeon in control of the organ harvesting."

"Is it possible that, at this time, the doctor could be alone with the patient?"

The nurse paused. "I guess it's possible. The pressure has dissipated by then. The organs have been removed and sent on their way. The retrieval teams have accompanied them. The only people left are the hospital staff rostered on for that shift. Because the rush is over, people are a lot more relaxed by then."

"So if a doctor suggested you take a break and he would finish up, would that sound reasonable?"

"Yes."

"Have you ever had a doctor suggest you take a break and leave him to finish whatever needs to be done?"

"Yes."

Rohan's breath caught and his heart began to pound. None of the staff he'd spoken to had answered that question in the affirmative. "And have you taken that break, leaving the doctor alone with the patient?"

"Yes."

"Who was the doctor who made such a suggestion?" he asked and could barely wait for the answer.

The nurse eyed him steadily. "It was Doctor Alistair Wolfe."

Bingo.

Rohan's blood pulsed loudly in his ears. His heart beat doubled in pace. "How often has this happened?"

The nurse shrugged. "I'm not sure. At least once or twice a week, I guess. It's usually after a late shift. I'm more than happy to take him up on his suggestion." Her features suddenly clouded with fear. "I hope I haven't done anything wrong?"

After reassuring the nurse she wasn't in trouble, Rohan thanked her for her time and saw her to the door. Slowly, he sunk into his seat and leaned his elbows on the desk. With his head in his hands, he released a heavy sigh. He should have been elated to finally have concrete evidence to confirm his suspicions, but all he felt was dread. When Samantha discovered what her brother had been up to, she'd be devastated, along with the rest of her family.

Knowing there was nothing he could do about it, Rohan pulled himself together and interviewed the two remaining nurses. Both of them told him that Doctor Alistair Wolfe had released them early from their shift after an organ recovery procedure on more than one occasion.

When the last nurse left the interview room, Rohan's thoughts turned to Bryce and he wondered how his colleague had fared. Reaching for his cell phone, he pulled it out of his pocket and checked the screen.

"Dammit." While his phone was switched to silent he'd missed two calls from Samantha. No doubt she wanted to talk about their magical night and set up another date. He thought of what lay ahead of him and was glad he hadn't answered her calls. As much as he wanted to hear her voice, now definitely wasn't the best time.

Once he'd conferred with Bryce and gotten the okay from their boss, he'd be searching the corridors of the hospital for Alistair Wolfe. He'd have a list of charges in one hand and a pair of handcuffs in the other. As much as it pained him to admit it, more than likely it would be a long time before he spoke to Samantha again.

With a sigh of resignation, he ignored the evidence that she'd tried to contact him and speed-dialed Bryce. It was time to put things into motion. After that, there would be plenty of time for Rohan to survey the carnage and see what could be done to resurrect what was left of his relationship with the woman he loved.

Alistair glanced over his shoulder, relieved to find the hospital corridor behind him was clear. Thanks to a loyal staff member, he'd been tipped off that the police were at the hospital, interviewing the theater nurses. Panic rose up inside him at the thought the net might be closing in, but he refused to believe they knew enough to arrest him.

Richard had assured him that the morgue's computer files had been deleted. Without that proof, there was no way of knowing if the paperwork matched up with the state of the bodies. It was just that he was feeling edgy and off balance after the phone call from his sister. Knowing Sam had probably guessed what he'd been doing unsettled him.

He hadn't planned to tell her. Despite the fact she believed as strongly as he did in organ and tissue donation, he didn't think she'd approve of his methods. It was best for all concerned that he keep his activities a secret. But now, it seemed the secret was out. He could only hope her loyalty to him would prove stronger than her ethics.

Striding out through the automatic front entry doors of the hospital, he breathed a sigh of relief. So far, so good. He had to get to the morgue and convince Sam to keep quiet before it was too late. Sliding behind the wheel of his Ferrari, he gunned the engine and sped off down the street. Within minutes, he'd pulled up outside the Glebe Morgue.

With his heart pounding, he forced a smile on his face and greeted the young receptionist.

"Hi, I'm Alistair Wolfe. I was wondering if I could see Samantha?"

The girl smiled back at him. "You're Sam's brother. I can see the resemblance. Just a minute and I'll let her know you're here. We've had some distressing news this morning about a colleague. I'm not sure if she's up to visitors."

Alistair nodded in understanding, his expression grave. "I know. Phillip Bond. Sam called me. Very, very sad. It's the reason I'm here. She asked me to come and get her. She doesn't feel up to driving herself home."

The lies rolled off his tongue and he was relieved when the girl appeared to believe him.

"Of course," she said. "I understand. Sam and Phillip were good friends." She stood and came around the counter and went up to a closed door. Punching in a security code, she held it open.

"Do you know where Sam's office is?"

"Yes. And thank you, I appreciate everything you've done. This must be pretty tough on you, too."

The girl drew in a deep breath and let it out on a sigh. "Yes, it's difficult for all of us."

Throwing her another sympathetic look, Alistair walked through the doorway. He'd only been to

Sam's workplace a couple of times, but it wasn't hard to locate the row of offices that opened onto the main corridor. His boots made a noise on the linoleum floor, but he didn't pay them any heed. He kept his attention focused on finding his sister and working out what he'd say to her when he did.

Richard stepped out of an office directly ahead. He froze at the sight of Alistair. "Wh-what are you doing here?"

Alistair took in Richard's swollen eyes and blotchy, red complexion and felt a stab of sympathy for his friend. The man had lost a work colleague in tragic circumstances. He deserved a little kindness and understanding.

"I'm sorry to hear about Phillip," Alistair said quietly. "It must have been an awful shock."

Some of the tension left Richard's face and he nodded jerkily. "Yes, it was. To all of us. What are you doing here?" he repeated a little more forcefully.

"I'm here to see Sam, but I'm glad I ran into you. I wanted to say thanks for coming through for me on our other...arrangement. The police have been interviewing hospital staff all morning. They think they're onto something, but they won't have any tangible evidence of wrongdoing without those files. I owe you one."

Richard nodded, but his face lost all color and fear flashed in his eyes. Alistair frowned. *What the hell was going on?* A sense of foreboding crept through his veins. He stepped closer to Richard and narrowed his gaze.

"You did destroy those files, didn't you?" he

said, his tone conveying a promise of menace if the answer was in the negative.

Richard took a step backward and wouldn't meet his gaze. Alistair's concern ratcheted up another notch.

"Richard, tell me you destroyed those files. You called and told me it was done. Were you fucking lying?"

Richard shrank back against the wall at the anger in Alistair's voice. "N-no! Of course not! I did! I deleted them off the database. But—"

"But what?" Alistair shouted, his temper getting the better of him. Christ, if the police had the files, it was only a matter of time before he felt the noose around his neck.

"I-I forgot about the hard copies—the paper files we store out in the back. And... And there's also a backup. It's possible the police might still get their hands on them."

For a moment, fury and disbelief left Alistair speechless. A moment later, he exploded. "Fuck! You idiot! Do you know what you've done?" Rushing forward, he grabbed Richard by the throat and shook him.

"*Stop!* Please, Alistair! Let me go! I-I can't breathe!"

The sound of Richard's pleading only infuriated Alistair further. He should never have trusted the incompetent idiot in the first place. Any moment, Alistair's world could come crashing down around him and it was all this bastard's fault. Drawing back his fist, he prepared to drive it into Richard's face. A shout from behind stopped him.

"*Alistair!* What are you doing?"

Alistair lowered his hand and slowly turned around to face his sister. She stared at him, white-faced with shock. Her gaze went to Richard and slowly her expression turned from horror to disbelief.

"Richard? No, not you. Not you, too! Please tell me you're not involved in this. I can't bear to think that both of you…"

With a gasp, she turned on her heel and ran back into her office. Alistair threw Richard a glare to let the man know this was far from over and then hurriedly followed Sam. She was bent over a desk with a phone in her hand when he came in.

"Please, I need the police. The Glebe Morgue. Fifty Parramatta Road. Hurry!"

Alistair stared at his sister, unable to believe what she'd done. Her betrayal cut him to the quick. "You called the *police*?"

She held his gaze, her eyes fierce with determination. "Yes."

He shook his head. "*Fuck.* Why, Sam? *Why?*"

The fire went out of her and all at once she looked stricken. "I can't believe you're asking me that! What would you have me do? Turn a blind eye and pat you on the back? You must be mad, Alistair!"

Hurt and disappointment nearly overwhelmed him. He'd been sure his baby sister would understand. After all, he'd done it for their mother and for all people like her who needed donated organs to stay alive. It wasn't about him. It had never been about him.

With another curse, he turned away and strode back down the hall. The police were already on their way. He had minutes to make good his escape.

———————

Rohan heard the dispatcher relay the emergency call over his radio only moments before he screeched to a halt outside the Glebe Morgue. Alistair's bright red Ferrari was parked close by. An earlier search of the hospital had failed to locate him, but Rohan and Bryce had been lucky when a security guard manning the car park had alerted them that Alistair had left the hospital.

Jumping out of the squad car, Rohan and Bryce charged toward the building. They'd barely made the first two steps when the front doors slid open. Alistair came barreling out toward them, oblivious to their presence. With a shout, Rohan drew his service revolver and pointed it directly at Samantha's brother.

"Police! Put your hands up!" Rohan shouted and waited for Alistair to comply. As soon as he had, Bryce shouted for Alistair to get down on the ground. Screaming obscenities, Alistair reluctantly did as he was told. Quickly, Rohan handcuffed him and then stood him on his feet.

"This is bullshit!" Alistair shouted. "Somebody call my lawyer! I'm innocent! I didn't do anything! Talk to the fucking deputy coroner! I'm not going down on my own for this!"

Rohan led him down the steps to the unmarked squad car and helped him into the back seat. Alistair continued to rant and rave all the way back to the station and Rohan began to listen...

The deputy coroner's name came up again and this time, Rohan frowned and considered it. Richard Davis had authorized the organ retrieval for every one of Alistair's autopsy patients. The man was worth a closer look.

CHAPTER 17

Sam stared at her phone and willed it to ring. She'd called Rohan three times, but the calls had gone through to voicemail. After her shock at finding Alistair in her building and placing the emergency call, she'd locked herself in her office, too distressed to go anywhere.

It was more than an hour since it had happened and she still couldn't believe what Alistair and Richard had done. The very thought was sickening. She didn't know that she'd ever get over it. As if the day hadn't already been grueling enough.

Earlier, she'd finished Phillip's autopsy and had entered her findings into the department's database. The cause of death was a massive heart attack. It must have happened while he was behind the wheel. He'd lost control of the car and hit a tree. He hadn't stood a chance.

Her findings ruled out suicide and paved the way for his family to collect on his insurance policy. That was little comfort and certainly wasn't going to bring their husband and father back, but Sam hoped that knowing they had some financial security would help a little in coming to terms with their loss.

A hesitant knock sounded on the closed door to her office. Sam turned with zero interest and even less enthusiasm and unlocked the door and told whoever it was to enter.

Angie appeared looking tense and pale. Sam wasn't the only one grieving over the tragic loss of a colleague and good friend.

"Hi, Angie," she managed quietly. "How are you doing?"

Angie trembled. "I came into the office as soon as I heard. I'm devastated, Sam. Like we all are. Phillip was such a good man! I can't believe I'll never see him again."

Sam sighed. "Yeah, me neither. It's going to be tough on everyone for a while. I guess we just have to accept his time was up."

Angie's eyebrow rose. "Do you know how he died?"

"A heart attack. He wouldn't have felt a thing. I guess for that we can be grateful."

Angie nodded somberly and then looked down. In her hands she held an iPad. She looked up at Sam and then back down again and Sam sensed there was more the girl wanted to say.

"What is it, Angie? Talk to me. It's better that way. We need to remember Phillip—how he was, and all the good things he's done. It's okay to reminisce and share—"

"It's not about Phillip. Well, it is that too... I

mean, I wanted to tell you how sorry I am. I know you and Phillip were close. But...there's something else. Something I think you should see."

She held the iPad out and Sam frowned. "What do you mean?"

"Open Safari and go to YouTube."

Sam did as she was told, wondering at Angie's strange request. The girl was once again fidgeting and had her gaze fixed firmly on the floor. A sense of unease took hold of Sam and all of a sudden, she didn't want to see. She thrust the iPad aside and shook her head.

"I don't think this is a good time, Angie. I'm sure it can wait until later."

"No! Please, Sam. You need to watch it. Trust me."

The girl stared at her with such an intense expression, Sam had no choice but to obey. Once again picking up the iPad, she opened Safari. The page loaded onto the YouTube website and a video appeared. It had been uploaded by a user less than half an hour earlier. Sam read the heading and gasped in shock tinged with sad resignation.

"RESPECTED DOCTOR ARRESTED OUTSIDE GLEBE MORGUE"

The video showed Rohan and his partner leading her brother down the front stairs of her building, toward a squad car. Alistair was shouting obscenities as he went. When the trio passed the videographer, Sam realized her brother was in handcuffs. She gasped again.

Helplessness and anger burst like fire through

her veins. It didn't matter whether Alistair was guilty or innocent. What mattered was that the man she'd so recently declared her love for, must have known all along what was planned. How else had he responded to the emergency call so quickly? His station wasn't the closest, by far.

Her call to the emergency operator had given no hint about the problem. She hadn't even mentioned her brother by name. For Rohan to have arrested Alistair, he must have had other evidence against her brother that she was unaware of. It made her wonder how long Rohan had been in possession of such information.

She didn't believe for an instant the arrest of such a high profile doctor had been done on the spur of the moment, or without considerable evidence gathered. Each detail would have been planned and discussed and reviewed from every angle and it wouldn't have been done in the past hour—or even earlier that day. That meant only one thing.

While Rohan had been making sweet and tender love to her, all that time they were together, he'd known what was in store for her brother. Rohan had left her bed and gone to work with the intention of arresting him and sending him to jail.

And he hadn't said a word.

Shoving the iPad in Angie's direction, Sam slammed her palm against her desk. The impact stung, but she barely felt it. Rage and hurt and remorse and regret all rushed through her head in a kaleidoscope of emotions until she didn't know where to turn. Snatching up her phone, she once again dialed Rohan's number.

As before, the call went through to voicemail. All of a sudden, it made sense why he hadn't returned her calls. The coward had known that sooner or later she'd discover what he'd done and then things would get ugly. He was right on that score.

"You asshole!" she sobbed into the phone. "You knew and you didn't say a word! How could you? You blinded me with declarations of love and all the while you were planning to arrest my brother! You're despicable! I hate you! I never want to see you again!"

She stabbed at the button to end the call and then threw the phone back onto her desk. She was so angry she wanted to put her fist through the wall, but what would that accomplish? She'd be left with a bruised and bleeding hand and Rohan would still go on his merry way. He was probably even now laughing at her as he locked her brother up in jail.

No, that wasn't fair. The Rohan she knew wouldn't be so cruel, but it still didn't change the fact he'd known what was going to happen and he'd kept it from her.

Was it a trust thing? Is that why he hadn't told her? Because he thought she might tip off her brother and help him disappear? Did he really think she'd condone illegal behavior? Particularly, behavior as abhorrent as what she suspected Alistair had done. The thought didn't make her feel any better. If anything, it made her feel worse.

She couldn't believe she'd fallen in love with a man who thought she was capable of such conduct.

Despite the time they'd spent together, growing closer by the day, it was obvious he didn't know her at all. After everything that had happened, now she'd lost Rohan, too. With a gasp and another sob, Sam dropped her head to her desk and cried like her heart had broken in two.

———————

Rohan stared at his phone where it sat on his old kitchen table and tried for the hundredth time to find the courage to return Samantha's call. After his stressful day he was totally spent, but it didn't seem to matter. His brain wouldn't let up on the images of her shouting and sobbing at him into the phone. Her parting words hurt most of all.

Of course, he'd told himself over and over to expect her to react that way. It shouldn't have come as a surprise. But somehow, he'd clung to the foolish hope that she'd realize he was only doing his job; that she knew him well enough to accept that he'd never arrest her brother if he didn't have hard evidence of Alistair's guilt; that she cared enough for Rohan to forgive him.

But it appeared those hopes were as substantial as a pile of ashes blown about in a stiff breeze. She said she hated him and she never wanted to see him again.

With a heavy sigh, he pushed away from the table and thought about finding something to eat. He'd skipped breakfast and lunch and all of a sudden, his belly reminded him he was hungry. Opening up cupboards, he found a tin of tomato soup and emptied the contents into a dish. He put it in the microwave to heat and when it was done, grabbed a spoon from the drawer and sat down at the table to eat.

The first mouthful had barely hit his tongue when his phone began to ring. His pulse jumped. His thoughts flew to Samantha. He hardly dared to look at the screen. When he did, his heart plummeted with disappointment. It was his mother. He thought about letting the call go through to voicemail and then changed his mind. It wasn't her fault his life had turned to shit.

"Hi, Mom," he said in the lightest tone he could manage. He was met with silence. Frowning, he opened his mouth to speak again and it was then that he heard the sob. Concern immediately rushed to the fore.

"Mom? What is it? What's the matter?"

"Oh, Rohan! It's your father! He... He's asleep in the armchair. I can't wake him up! I... I think he might be dead!"

Rohan's blood ran cold and fear clutched at his heart. "Stay where you are and call an ambulance. I'm on my way." Tossing the bowl of soup down the drain, he snatched his wallet and keys from the table and headed for the door.

Dinner would have to wait.

CHAPTER 18

Rohan sped through the night with lights and siren blaring and prayed desperately his dad was all right. For months, he'd been worried about his mom and all along... He shook his head, still in shock. Cursing at yet another red light, he eased his way through the pack. It was at times like this he wished he lived closer to his parents. With the heavy traffic, even with the aid of the lights and siren, it would take him the best part of half an hour to reach home.

He'd barely finished the thought when his phone rang again. He checked the screen and tensed. "Hi, Mom, I'm on my way. Just stay there and try and keep calm. Has the ambulance arrived?"

"They've taken him away, Rohan! They've taken him away!"

"Where, Mom? Where have they taken him?" He held his breath and prayed that she wouldn't say the morgue.

"To the Sutherland Hospital."

"Okay. Where are you now?"

"I'm following them. They told me to hurry."

He sucked in a deep breath and blew it out and tried to get his panic under control. "Drive carefully, Mom, and watch where you're going. I don't want both of you in the hospital."

"I will, son."

"I'll meet you there as soon as I can. Have you called any of the others?"

"No, there wasn't time. I had to leave. I had to follow your dad. They told me to hurry." Her voice cracked on the last word and Rohan's gut tightened in agony. He stepped on the gas and wove in and out of the traffic like the devil was on his tail. He needed to call his brothers and sisters, but that would have to wait. Most of them lived hours away, so it wasn't like they could get there anytime soon, even if this were really serious.

Denial, fierce and hot, burned through him and he wanted to howl out his pain. His father was fit as a fiddle, in the prime of his life. He'd never had a day off sick. It wasn't fair that this had happened. It just wasn't fair his father was now fighting for his life.

How would his mother cope if his father was no longer around? She relied on her husband for so many things—things Rohan hadn't even thought of. And then there was the emotional hole her husband's dying would leave in her heart. They'd spent more years together than they had apart. He couldn't begin to imagine what it would be like to lose the love of your life.

He thought about the pain he felt after he'd

listened to the message from Samantha. It was like his heart had been ripped out and they hadn't even officially been together as a couple in the world. He shuddered to think how much worse it would be for his mother.

Forcing the terrible thoughts aside, he concentrated hard on thinking positive. His father was obviously still alive. Paramedics didn't rush to the hospital with a corpse. He had to believe his father would pull through and that his morbid thoughts were simply an overreaction.

It was no surprise his mind was all over the place. He'd started the morning in Samantha's bed after a magical night with her in his arms. All the while, he'd been weighed down by the knowledge that it would likely be over between them before the next day was out. He never imagined his father would fall ill, once again turning Rohan's life upside down.

Thinking of Samantha and how much she meant to him made him yearn to give her a call. He desperately needed her support and comfort for whatever lay ahead. He swung into the car park of the Sutherland Hospital and quickly pulled to a stop. Across the way, he saw an ambulance outside the Emergency Department with its back doors wide open. He glanced around for his mother's car, but it was nowhere in sight. He took off at a jog.

A moment later, he burst through the automatic doors that opened up into the ED. His gaze fell on his mother. She sat in a hard plastic chair hunched over with her head in her hands.

Her shoulders shook with the weight of her distress. He made his way over to her and touched her gently on the arm. Her head snapped up. When she saw him, she crumpled over again.

Sitting down beside her, he threw his arm around her and gathered her to his side. Tears continued to pour down her cheeks.

"Oh, Rohan! They won't tell me what's happening! All I know is that he's been taken away!"

"Where, Mom?"

"To the operating theater."

"Did they tell you why?"

"No, but they mentioned something about a bleed. I don't know what's going on! I don't know if he's dead or alive! Nobody will tell me anything!"

She sobbed harder and Rohan did his best to comfort her with murmured words. Inside, he was just as distraught. Gently, he disengaged his arm from around her and propped her up against the chair.

"I'm going to talk to one of the nurses, Mom. I'll find out what's going on."

She merely nodded, as if any other response was beyond her. Torn between reluctance to leave her alone and needing to obtain information, he slowly walked away. A nurse with shiny blond hair and a kind smile acknowledged him as he walked up to the counter.

"What can I do for you?"

"I'm Rohan Coleridge. I'm asking about my dad, Bill Coleridge. He was brought in by ambulance not long ago and was apparently rushed to surgery. Do you know anything about his condition?"

The nurse regarded him seriously. "Yes, he's been taken to the operating theater. They're trying to save his life."

At her solemn words, Rohan's heart sank like a stone to the bottom of his chest. A part of him rejoiced that his father was still alive, but it terrified him to realize the situation was so grave. He forced himself to continue. "Do you know what happened?"

"I understand he's suffered a brain aneurysm. It's a bleed on the brain," she added.

The words bounced around inside Rohan's head. "A *bleed on the brain*." It sounded bad. "Is he... Is he going to be all right?"

The nurse's eyes filled with sympathy. "I don't know. I'm sorry, but that's all the information I have."

Rohan's nod was curt, but he understood the nurse's position. She didn't know what the hell was going on in the theater.

"Is there somewhere closer to the operating room where we can wait?"

"Yes. Go down to Level Two. Turn to your left as you step out of the elevator. You'll find a waiting room down the hall."

"Can you let the theater staff know where they can find us?"

"Yes, of course. I'll phone down there now."

"Thank you," Rohan said and meant it. Then he turned on his heel and strode back to his mom.

Taking her by the hand, he gently pulled her to her feet.

"Come on, Mom. I've found out where they've taken Dad. Let's go."

Matching his steps to her much slower ones, Rohan tried hard to curb his impatience. He wanted to race through the corridors, shouting for someone to take him to his dad, but he couldn't and wouldn't do that. Instead, they found the elevator and punched in the button for the second level.

A moment later, the doors slid open and he and his mother stepped out. It was cool and quiet and there didn't seem to be another soul around. He guessed that all of the theater staff were busy in the operating rooms. He only hoped someone would come out and find them and give them an update before he was driven mad.

The phone in his pocket chirped and he tugged it out and checked the screen. It was a text from his boss congratulating him and Bryce on the good work they'd done that day. Ignoring the message he went to put his phone away and then once again thought of Samantha. It would be nice to have her here with him, adding support. Yesterday, he'd been sure they loved each other enough that she'd want to be by his side in times of distress. Now, he wasn't so sure.

With a sigh, he found the waiting room and settled his mom in a comfortable chair. Coming to a decision, he excused himself and left the room. He dialed Samantha's number before he changed his mind and then paced the corridor, waiting for her to answer. When the call went through to voicemail, hot tears burned behind his eyes.

"It's me. I... I just wanted to let you know I'm at the Sutherland Hospital. My dad's suffered a brain aneurysm. He's in surgery now. We not sure if..." His voice cracked, but he forced himself to continue. "We're not sure if he's going to pull through."

Biting his lip against another surge of emotion, he ended the call and slid the phone back into his pocket. With the weight of the world on his shoulders, he made his way back to his mother and the task of calling family members with the sad news.

Sam heard her phone ring and a few moments later, it beeped, indicating the caller had left a message. She had left work immediately after watching the YouTube video and had headed straight to her mom's. It would only be a matter of time before Enid Wolfe saw Alistair's arrest on the news and Sam wanted to tell her before she found out that way.

Telling her was one of the most difficult things Sam had ever done. Her mom stared at her in shock and confusion and then collapsed in a fit of distress. "I don't understand how the police could think Alistair capable of something like this!" she cried.

Sam thought back to the last conversation she'd had with her brother and remained silent. She didn't want to believe he'd done it, either, but she was terrified it might be true. He'd as much as admitted to forging signatures on consent forms and she knew Rohan well enough to know he was a good cop. He would never have acted rashly, without substantial proof.

A fresh wave of anger and helplessness washed over her. *Why, oh, why did it have to be Alistair?* A brother she admired and respected and loved with all her heart. She wanted so desperately to believe it was all some horrible mistake; that someone else was to blame. Perhaps Richard was the brains behind it? From what she'd seen and heard, her boss was most definitely involved.

She thought about the angry confrontation she'd interrupted between her brother and her boss. Alistair had been furious; Richard looked scared and appeared to be doing his best to pacify him. Their body language spoke volumes. No matter how much Sam wanted to believe otherwise, it was obvious her brother was the one in charge. Rohan must know it, too.

So why had she treated him so badly, ranting at him over the phone? He was only doing his job. Along with Hannah, Sam had been the one who'd drawn the whole terrible situation to the attention of the police. Then, when the investigation hadn't panned out the way she hoped it would, she'd laid the blame squarely on Rohan. She couldn't help but wonder if she'd have reacted so angrily if the alleged perpetrator had been anyone other than her brother. It shamed her to admit the answer was no.

With a sigh, she stood and moved across the living room to retrieve her phone from where she'd left it on the coffee table. There was no doubt about it: She owed Rohan an apology. Glancing at the screen, she noticed she'd missed his call. Keying into her mailbox, she listened to his message.

A second later, she gasped. Her heart went into double time as images raced through her head. His father was gravely ill; possibly dying. She had to go and be with him; to offer comfort and support to the man she loved. Turning to face her mother, Sam opened her mouth to tell her she was leaving and then closed it again. Enid was in no state to be left alone. Panic tightened Sam's chest until all of a sudden, she came up with an easy solution.

Dialing her sister's number, she waited for Ava to pick up.

"Have you heard?" her sister said by way of greeting.

Sam drew in a breath and eased it out. "Yes. I'm just as shocked as you."

"I can't believe it! It's all over the news! The police must have gotten it wrong! There's no *way* Alistair could be guilty of what they're saying."

"We need to talk, and Jessie, too, but right now, I need a favor." Sam explained her situation and was relieved when Ava agreed to come over and sit with their mom. She lived only a short distance away and it wasn't long before Sam's sister arrived at the house. They greeted each other with fierce hugs.

"Thanks for doing this, sis. I really appreciate it."

"No problem. How long will you be gone?"

"I'm not sure, but it might take all night. Are you all right with that?"

Ava pointed to an overnight bag by her feet. "I came prepared. I figured you'd want to stay with your friend as long as he needed you and you could do without having to worry about Mom and whether she was okay."

Tears burned behind Sam's eyes and she swallowed a lump that had lodged itself in her throat. Hugging her sister again, she led her into the living room to their mother.

"Mom, there's been an emergency at the hospital. I have to go. Ava's come to stay with you. Is that all right?"

Enid looked up from her position on the couch and nodded vaguely. "Will you come back?"

"As soon as I can, I promise." Kissing her mom on the cheek, she collected her handbag and hurried toward the front door. With a last hug and a whispered thank you to Ava, Sam left.

The hard plastic chair dug into Rohan's butt, but he was beyond caring about the discomfort. With his forearms on his thighs and his head in his hands, he stared at the worn linoleum floor of the waiting room. It felt like hours since he and his mom had arrived at the hospital, with fear and panic in their hearts. He'd called his brothers and sisters. Shocked and tearful, they were all on their way to the hospital. For some of them, it involved a twelve-hour drive, but every one of his siblings had expressed their desire to be there; to see their dad; to lend their support, no matter the outcome.

As far as Rohan knew, his father was still in surgery. Nobody had come near them to tell them any different. He tried hard to believe no news was good news, but his heart wasn't buying it.

As if his thoughts had conjured up the doctor, a middle-aged man dressed in blue surgical scrubs appeared in the open doorway. Rohan stared at him for a second and then jumped to his feet. His heart thumped hard in his chest. He glanced across at his mother where she sat in another chair. She'd also noticed the surgeon and stood and rushed to Rohan's side.

"Doctor, can you tell us what's happening?" he asked.

The man looked drawn and tired. A surgical mask hung loosely around his neck. His hair was still covered by a scarf.

"Are you the relatives of William Coleridge?"

Rohan's arm went instinctively around his mother and drew her close. He nodded in response to the doctor's question.

"He's my father. And this is my mother."

"Please, Doctor," his mom whispered. "Please, tell us what's happening. We... We've been here so long. Please, we need to know."

Her voice hitched and Rohan's throat went tight. He squeezed her shoulder in wordless comfort.

The doctor looked at them kindly. "Please, why don't you take a seat?"

He indicated the chairs they'd recently vacated. Rohan guided his mother over to one and sat beside her. The dread in his gut increased.

"I'm afraid I have bad news," the doctor murmured and pain stabbed through Rohan's heart.

His mother began to shake her head from side to side. "No! No! No! It can't be." She implored the surgeon. "Please, tell me he's still alive."

The doctor's lips compressed and his face filled with sadness. "I'm sorry, Mrs Coleridge. We did everything we could, but...your husband didn't make it."

A keening howl of pain came forth from Rohan's mom and she buried her face against his shoulder. Sobbing uncontrollably, she clung to him like she'd never let him go. The realization that his father had died slowly sank in. Tears pricked his eyes and his chest went tight. He'd never felt so helpless.

"I'm so sorry," the doctor continued. "He had a bleed on his brain and..." He shook his head. "It was left unchecked too long. We tried so hard to save him, but there was nothing we could do."

Despite Rohan's shock and grief, he could see how hard it was for the doctor to speak to them about the terrible news. With his jaw clenched against the pain in his heart, he offered the doctor his hand.

"Thank you for telling us, Doctor. We appreciate everything you've done." He glanced across at his mom who was still quietly sobbing. "What... What happens now?"

The doctor drew in a deep breath and exhaled slowly. "He's still on the respirator. Though his brain is clinically dead, the machine is keeping his other organs alive. I'd like to have someone come and speak to you about organ donation. Was William a registered donor?"

Rohan froze. A moment later, his heart pounded in his chest. After all that had happened over the past few months, he couldn't believe he was facing this decision. His mom pulled away and wiped at her eyes and then looked somberly at the doctor.

"Yes, he was."

Rohan reared back in surprise. He'd never discussed organ donation with either of his parents. He turned to his mom. "Are you sure?"

"Yes," his mom said quietly. "We saw a show about it a few years ago on TV. It was one of those hospital dramas, but we started talking about it and we both agreed it was something we'd like to do. They aren't going to be any help to us after we die, we thought someone else might as well have the use of them."

Rohan sucked in a breath and held it deep inside his lungs. Exhaling on a heavy sigh, he once again drew his mother close. Pressing a kiss against her hair, he whispered, "I never knew."

His mom offered a tiny, sad shrug. "We should have told you. I guess it just never came up."

———————

An hour later, after driving as fast as the traffic allowed, Sam made it to the car park of the Sutherland Hospital. She'd sent Rohan a text while she was stopped at a set of traffic lights. The message simply read: *I'm on my way.*

She found a vacant parking space and hurried from her car. The lights of the hospital beckoned and she sent up a silent prayer that Rohan's dad would pull through. The automatic doors opened upon her approach and she moved as quickly as she could. A brief enquiry at the patient information booth gave her the information she sought. She half-ran to the elevators and then punched in the button for the second level. She stepped out a moment later and almost collided with Rohan.

"Rohan!" she gasped, clutching at his shirt. His arms came out automatically to steady her.

"Sam! Thank God you're here."

She stared up at him and couldn't help noticing the bleak expression in his eyes. She tightened her fingers on his arms. "How is he?"

Rohan closed his eyes and his shoulders slumped. Slowly, he shook his head. Sam's hand came up against her mouth in an effort to hold back her shock.

"Oh, Rohan! Don't tell me..."

"He didn't make it, Sam. The doctors came out a little while ago and told us. The bleed was left unchecked for too long. There was nothing they could do."

"Where's your mom?" she asked quietly.

"She's still in the waiting room with the doctors. They asked us to consider organ donation."

For the second time, Sam gasped and this time she didn't know what to say. After all that had happened with her brother, having to contemplate donating his father's organs must be the last thing Rohan wanted to do. She understood why she'd found him by himself, near the elevators.

"You don't have to say anything, Samantha. I know how you feel about it and that's okay. Your mom's facing certain death if she doesn't get a transplant. I get how important organ donation is to you and your family."

"It *is* important to me. I won't pretend it isn't, but if there was a worst day to consider the question seriously, today is probably it. My brother..." She shrugged helplessly, unable to find the words. "All I ask is that you think about how you felt about organ donation last month, last year... Don't base your decision on my brother and his actions. He... I don't know what he was thinking or why he went so far off course, but there are so many other wonderful, dedicated medical staff working in this area who make such a difference to people's lives." She paused and then asked softly, "How did your father feel?"

He stared at her, his expression inscrutable. "My

father was a supporter of organ donation. Mom's going to consent to the recovery."

Her heart skipped a beat. "Oh, my goodness! Are you sure?" She gazed up at him, searching his face for the truth.

His eyes filled with tears, but his nod was firm in response. "Yes. Mom told me tonight Dad was a registered organ donor. I never knew. We talked about it. Mom's sure it's what Dad would have wanted. He was the first to offer help to a friend, or even to a stranger. If donating his organs can help someone else, she's certain she has his blessing."

He dragged in a breath and continued. "During the course of the investigation, I spoke to a lot of people involved in the industry and I'm also convinced it's the right thing to do."

Sam put her arms around him and hugged him close. She was relieved to feel him relax against her. Resting his chin on the top of her head, he sighed heavily. His arms tightened around her— like he never wanted to let her go. She was content to stay there for as long as he needed her.

So much had happened in such a short time. She'd started the day on top of the world and had quickly come crashing down. Phillip's death had shocked and saddened her, but discovering what her brother had done to him and countless others had rocked her to the core. She could only imagine the distress Alistair would no doubt cause to the grieving relatives when the news got out. And through all that, a little voice in her head reminded her that his actions had also saved many others.

That the increased number of people who'd received lifesaving transplants was a direct result of what Alistair had done, couldn't be discounted. It didn't mean she condoned his actions, but neither would she judge him. Their mother was one of the very people needing such a lifesaving gift.

How would Sam have felt if one of the harvested organs had been a match? Would it have mattered that the organ had been obtained illegally or did saving her mother's life trump everything? Sam didn't know where the answer and the truth was, and for now, she preferred it that way.

Eventually, Rohan's hold loosened and he lifted his head. "I need to go and be with Mom."

Sam nodded and let him go. She went to step away, but he reached for her hand. "Will you come with me when I say good-bye?"

Her breath caught in her throat. She blinked back a surge of tears. Squeezing his hand, she nodded. "Of course."

Hours later, surrounded by extended family, Rohan and his mom took their time to say good-bye to a man they obviously loved and held in high esteem. Sam didn't have to meet Bill Coleridge to know he'd been a great man. Though she kept in the background, the love in the room was overwhelming and the support Rohan showed his mom touched Sam like nothing else could.

Her phone vibrated in the pocket of her skirt and she surreptitiously glanced at the screen. It was Ava. A wave of concern washed over Sam and she quietly removed herself from the group. Moving out of the room, she quickly answered the call.

"Ava, what is it? Is Mom okay?"

"She got the call, Sam! Mom finally got the call!"

Sam frowned in confusion. "What are you talking about?"

"The transplant unit at the hospital! They think they've found a donor kidney!"

"Oh, my goodness!" Sam gasped in disbelief, her heart pounding like a hammer against her chest. "Are you sure?"

"Yes! I was sitting right next to Mom when she answered the phone! It's real, Sam and it's happening! After all these years, it's finally happening!"

Sam heard the happiness and relief in Ava's voice and blinked back tears as she listened. She was in as much shock as Ava was. She only wished she could call Alistair and let him know the good news. He'd devoted his life to saving others, including their mother. The day had finally arrived when she was to be given another chance at life and he was locked up in a jail cell, awaiting a fate that was as yet unknown.

"Where are you taking her?"

"They're going to prep her for surgery at Westmead. The donor kidney is apparently already on its way. We have to get there as soon as possible. Mom's in the car. I've thrown a bag together for her and I'll be leaving just as soon as

I've locked up. How long will it take for you to meet us there?"

"Give me an hour. I'll explain to Rohan what's happened. I'm sure he'll understand."

"Okay, sis. Drive safely. Oh, my goodness, I can't believe it's finally happening!"

CHAPTER 19

Dear Diary,

I can't help but wonder as I lie on my uncomfortable prison bed, smelling of body odor and sweat, whether I would have done anything differently if I'd known I'd be caught and tried. Would I have done it at all?

I might have quit sooner or gotten better at covering my tracks... I'll never know because I was outsmarted by a cop and betrayed by my sister—between the two of them, my choices were taken away.

I lie here and think about all the lives I have saved. I helped the lame walk again; I helped blind people see. I breathed new life into people who were facing certain death and I couldn't have done any of it without the sacrifice of the dead.

But in the end, I was the sacrifice. I gave my life, my freedom, my everything and I did it all for them.

Or did I...?

Sam wasn't at work when the police attended the Glebe Morgue to arrest Richard Davis. She was sitting beside her mother's hospital bed in the ICU, waiting for her to wake up. A television near the nurses' station was on low and she looked up at the screen in time to see her boss being led away by the police. A suit jacket tossed over his face concealed his expression, but reflected light from the news cameramen glinted off shiny, metal handcuffs. Sam stifled a gasp of shock, even though the scene didn't come as a surprise. The argument she'd partially witnessed between her brother and her boss had made it all too clear.

She shook her head, overwhelmed by the tragedy of it. Two brilliant men, kind and compassionate, had succumbed to the dark side and she wasn't even sure what had motivated them. No doubt it would be revealed in time as the whole sordid mess played out in the courts and in the media. She shuddered at the thought. Catching a movement out of the corner of her eye, she saw Rohan walking toward her. She offered him a weak smile.

"How is she?" he asked quietly, coming to a halt beside her mother's bed.

Sam lifted her shoulder in a half-shrug. "The doctors are happy with how it all went. Now it's a waiting game. They'll keep her in the ICU for the next several days until they know the kidney's going to take. Rejection's more likely to happen during that time. She's taking a cocktail of immunosuppression drugs to aid in her body's acceptance, but of course, there's no guarantee."

Rohan nodded and his attention turned to Sam. "How are *you*?"

The concern and compassion in his eyes was enough to undo her. Tears welled up and she stifled a sob, but the stress and anxiety of the past few days had finally caught up. Another sob escaped, followed quickly by more. Tenderly, Rohan drew her into his arms and she leaned into him, grateful for his support and the comfort only he could give.

He stroked her back and held her close and whispered soft, soothing words against her hair. She cried quietly against his shirt. A long while later, she lifted her head and gave him a shaky smile.

"I got your shirt wet." She hiccupped and drew a deep breath.

"I have plenty of others."

She tightened her arms about his waist and once again rested her head against his chest. His heart beat slow and steady and strong beneath her ear and made her feel safe and secure and loved. She never wanted to leave. As if he could read her mind, Rohan loosened his arms and tilted her chin up with his fingers. His head came down and his lips found hers. The sweetness of his kiss brought forth another rush of tears.

"I love you, Samantha Wolfe."

She stared up at him. "I love you, too, Rohan Coleridge."

He kissed her again and Sam responded with all the love in her heart. It was a kiss filled with gentleness, kindness and compassion. It acknowledged wrongs and it offered forgiveness and it promised a bright new start.

EPILOGUE

ohan pulled over next to the curb outside Samantha's apartment building and swallowed the bundle of nerves that threatened to block his throat. Wishing he'd bought a bottle of water to ease the dryness in his mouth, he felt around in the pocket of his jeans. His fingers closed around the jewelers's box and relief surged through him. *It was still there.* The thought was immediately followed by another rush of nerves.

Samantha's mom had undergone her transplant a month ago and from all reports, she was doing fine. Tonight, Sam had invited her family around to celebrate the milestone. While Rohan had met Enid in the hospital, he had yet to be introduced to the remaining two siblings who made up the Wolfe family. The thought of meeting the sisters of Alistair Wolfe only added to his nerves. While Samantha had shown remarkable understanding and had accepted Rohan was only doing his job, he had yet to see if the remaining Wolfe children would be as forgiving.

Knowing he couldn't put it off any longer, he grabbed the six-pack of beer on the seat and collected the bottle of wine. Samantha had told him her mom adored a glass of Merlot at night and although she now limited herself to one or two glasses a week, it was a habit she still indulged.

With the wine in one hand and the six-pack in the other, he made his way into the building's foyer and up the short flight of stairs. With the back of his knuckles, he knocked on Samantha's door. It was opened almost immediately and she stood before him, gorgeous in crimson silk. It floated around her body like a living thing and set off her olive skin. Her black hair was loose and curled around her lovely face.

"Rohan!" she exclaimed with a smile and threw her arms around his neck. He stood a little awkwardly with the alcohol in his hands and tried to maintain his balance.

"I'm sorry." She laughed and pulled away. "I almost bowled you over!"

"Oh, you bowled me over, all right. You bowled me over the moment I saw you again." He grinned and set the bottles on the floor and swept her into his arms. Unmindful of smudging her ruby-red lipstick, he kissed her thoroughly before setting her aside.

"That's a lovely way to say hello." She laughed a little breathlessly. "Come in and meet the rest of my family."

Rohan collected the bottles off the floor and

then Samantha took him by the arm. Depositing the beer on a nearby counter, he followed her into the living room. He'd expected a crowd, but there were only two other couples, along with Hannah Langdon and Enid. Sam's mother sat alone, a little ways apart from the others in pride of place in a large armchair.

"Sam, can you help me with something in the kitchen?"

The question had come from one of the women who looked so much like Sam she had to be her sister. Sam flashed him a quick smile of apology and turned away. Rohan moved toward Enid and she smiled and waved him over when she saw him.

"Rohan! How lovely to see you again!" she cried, reaching out to him.

Rohan stepped forward and took her hand and then leaned in close to press a kiss against her cheek. "You're looking great, Enid. It's fantastic to see you."

She nodded and squeezed his hand. "I feel like a new woman. I never imagined a donor kidney could make me feel so good. The doctors are pleased with my progress. So far, there haven't been any signs of rejection."

"That's great news!" Rohan replied, genuinely relieved. Samantha's mother and her family had been through enough over the past little while, and it wasn't over yet, not by a long shot.

Alistair's trial had yet to begin and with it, more hardship for them would follow. Rohan could only imagine the media circus the trial would cause.

Not to mention the devastation if a guilty verdict were handed down. The Wolfe family would need all the support they could get over the coming months.

"You've had a hard time of it lately," Enid said softly, as if reading his mind. "Almost as hard as me. I know you're feeling bad about the arrest, but I don't want you to feel that way. Alistair made his own choices; you did what you had to do."

Rohan sucked in a breath and then eased it out on a sigh. He nodded, acknowledging her generosity of spirit. She patted his hand in comfort and he was grateful for it. Silence fell between them. After a while, she broke it.

"I haven't had a chance to thank you," Enid said softly, her gaze intent on his.

Once again, Rohan tensed and then a moment later, let it go. *What did it matter if Enid suspected she carried his father's kidney?* Rohan knew the truth.

Samantha had come and told him about her mother receiving the call long before his dad's organs had been recovered. He couldn't possibly be the donor. He'd heard from police sources that there had also been two motor vehicle fatalities the night Enid had received her transplant. One was a twenty-three-year-old triathlete; the other, a thirty-six-year-old father of two. It wasn't possible to find out the truth about the donor and he didn't want to and if it made Enid feel better that there was a possibility she might have received the gift of life from his dad, who was he to argue?

As if able to read his thoughts, Enid squeezed his hand again. "I'm so sorry for the loss of your father. Nothing can replace our loved ones who have gone on ahead of us, but I promise you this. As long as you continue to love my daughter, with all your heart and soul, you'll be a son to me."

Tears appeared in Enid's eyes and Rohan felt them, too. He swallowed a lump and tried to speak around the emotion that clogged his throat. It had been a month since his dad had passed, but he still missed him every day. He thought briefly of the other two people who had died that day and said a silent prayer for their families.

"You're a remarkable woman, Enid Wolfe. I'm so very proud to know you."

"You're a special man, Rohan Coleridge, from a very special family. Take care of my daughter. Love her with all your heart. Protect her and keep her safe from harm, even in times of doubt. She loves you with everything that she is and she deserves to have you in her life. Make her happy, make her sad. Show her how to live."

Rohan nodded and for a moment he was beyond words. "I will."

The rest of the party sped by in a blur. Rohan was introduced to Samantha's sisters. Though the girls were polite, he couldn't fail to note their reserve and he understood it. He could only hope over time, they'd come to forgive him for his part in their brother's downfall. The girls' boyfriends were also dutifully introduced, but Rohan paid them little heed. As the night wore on, his hand returned to his pocket over and over again.

He'd bought the ring a fortnight earlier and had been trying to find the right time. But was there any such thing as the right time to ask the love of your life to marry you? He was beginning to wonder. He wandered out onto the balcony to clear his head. A few moments later, he heard the sound of the sliding door opening behind him.

"There you are!" Samantha laughed, appearing by his side. She linked her arm with his. "I've been looking for you everywhere!"

Rohan smiled and pulled her close. "I thought I'd step outside and catch a breath of air. It's a beautiful night."

Samantha nodded. She leaned over the balcony and breathed in deeply of the fresh spring air. "You're right. It is beautiful. I love this time of year."

Lights from the surrounding houses and apartment buildings twinkled gently in the night. A soft breeze brought with it the smell of frangipani or something equally sweet and pungent. Once again, Rohan felt in his pocket and his heart picked up its pace. Feeling his way, he opened the box and took hold of the ring. Now was as good a time as any. In fact, now was perfect.

Taking her hands in his, he took a deep breath and then dropped to one knee. Samantha stared at him in surprise, her eyes going wide.

"I love you more each day and I yearn to make you mine. Samantha Wolfe, will you do me the honor of becoming my wife?"

The words fell out in a rush, not at all in the way

he'd planned. For half a second, she looked almost stunned and then her face broke into a wide smile. She laughed and hollered and cried out with joy.

"Is that a yes?" he asked, waiting for her to say the word.

"Yes! Yes! Yes!" she cried and tears ran down her cheeks.

Rohan came to his feet and took her left hand and slipped the one-carat diamond ring onto her finger. She gasped and cried and stared at it, turning it every which way in the light. At last, she threw her arms around him and kissed him like forever was in her sights.

Together, they looked up at the starry sky. Rohan's heart filled with love and hope for their future.

Note to Readers

I do hope you have enjoyed reading Samantha and Rohan's story. If you've enjoyed this story, please feel free to leave a review for The Body Thief at Goodreads and your favorite digital retailer. Every review is very much appreciated.

If you would like to receive news on upcoming stories, release dates, book launches and other snippets, please feel free to sign up for my newsletter. You can do this by visiting my website at www.christaylorauthor.com.au and clicking on the "Subscribe to my Newsletter" link on the right.

The Baby Snatchers is the next book in the Sydney Harbour Hospital Series. Here's a sneak peek:

Between heaven and hell...
Georgina Whitely loves her job as a midwife at the prestigious Sydney Harbour Hospital. The joy and excitement of helping to deliver babies never fails to bring a smile to her face. But the job is not without its challenges...

Ward Seven is where pregnant, drug and alcohol addicted women go to have their babies. It's Georgie's job to not only manage the births, but also to manage the addictions. It breaks her heart to watch tiny newborns suffer from the harsh effects of drug withdrawal. And then there's the stress of dealing with their mothers.

But, despite the emotional and physical upheavals a day on Ward Seven can bring, Georgie relishes the challenges. The new mothers look up to her and respect her; they want to keep her close. But babies are dying on Ward Seven and nobody can figure out why.

Detective Sergeant Cameron Dawson has spent a decade putting his troubled childhood behind him. Just when he thinks his life is back on track, his sixteen-year-old sister, Cynthia, arrives on the scene. Not only has she run away from home, she's also just given birth at the Sydney Harbour Hospital. When Cameron arrives at Ward Seven, the midwife who introduces herself as Georgie Whitely, informs him Cynthia's baby has died.

Shocked and saddened, Cameron does his best to help his sister through her grief. Within a fortnight, he hears of another infant death on the same ward. The hospital staff say the deaths are sudden and unexplainable, but Cameron isn't so sure. And what in the world do they have to do with Georgie Whitely…?

The Baby Snatchers will be released on 28 February, 2016 and is available for pre-order from your favorite digital retailer.

ABOUT THE AUTHOR

Chris Taylor grew up on a farm in north-west New South Wales, Australia. She always had a thirst for stories and recalls writing her first book at the ripe old age of eight. Always a lover of romance and happily-ever-afters, a career in criminal law sparked her interest in intrigue and suspense. For Chris to be able to combine romance with suspense in her books is a dream come true.

Chris is married to Linden and is the mother of five children. If not behind her computer, you can find her doing the school run, taxiing children to swimming lessons, football, ballet and cricket. In her spare time, Chris loves to read her favorite authors who include Richard North Patterson, Sandra Brown, Kathleen E Woodiwiss and Jude Devereaux.

You can find out more about Chris and sign up for her newsletter at her website:

http://www.christaylorauthor.com.au

www.ingramcontent.com/pod-product-compliance
Lightning Source LLC
Chambersburg PA
CBHW061623210726

48287CB00001B/256